Praise for Teri Terry's previous books

'Teri Terry is a master of the thriller, and the pace of this book rivals the deadly infection itself'
Scotsman

'Flame-hot dystopian thriller ... sizzles with sinister science and supernatural intrigue'
lovereading4kids.co.uk

'Keeps the reader on the edge of their seat ... ch[...] believable ... Can't wait for the next on[...] in this trilogy'
readingzone.com

'I loved *Contagion* ... the story is told with gre[...] and a breathless pace'
thebookbag.co.uk

'A gripping dystopian debut'
Bookseller

'A terrific read which doesn't give up its secrets lightly. From the first pages it grips. Highly recommended'
School Librarian

'There is an Orwellian harshness about this dystopia that makes for disturbing and provocative reading'
Books for Keeps

'A thrilling futuristic drama ... compelling and well written'
Bucks Herald

Also by Teri Terry

F**A**TED

FATED

TERI TERRY

ORCHARD

ORCHARD BOOKS

First published in Great Britain in 2019 by The Watts Publishing Group

1 3 5 7 9 8 6 4 2

A CIP catalogue record for this book is available from the British Library.

ISBN 978 1 40835 066 9

Typeset in American Garamond by Avon DataSet Ltd,
Bidford-on-Avon, Warwickshire

Printed and bound in Great Britain by Clays Ltd, Elcograf S.p.A.

The paper and board used in this book are made from wood from responsible sources.

Orchard Books
An imprint of Hachette Children's Group
Part of The Watts Publishing Group Limited
Carmelite House
50 Victoria Embankment
London EC4Y 0DZ

An Hachette UK Company
www.hachette.co.uk

www.hachettechildrens.co.uk

To readers everywhere,
who hope and dream of a better world:
it is yours. Make it so.

Part 1: Chaos

Order is artificial, imposed by government:
nature strains for chaos!
Who do you trust?

A4A,
Public manifesto

It is human nature to both create and destroy.
But let your enemies knock things down, and then
step in to save the day when they are done — they get
the blame, you get the credit.
Besides, it saves energy.

Opposition MP Astrid Connor,
private diary

1

Sam

We're trapped. Thin glass and steel are all that separates us from hate and fury, and fear grips my guts inside, crushes breath from my lungs.

Dad is saying something, harsh instructions to our driver to get us away, but there is nothing he can do – we're surrounded.

Faces twist with rage and scream obscenities. A hand smashes a brick against the window by my seat and a scream of my own works its way up from inside me, but the glass holds – it's bulletproof; they can't break it, can they? But what if they strike at it again and again?

Now our car is rocking. They're pushing on all sides, and it's rocking.

Sirens are closing in; people around us start to pull away and run. Riot police rush forwards and form a wall of shields and batons that strike out. There is a blur of people and blood.

A girl falls by my car window and people just keep coming – she'll be trampled, hurt. I'm up against the glass but lose sight of her ...

'Get *down*, Samantha,' Dad says.

Our tyres screech. Somehow our driver spins us around, half on the pavement, pushing through the screaming mob.

Once back on the road we go fast; as fast as we can when everyone is trying to rush down crowded London streets the same way – away from what happened.

Dad is on his phone, demanding to know how we could be ambushed like this without warning.

He ends the call. 'Samantha?' he says. 'I need to go straight in. You'll have to come with me for now.'

We get green lights all the way – do they make that happen just for us? When we near Westminster, guards open the new gates in the high fences that surround the buildings, and we drive into the courtyard. The doors are opened and we're rushed out of the car with guards all around – it's an alert thing, I remember now; when it's high enough they do this – and up the steps to inside.

Dad is hurried off and I'm left standing there, blinking, mind curiously blank and still – it's an odd feeling, like time is moving *wrong*, or I'm outside it, watching the scene spin fast around me but not taking part. Like I am still in the car in the middle of a riot.

A cool hand touches my shoulder. It's Astrid Connor – an opposition MP and shadow minister for something or other. I know her through her daughter, who goes to my school.

'Samantha, dear. Are you all right? That must have been frightening.' Her lips curve into what is probably supposed to be a reassuring smile, but somehow misses the mark.

I swallow, not sure what to say. 'Can I go home?'

I finally ask, hating how my voice sounds – small and weak.

'I don't know. We'll have to check the cordon and see if someone can take you.' She looks around and then gestures to an aide, who hurries over. 'Go and have some tea, and I'll make sure someone comes for you when they can.'

The aide takes me to the café, has me sit down at a table and brings me a cup of tea. I reach out, hold it, using both hands so I don't spill it: my hands are shaking.

There's a TV up on the wall. The BBC is showing scenes from where we were – they're calling it an *incident*. They like that word. Seeing it on the screen now – the surging mob, our car almost lost in the midst of it – I feel like I'm back there, like it is happening over again now. It's weird, like I'm watching from outside my own body.

Then they add that the car of Deputy Prime Minister Gregory was caught up in the protest, that his daughter was with him. An image of us appears on the screen. It's an old shot, from just after the election about a year ago – I was fourteen – I hated the dress they made me wear. It was blue to go with my eyes, Mum had said, but between that dress and the way they'd done my pale blonde hair, in *ringlets*, I looked much younger. Dad had his serious politician face on. Then it seemed to be something that he could put on and take off, but now it seems more like it is always there – just like his short dark hair has more grey creeping up the sides with every *incident*.

I count slowly in my head from when we were named.

One – two – three – four ... and it begins. My phone vibrates with texts.

R U OK Sam?

Yes.

What happened?

Watch the news! Just like that but louder

Where R U?

Hauled to WM to drink tea

Did u get any vid?

No, actually that wasn't first on my list

U OK babes? School is closed today – fingers crossed for tomorrow, too

Yes. Yes!!!

What did you see? Were you scared?

I hesitate. One minute we'd been driving up the road to drop me at school, and the next minute – well ... All hell broke loose. Jumbled images – hate-filled faces, the screaming, the brick against my window, then the police and the blood – fight in my mind. The terrified face of that girl who disappeared under the feet of the crowd by my window.

And then, I lie:

I couldn't see anything.

Texts continue to come: from friends at school, my art teacher, my cousins, even Sandy, the opposition leader's little daughter. Most are variations of *Are you OK? Are you all right?* I answer *Yes*, *Yes*, and *Yes*, and I guess I am. At least, I'm ... intact; the glass didn't break. What if it had? But it didn't. Yet I'm *not* all right at the same time.

As I answer the ones I want to and the replies that

come back again after, I watch for the call or text that doesn't come, until finally I can't stop myself from sending one of my own: *Hi Mum, I'm just fine, thanks for not asking.*

There's no answer.

2

Ava

I sink gratefully on to my favourite place – this one bench, in Kensington Gardens. The new security fences around the palace mar the view the other way, but they can't be seen from here, and it is far enough from the fading late summer flowers and main paths that it is rarely invaded by others.

Late September sun warms my arms; the grass is that perfect shade of green that only comes with care. The breeze is soft, the sirens distant. I can almost pretend they don't exist, though if it wasn't for them I'd be in school right now.

In London there is always this backdrop to beauty. An edge, one that is becoming sharper. One that has pierced my heart before, but I shy away from thinking of that now. It is time to block out the world and open my books. To lose myself in words – my other favourite place.

But when I try they are dancing on the page, and it isn't pain – old or new – distracting me now; it's something else completely. Finally I give up, close the books. Lie back on the bench with my knees up, liking the feel of the warm wood through my thin dress, against my back and arms. I close my eyes against the sun, but still I shiver.

Why does it have to be her?

I couldn't say no. Even with the full scholarship I have, there are always all these extra costs of going to that school. My dad can't do more shifts than he does already. I must tutor this girl; there is no choice to be made.

But why does it have to be *her*?

3

Sam

Three cups of Westminster tea, two chocolate bars and endless news bulletins later, the aide comes back and tells me I can go soon. I've been drawing on napkins with a borrowed pen, having left my stuff in the car – drawing images from this morning. But they're not clear enough, real enough. What happened was terrifying, senseless and violent – but real. Not cleaned or covered up.

The aide looks over my shoulder. 'Wow,' she says. 'You're really very good.'

When the driver comes to get me I crumple them up and land them first try in a bin across the room.

Late that evening, pencil on sketch paper, I'm sitting up in bed and trying to draw what I saw again – from my memory, not what was on TV. That's not the same somehow, as if a reporter and a camera between me and what I saw puts a filter in the way, like when the bodies are blurred on the news so you can't see who they are. Now I'm wishing I *had* got my phone out and taken some images of my own.

The next time I'm caught up in a riot I'll try to remember.

Then there is a knock on my door.

'Yes?'

Dad looks in. 'I saw the light under your door, Samantha. It's late. Shouldn't you be asleep?'

I shrug and he comes in, sees the drawings spread across my bed. He pulls the desk chair across and sits next to me, and takes my hand. It's been a long time since he's come to my room to say goodnight, something he always did *BE*: before election, and I know he didn't just happen to spot the light under my door. In a house this size he doesn't come past this way unless he makes a special trip.

'I'm sorry I couldn't stay with you this morning,' he says. 'Are you all right?'

I answer the question truthfully for the first time. 'No. Not really.'

'Me neither. But don't tell anyone.'

'You see stuff on TV, but being there ...' My voice trails away.

'I know. It's different.'

'What was it about? I mean, I saw what they said on the news: there was a protest about housing and jobs and stuff. But they were so *angry*.'

'I understand it was peaceful to start with, but there is always an element that seeks these things out and twists and uses them for their own purposes.'

'Who was it this time?'

'Investigations are—'

'Continuing. Yes, that is what they just said on the

news. But don't *you* know?'

'You know I'm not at liberty to discuss—'

'I'm not the media, and I have a right to know: were they targeting us?' I say, finally asking the question I'm afraid of.

His face softens. 'I don't think so. They saw a government car, that's all. Likely we were just in the wrong place, wrong time. Now, it is time for you to go to sleep; I need to get back to work.'

'Shouldn't you get some sleep, too?'

He smiles. 'Soon. I've got some boring stuff to do first. And don't worry: security is increasing their road surveillance, so nothing like that can happen again.'

But every time something happens or almost happens they take measures – they increase this, guard against that. But what about the things that have never happened, the ones they haven't thought of yet?

There was a time when he could say *don't worry* and I wouldn't. I thought my dad could do anything, and it feels weird to think that isn't true any more – to not just think it, but *know* it. The world is shifting and changing around us – nothing is completely safe and sure. London is quicksand.

'Where's Mum?'

'She stayed at her sister's. Sensible, rather than crossing the city tonight. Now. What are you going to do when I close the door?'

'Sleep.'

'Good girl.' He gathers my pages, puts them on the desk and walks to the door. 'I'm sure there was something else ...' His eyes defocus for a moment, then he nods. 'Ah, yes. I meant to tell you in the car this morning, but events overtook us. I'm concerned about your schoolwork with the days you've been missing.'

I roll my eyes. Seriously? After what happened today – we're having this conversation?

'Don't give me that look; you know your GCSEs are important. I've had someone ask your head teacher for suggestions. There's a girl in the sixth form who does some tutoring. You would have met with her after school today; it'll be tomorrow now, I expect.'

'What? Tomorrow? But I've got plans. Who is it?'

He shrugs; if he ever knew her name he's forgotten it. He turns on my night light before switching off the main lights, and then shuts the door.

At least I've got something else to think about now. I really can't believe he's done this without talking to me first.

Who could it be?

4

Ava

She's singing softly.

> Sov, du lilla videung,
> än så är det vinter ...

The tune is familiar and warm, a comforter that wraps around me with her arms. I snuggle in closer to a cosy nest of wool and that mum-smell, some mix of flowery fragrance and spice from cooking. Her long hair is soft on my cheek.

> ... sov, du lilla vide,
> än så är det vinter ...

I don't know all the words. I am forbidden to learn them, but some of the willow song seeps into my awareness just the same. And I know Dad wouldn't like that; if he could hear her he'd say to stop. She agrees that with all the English-only laws now it is better if I don't learn the words, but her voice still finds its own way in Swedish sometimes when he's not here.

> ... Solskensöga ser dig,
> solskensfamn dig vaggar

Then the song ends, and changes.

Harsh notes jar through my skull. Fear and then sadness creep inside me; I know the words now, but stuff my hands tight against my ears.

No matter what I do, I can still hear it.

She's gone, and I scream to make it stop.

I force my eyes open. My heart races against my ribs in the darkness and I reach for the lamp by my bed, forgetting that the bulb is gone – latest on the list of shortages. There are sirens in the distance, getting closer; it may be that their sound found a way into my dream and changed it. And I want to go back to the start – to my mother's arms.

Then I'm angry at myself.

She *left*. What was it – six years ago now?

Get over it.

Then another sound joins the sirens: my alarm. It's time to get up for school.

I pause by the chess set on the table on my way out. Dad's next move has been made, and it's both an interesting one to counter and the only evidence that he was home at all while I slept.

When I see the solution, it's obvious, really: a bishop slid along two spaces to both block the threat and impose my own. A sign he's tired. I move the piece, change the little flag to his side to show it is his move next.

My phone vibrates with a text – Dad. *Are you out the door yet? *stern face**

I smile and step through, juggling my books in one

arm to pull the door shut behind me before answering. *Yes, of course.*

Take care. Go the long way.

I slip my phone into my pocket; I can pretend I never saw that one, or that I'm already on my way and he's too late. Then it beeps again and I can't resist a look.

I know you got my text. I have Super Dad magical powers, remember?

I sigh. *Yes! OK, I will.*

Soon I'm not sure the long way is better than the short any more; I walk fast, both to avoid being late and to leave it behind. The homeless have found another street, and it's not just one person, or two, who have somehow lost their way, but whole families. Dad would say don't look, that making eye contact might be dangerous, but how can I not see children sleeping huddled together in cardboard boxes?

Yesterday's sunshine is a memory and now it's cold, damp. Winter's icy fingers will be coming soon, and those of us walking go quickly, most averting their eyes like Dad says I should.

But it's not as it used to be. Those who rush along to work or school don't refuse to see to avoid their guilt — why they have more, why they don't help. Instead it is *fear*: that could be me. One day, it might be.

To see these people as human would be to acknowledge what they are afraid of.

5

Sam

School isn't cancelled the next day, and I wish it had been for more than the usual reasons.

I'm uneasy in the car on the way; I can't help it. Maybe it doesn't help that Dad went early and I'm on my own. He said we weren't targeted yesterday, but then why are we going a different way? At least if he were here I could ask him.

But nothing happens, and when the school gates open for our car a knot loosens inside me. The gates close behind us before the next ones open.

The driver tips his hat when he opens my door. He's the same one as yesterday – the one who drove through a crowd of people, maybe not slowly enough for everyone to get out of the way. I shudder inside but don't let it show. The news this morning said two police officers were injured but nothing about anyone else, and from what I saw there's no chance all the protestors walked away.

I head for the usual place before bell – art block. A group of sixth formers go past on the way – no uniforms for them, not like this hell of a dark blazer and skirt the rest of us have to wear – and I wonder if one of them is this tutor Dad lined up. I may just conveniently forget all about it.

'Sam, wait!' It's Anji. She slips her arm in mine when she catches up. 'All right?'

'Course. Could have done with another day off, though.'

Her face quirks with sympathy. 'I'm sure, in the circumstances, you could have stayed home today?'

'No chance. Seriously.' I roll my eyes.

We reach Ruth and Charlize, leaning against the radiator. These old buildings are always freezing – even if the sun shines outside it doesn't reach in here.

'Next time you get caught in a riot could you do something to escalate the situation?' Charlize says. 'So we can get more time off?' And she winks. She doesn't mean anything by her words and I know it, but I'm still uneasy from the drive in. The restless night that came before it.

'So them rocking our car and smashing bricks against the windows wasn't enough for you? Would you rather the glass had broken?'

Round eyes and matching unease are the answer. Do I want to take the words back? No, not exactly – I want to take *time* back. Make it not have happened.

'Why would anyone behave like that?' Ruth says, breaking the silence, and this is it, exactly – the reason I couldn't sleep. The *why*.

'My dad says they must be Euros,' Charlize says. 'That they should *all* have been kicked out before the borders closed. That they still could be, if the government has the nerve to do what is right.' She looks at me like I have a say in it and should agree, but before I can decide how to answer, more of our crowd arrive. After a quick check that I've got my usual complement of arms and legs, talk turns to important stuff: Charlize's birthday party. She's sixteen soon, and her birthday party – the catering, what she is wearing, what everyone else is wearing, and which boys from which schools are coming – takes over until the bell goes.

English first. A subject I don't mind that much most of the time, but my mind is drifting – and seriously, what do Romeo and Juliet have to do with *anything* in my life right now, stuck in an all-girls school? And they were such idiots. Being ready to die for any boy I've ever met seems way beyond impossible. The teacher must notice me staring out of the window but doesn't call me to task. Maybe today I get some latitude.

The bell goes and she asks me to stay back: maybe I don't.

'Yes, Miss?' I say.

She waits until the others file out of the room and the door swings shut.

'How are you, Samantha?'

Does she really want to know, or is this teacher-speak for something else?

'All right,' I say, opting for vagueness.

'Is there anything you want to talk about?' I shake my head. 'I often find if you talk something through it's the best way to move on. You need to concentrate in class, particularly this year. *Bleugh bleugh bleugh* exams *bleugh bleugh bleugh …*'

I nod, and pretend to care enough about exams to be allowed to leave before I'm twenty.

Art is next. I find my work from last week, set it up. We're painting still life. Even with a bowl of fruit I was losing myself in this piece last week – in getting the shading and perspective exactly right.

'Miss?' Charlize says.

'Yes?' Mrs Jenson answers, a resigned look on her face.

'When will we get something more interesting to paint?'

'What do you have in mind?'

'Life drawing.'

'I see.'

'You know – using models. *Male* models.' There are giggles and smirks around the room.

Mrs Jenson pretends to consider the request, then holds up a peach from the reserves that didn't make it into the bowl. 'Use your imagination, Charlize.'

'Miss!' she says with fake shock; there are more titters around her.

'Baby steps, Charlize. Master light, perspective, shade, colour – *then* we'll talk about life drawing.'

'She didn't say no,' Charlize says, an aside to Ruth and me behind her.

'Dream on,' Ruth answers.

When Mrs Jenson makes her rounds towards the end of the lesson she stops by my shoulder. 'Good work, Sam,' she says, in an approving tone.

I can look at this and know it's not a bad representation of what my eyes see on the table. But it's a *copy* – it's not anything on its own. You can't bite this apple.

Or throw it at anybody.

Neither food nor a weapon, so what is the point?

6

Ava

I thought she wasn't coming, and was about to give up and leave – probably too soon to do so, but I'm nervous, or something like it. I hate feeling this way.

But there she is through the glass of the door. The deputy head is at her shoulder: escorting her to make sure she attends? She opens the door and gives her a nudge.

'Good afternoon, Ava. Do you two know each other?' Samantha shakes her head no, but I know her. Everyone does.

'Samantha, this is Ava Nicholls. One of our top students in the sixth form!' She beams with a sense of astonishment and I wait to hear if she adds *so amazing for a scholarship student, especially with* her *background*. I've heard this before over my head at orientation for new students, as if I'm not there: if *she* can do this, imagine what *you* can achieve? But she leaves it unsaid today. 'And *this* is Samantha Gregory.' She says it rather like she is presenting a priceless work of art.

'It's Sam, really,' she says, shifting her weight from one foot to the other.

I nod, smile a little. 'Hi, Sam.'

'Well, I'll leave you two now. Make sure you make good use of this time, Samantha,' the deputy head says. Sam rolls her eyes when she turns to go.

Once the door shuts behind her, Sam walks around the tutor room. She looks at books on the shelves, stationery supplies on the table; touching them, ignoring me. She moves like a cat: she's not very tall and every movement is fluid, precise.

'This might work better if you sit down?' I say.

She sighs, then sits down across from me at the table with elbows on the table and her head in her hands.

'What do you want to get out of these sessions?' I ask.

'An early exit?'

I raise an eyebrow and she looks embarrassed. She sits up and crosses her arms. 'I'm sorry; it's nothing to do with you. It's just it wasn't my idea, and I had plans. I'm sure there is something you'd rather be doing, too.'

'Maybe, but I need the money.'

She looks intrigued, as if needing money is a strange concept. 'How much do they pay you?'

'Standard minimum for a seventeen-year-old: £20 an hour.'

'How about this: I'll pay you £25 an hour to *pretend* to tutor me, and pass along glowing updates. That's a win, isn't it? Then you'd get £45 an hour altogether without doing a thing, and I'd get some free time.'

I pretend to consider her offer and at the same time hide the shock. She has that kind of money that she could give me, just like that? And maybe there is a tiny part of me that is tempted – but more to get out of this than for the extra money, as handy as it would be.

I shake my head. 'You're asking me to lie. I can't do that. Besides, I'd probably get expelled if I got caught.'

'Damn. I was afraid you'd say that.'

'Look, all they want is for you to do better at your exams. Don't you care about your results?'

Sam shrugs. She looks down and her hair falls over her eyes. Can it even be natural, that pale blonde colour? I doubt it, but there are no dark roots I can see. She pushes it back and looks up.

'It's not that I don't care, exactly. It's just that it doesn't seem important.'

'What does?' And I'm genuinely curious: what would seem important to someone like her?

She hesitates as if she might answer, her eyes on mine. Then she looks away and shakes her head. 'Look, if we have to do this, let's get it over with. All right?'

'Of course.' I open the files from her teachers. 'I've been given work from all your subjects. Except for art.'

'And here was me hoping we could paint a bowl of fruit.'

'That I couldn't help you with. You can choose where we start if you want to?'

She looks through the folders and picks the one with the shortest assignment. 'Maths,' she says.

It's soon obvious that she's able enough to handle this work, just like her teacher said – if she can be bothered. Maybe she'd never be an A student, but she should be doing better than she is.

But why should she be bothered? She has everything. She won't ever be afraid of sleeping in a cardboard box if she can't get a job.

7

Sam

I'm barely through my bedroom door when there is a light knock. It opens: it's Mum. She looks … amazing: blue satin dress, fair hair so like mine swept up, makeup all done – smoky eyes that shouldn't work with her colouring but somehow do.

'Darling,' she says, and holds out her hands, pulls me towards her. 'Careful of my face!' she says. Air kisses.

'Hi, Mum. You made it home OK then?'

'I did. Oh, that dreadful business yesterday! Are you all right?'

'I'm fine.' Better late than never, I guess. 'It was kind of—'

'Where have you been? I've been calling.'

'Ah, school? You know, the place they make you go until you're eighteen. To learn stuff.'

'Don't be cheeky. Why are you so late, today of all days? We're going to the charity dinner for the Tate tonight, remember?'

'I was with a tutor for my exams; Dad set it up. I forgot to take my phone off silent when I left – sorry.'

She shakes her head impatiently. 'What was he

thinking? Now you really must hurry. I've had Penny set out your clothes, and Francesco is here for hair and makeup: he's in a state about how little time he'll have. There's only twenty minutes before our car.'

'I didn't sleep well last night; I'm really tired. Could you make excuses for me?'

'No. Samantha, darling, you *must* remember how lucky we are; this is an important charity for us to support. And I particularly want you to come along to this one with me since your dad is in meetings. Get dressed – now. And then hurry along to my dressing room for Francesco.'

She sweeps out of the room, and I lean against the door. There is indeed a dress on my bed. It's pale blue, almost a mirror of Mum's but shorter and not as low cut. I don't remember seeing it before.

I shimmy into it: it fits, but only just – they've got my measurements at the place Mum uses. Mental note: go and get measured again.

I *hate* wearing tights. For about a nanosecond I wonder if I can get away with bare legs, but no chance – the dress is too short. Then matching shoes – oh my God, what are they: like, four inches? Another night in heels.

There's a tapping on the door. This time it's Penny peeking in, come to hurry me along.

'You look so beautiful,' she says.

I glance in the mirror on my way out of my room. It's a lovely dress, but I won't be able to eat anything in it; I couldn't run a step in these shoes. Francesco will do something simple to my hair and face and maybe there will be something beautiful about what I see by the time he's done, but it won't be real. It'll be as fake as the smile I'll wear tonight.

There is a double security detail today, with cars both in front and behind us; and the latest? They're not standard government cars. Do they really think anyone will be fooled just because they haven't got government plates? Three shiny new cars in a row with opaque back windows – hmm.

I feel uneasy as we head out of our gates, but traffic is light and we speed along without *incident*. We should even be 'on time': about twenty minutes late is exactly right in Mum-land.

When we arrive and go through the security gates, we're helped out of our car, umbrellas held up as it's starting to rain. There are flashes again and again in our eyes: the press are out in force. No wonder Mum wanted me to come.

Inside there's the usual line of important people's hands to shake; some I know, some I don't. Tonight's charity is a new Tate initiative to support up-and-coming artists. There are a few of them here, looking out of place but in the right way – interesting hair and clothes – being chatted to by adoring women and giddy girls. I roll my eyes; Mum must notice, she digs my ribs with a finger. I guess they couldn't find any female artists, or maybe the charity committee – all friends of Mum – were more interested in other attributes.

Charlize is here with her parents. She sneaks us a glass of champagne, pulls me on to a balcony. A few sips of fizz and my head is spinning, but smiling is easier.

'Did you see what Stella is wearing?' she says. 'Oh my

God. And did you meet that Lucas somebody? He came with one of the artists. He's hot, isn't he?'

'Well, thanks,' a voice says and we turn around. I'm guessing the person standing behind us and laughing must be Lucas.

Charlize goes an interesting shade of scarlet, even under all her makeup.

I shake my head. 'You broke the first rule of gossip, Charlize. Always look around *before* you talk about somebody.'

He's grinning, and he *is* hot – I can see why Charlize said so, at least – wavy, too-long dark hair, warm brown eyes, tall.

'Who are you?' he says to me.

'Sam. And you must be Lucas somebody.'

'The one and only. It's my uncle Gil who is one of the artists; I came with him.'

'Sam is an artist, too,' Charlize says, having recovered enough to speak.

I shake my head. 'No, I'm not! I just draw a bit sometimes.'

'She paints, too.'

'Would you girls like some more champagne?' he says.

I shake my head again. 'Yes, please,' Charlize says, and he goes back through the door to inside.

'He was flirting with you!' she says. 'I'm going to do you a favour and let you have first chance.' Before I can protest he's stepping back through the door, two glasses in hand.

'Sorry,' Charlize says. 'I've just remembered I promised

to, um, do something.' And she's gone.

I thunk my forehead with my hand, shake my head. 'That was totally her idea. Not mine.'

'Damn.' He grins again, and holds out one of the glasses. 'It'd be a shame to let it go to waste.' And I find myself taking the glass and having a sip – just a sip, no more, I promise myself.

'So, how'd you end up coming with your uncle tonight?'

'I paint a bit, too, so he invited me along as his plus one.'

'How old are you?'

'Sixteen. Do you always ask this many questions?'

'No. Actually, I don't. It must be the bubbles.' I frown at my glass and have another sip, just to be sure.

'And you?'

'What?'

'How old are you?'

'Nearly sixteen.'

'Do you go to parties like this a lot?'

'Now who is asking all the questions? Only when my mother makes me.'

He really laughs then.

'What?'

'My uncle may have invited me but it was my mother who made me come tonight, too. Here's to getting through it.' He holds up his glass, clinks it against mine, and then I have to have another sip, don't I? It's a toast. It'd be rude not to.

I frown at my glass again. 'My champagne glass is mysteriously empty.'

'Another?'

'NO. No way.'

Movement inside catches my eye through the glass doors. 'Uh-oh. Looks like everyone is moving in to dinner.'

'Can we sit together?'

I shake my head. 'There'll be a seating plan. I'm bound to be on the most boring table in the world.'

'It's been fun to chat, Sam,' he says, and I find myself smiling back at him, not saying anything.

Back inside I find Mum and our boring table of important people. Lucas is halfway across the room, turned the other way, and – oh, that figures. He's at Charlize's table, and seeing them sitting together gives me an uneasy feeling inside, one that is hard to label. Either she'll decide he is open game now and he'll be next on her list of madly-in-love-withs, or that she's my second and tell him cringeworthy things about me endlessly.

At least the former is more likely. He was fun to talk to – with the fizz – and that's as far as it goes for me.

Just in case she's having an uncharacteristic moment of conscience, I text Charlize under the table: *he's all yours, babes*.

Dinner looks good, even if along the lines of weird and arty – just as well I'm hungry enough to eat anything – but I already can't breathe sitting down in this dress. I giggle to myself; imagine the press photos if I literally popped out of the seams? But after a few bites of the first course I feel sick, and just push the next ones around my plate.

Finally it is time to head home. There is much air-cheek-kissing on the way out the doors and to our car.

I see Lucas standing off to the side; he nods, smiles.

There are more flashes from the press. Our doors are held open and as soon as they shut behind us I kick off my shoes, then snuggle my wrap around myself and surreptitiously undo a few buttons on the back of my dress. Mum notices and shakes her head.

I lean back against the seat, eyes closed. My head is pounding from too much champagne with not enough to eat, and I start fantasising about what I might find if I sneak into the kitchen when we get home: I'm starving.

I'm almost drifting to sleep when the driver's microphone clicks on.

'There's a road traffic accident ahead so we're going to divert. The route has been cleared as safe, but it may be a little … colourful.'

Mum sighs. 'Whatever next?' she says.

My eyes are open now: colourful? Whatever that means, I want to see it.

At first it looks like everywhere else, but gradually the streets are narrower, the shops smaller – some with broken windows or boarded up. Rubbish is piled up against buildings. There are symbols painted on some of the walls – I can almost make them out – something like 'A4A'? Slogans are painted alongside but we go past too quickly for me to read them. On one corner, there is a group of people on the street, drinking something out of a bag. They look at our cars with a mixture of curiosity and contempt.

Another turn. There are people huddled in doorways, lying down. Are they *sleeping* there, on the street? My eyes widen.

We stop at a red light.

A woman gets up and comes to my door. She knocks on the window: it's two-way glass, so I can see out but she can't see in. She's holding a small child; another one clings to her leg.

'Please. Help me feed my children,' she says. 'Please!' And the child in her arms – his or her eyes are half open, staring, in skin and bone and shadows, like the woman and other child. I'm horrified, sick, unable to believe what my eyes are seeing.

'Mum?'

She doesn't answer.

'Mum!' I turn to her and her face is blank, eyes fixed straight ahead. 'Didn't you see them? Can we do something?'

But then the lights change to green and we're gone.

8

Ava

Sam is already there when I get to the tutor room. She's half lying down on the table, head on her arms. Eyes closed.

I open and shut the door again, this time more loudly.

She jumps, sits up. Yawns. She's pale, with faint shadows under her eyes.

'Are you all right?' I say.

'Hmm? Yes. Just tired, and I've got a bit of a headache. Didn't get much sleep last night.'

'I saw the photos in the newspaper. A charity dinner?'

'Something like that.'

'Does that mean you didn't start any of your other homework?'

'Nope. Not my fault, though; I didn't want to go.'

'No matter whose fault it may be, your English assignment is due tomorrow, isn't it? Let's have a look at that first. Then there's some science coursework, also due tomorrow.'

She groans. 'Nooooo. That's too much. Just one subject, and then I need to take a break.'

'Maybe a short one.'

'How about this: we do some boring stuff, then we'll draw each other?'

I'm surprised, but I have heard she's really good at art — or maybe that has been exaggerated because of who she is.

'I can't draw at all,' I say, but I'm curious how she would draw me.

'Well, then; you can try and I'll give you some pointers. So that way I can teach you something, too.'

I hesitate. I'm not sure the approval would be there for spending part of this hour doing anything other than schoolwork, but will it help convince her to do more of it?

'All right,' I say. 'But only if you *finish* the English assignment first.'

I open the folder and Sam makes a gagging noise. 'Seriously, though, write a love sonnet about Romeo from Juliet's point of view? They're both bonkers: no boy is worth dying for. And that love at first sight stuff is such a crock.'

I'm surprised to hear Sam say these things: most of the girls in this school are always mooning around about some boy or another. 'Some might say that maybe you feel that way because you've never met the right one.'

'Another myth: *the* right one. Like there is only one person in the entire world exactly right for each of us. What would be the odds of finding them? I'd say so close to zero there'd be no point in even trying.'

'You don't have to believe it; just *pretend* that you are Juliet, and you've just seen Romeo, and you believe in love at first sight and that this is it.'

'And make it into a sonnet.'

'Only fourteen lines. Maybe it would help if you pretend that you want to draw him?'

Sam tilts her head to one side, thinking. 'Do you mean making the sonnet like a drawing in words?'

'Why not?'

She stares at the blank pages of her notebook, then picks up a pen.

9

Sam

So much of my life is pretend. I've become so good at being what I'm supposed to be, that who I really am seems lost.

I try to put myself into Juliet's mind, imagine how she feels, and then begin both: a drawing on one side of my notebook, words on the other. Actually, it does help, connecting it with drawing in this way. Ava watches, making suggestions of things to think about when I get stuck; she reminds me of the correct rhyme scheme for a sonnet when I wouldn't bother.

She touches my drawing of Romeo when it's done. It's sort of Lucas, but I've made him so perfect he's almost repulsive: will the teacher get the joke? Does Ava?

'He's a caricature,' she says: she does, and I'm pleased.

'That's done: it's time for a break,' I say, but as I say it the lights go out. No warning, no flickering, just one second the room is brightly lit and the next, dark. The doors are shut, there are no windows in this small tutor room – it's completely pitch black.

Panic – automatic and stupid – kicks in, my heart racing, my stomach clenching, and I fumble in my pocket for my phone. I get it out and put the torch on. With its thin light in the dark room I start to breathe easier.

'What's going on?' Ava say.

'Maybe the power is out?'

I open the door and look out into the darkened hallway. No one is there. I turn back to the room and Ava has gone through an adjoining door to the room next to ours: it has a window.

'It's not just the school,' she says. 'The lights are off all around.'

I check the charge on my phone: I forgot to plug it in last night. It's only got eleven per cent. How long will that last? These old buildings don't have many windows and I want to get outside, *now*; into the air and light.

'I think this is a sign that we're done for the day,' I say.

'Agreed,' Ava says.

We gather our things, head down the narrow hall with the thin pool of light from my phone the only thing to show the way. We open the door and step out into the courtyard between buildings. There are other people emerging, too – teachers, a few students who've stayed late for one reason or another. We walk towards the offices and main exit, but before we reach it the deputy head comes out.

'We've been asked to keep everyone here for now,' she says, and before she finishes her sentence there are sirens sounding – not that far away.

'What's happening?' one of the teachers asks, a note of apprehension in her voice, and the deputy head gives her a look.

'I'm sure everything is fine. Maybe it's just because the roads will gridlock without the lights working? We're looking into it. For now, either stay here in the courtyard or go into the library. The caretakers have started to sweep the buildings; we'll get everyone to go there.'

The others go through the doors to the library, but I head for a bench by the entrance – wanting to stay outside in the daylight. Ava hesitates.

'Go in if you want to,' I say.

She sits next to me instead, and I'm both relieved not to be alone and annoyed to feel that way.

'You finished your English homework,' she says. 'A deal's a deal: we could draw each other out here? But I'm not very good, so don't be offended.'

'I won't be.' And I get out the pencils and sketchpad that are always in my schoolbag, tear off a few sheets and give them to Ava. Something else to do will take my mind off the time. How long until the natural light is gone? The sun is low in the sky already.

'I don't know where to start,' Ava says.

'Try one thing – like, say, a lock of hair. Doesn't have to be the whole face. Focus on the detail – you can make it is as exact as possible, or change it if you see it differently with your inner artist's eye.'

'Not sure I have one! But I'll try.'

She's staring at me intently now, pencil in hand, looking down to her page and making a start, looking up again. I'm still studying her face – the proportions. She is … arresting, rather than pretty: she draws the eye. High cheekbones: she has good bone structure. Slightly wide-set eyes; long lashes – but not a trace of makeup to make them that way. Her dark, straight hair is tucked behind her left ear and falls forward on the right, down past her shoulders. Her gaze is intense, always: she's in the moment, concentrating completely on what she is doing. To capture her, *this* is what I have to show on the page. Pencil to paper, I begin.

I lied yesterday. We may not have spoken before but I did know who she is, and this isn't the first time I've drawn her. In the sea of made-up faces and carefully arranged hair in this school, she is somehow different. I was so surprised to find her in the room when I was dragged there yesterday that I had to compose myself before I sat down. There is something about her that I've tried to capture before and not quite got. Now that she is in front of me, I'm determined.

She isn't really part of the social scene of this place and doesn't have any close friends that I've noticed: she is somehow her own separate person amongst all the cliques. She's quite isolated. Is she lonely? She doesn't seem to be. She's more … self-contained, like the rest of us don't matter that much, or even register. And no one seems to target her with the usual bitchiness, even though she's a scholarship student and dresses, well, not the best. This place can be unforgiving of that sort of thing, with students like Charlize and Ruth who basically have wardrobes as big as most houses. If I dressed like Ava does the claws would be out; I'd end up in the newspapers on the Worst Dressed list. I'm curious; wistful, even. How does she get away with it?

I'm aware she's stopped drawing now, that she's

waiting for me to finish. She leans forward a little to look but I angle my sketchpad away.

'Not yet!'

She sits back again and I continue working on her eyes, smudging the dark lines a little ...

I'm concentrating so much that when she clears her throat I jump.

'Can you even see what you are doing any more?' she says.

The light is almost gone and I hadn't noticed; my fear rushes back now that I do. The power isn't on yet in the buildings around us, but there are flickering lights through the library windows. They must have found candles or something.

'Let's go in now,' I say, and close my sketchbook.

'Can I see?'

I hesitate, wanting to get it right first, so I stall. 'Yes, but later? Here it's too dark, and I'd rather not have everyone inside looking at it like they will if I show you in there.'

'All right. Just a moment; I'll call my dad before we go in.'

She gets her phone out of her bag and it is practically an antique; it's hard to believe it'll even work. But then she is saying hello, that she's still at school and about the power. She's listening, says goodbye. Turns back to me, and her eyes are wider.

'Dad says this whole area of London is in lockdown.'

'Is he in the police?'

She shakes her head, hesitates. 'He's a taxi driver.' She says it almost defiantly, as if waiting for me to react.

I didn't know that, and I'm sure if anyone at school did the word would have got around – even if she is under the radar that isn't the kind of thing that would be ignored here if known. Has she told me something she doesn't usually say? 'He always knows what is happening, and where,' she says.

I take out my phone: it was on silent. There are missed calls from Dad's assistant, then one from Dad, then his text: *are you still at school? Stay there*.

I dial.

10

Ava

Nervous faces are lit by candles in the library. Sam draws away from the edges, close to the wavering light and into the centre of the circle of people. Her eyes flick to the darkened corners of the room as if afraid what might lurk in the shadows.

We sit down. There are a few dozen teachers, half as many students. They are scattered around, some chatting, some reading or staring at their hands with the ghostly light of their phones reflected in their eyes as they text or do whatever it is that they endlessly do.

The deputy head comes over to us. 'We're just waiting to hear from the police when we can leave.' She doesn't ask Sam anything, but there is an almost-question in the pause at the end of what she said. Others are looking over, listening.

Sam shrugs. 'All I know is that the roads are shut.' She doesn't say the rest of what she told me outside after she spoke to her father: that the police are checking the area, that they think the power grid was sabotaged.

Then the overhead lights flicker and come back on, and everyone cheers.

A moment later, Sam's phone rings.

'Yes … uh-huh … twenty minutes? Can we take Ava home, too? … OK, I'll text the address in a minute.'

She hangs up. 'Driver is on the way.'

'We haven't been told anyone can leave yet,' the deputy head says, but then her phone rings; she confirms it. People start putting on coats, saying goodbye, wondering aloud what was going on, why they had to wait so long to leave. Teachers check with all the students that they have someone to collect them.

'We'll take Ava,' Sam says when someone gets to us.

We're putting our coats on now, too, then we walk to the gates.

'What is your address?' Sam says.

'I can get myself home, it's all right.'

'Don't be daft; it's late, and who knows what has been going on out there. I just need your address as they have to clear the route or some nonsense like that first.'

'Thank you, but no.'

Sam looks concerned, then glances back the way we came; is she looking for the deputy head? I say goodbye and make my way to the side gate of the school quickly before she can tell her, or argue any further.

I key in the code to exit the gate, then walk fast up the road to the turn to the bus stop.

The road is quiet, few people are about. Part of me thinks I was crazy not to get a lift. What if the bus isn't running this late, or doesn't turn up?

Why didn't I? I sigh. I know, but I don't want to admit it to myself.

I didn't want her to see where we live. That's it, isn't it?

Just when I think I've finally managed to stop caring what they all think, now this. And it's even worse than that. It's not just anyone, it's her.

11

Sam

One set of gates opens; it shuts behind the car, and then the next opens. These probably wouldn't even have worked with the power out. We could have been imprisoned by all the safety measures – huh! Though surely they must have emergency releases?

Why was the power sabotaged? Around our school it's all big houses, expensive shops and restaurants – all places that have security: gates like these ones, alarm systems, cameras.

It's almost all electronic stuff. Some of it might have battery backup, but anything without backup must have emergency releases when the power is out – you couldn't have gates that locked you in during a blackout. What if there was a fire or something?

I'm uneasy. The police know all this; is that why they closed the roads, told us to stay where we were while they checked everything?

Traffic is light, and the knot of tension inside me eases as we move further from the school, closer to home.

Then there are sharp sounds, somewhere behind us –

like a car backfiring? But again and again. Is someone *shooting* at somebody?

I hit the sound button to the front of the car.

'What's happening?'

'Police operations. Not a concern for our journey.'

Is Ava all right? The sounds were roughly back the way we came, but I don't know where she lives, where she was headed or how she was going to get there, so I can't even check. I'm sick with fear for her. Why wouldn't she come with us?

These first few tutoring sessions haven't been what I thought they'd be. I mean, Ava has made me work – somehow – but it's the other stuff, too, like the things we talked about. And drawing her.

Today I was more open with Ava than I can remember having been with anyone in ages, and I'm not sure why. Maybe it was just because I'm so short of sleep that I didn't know what I was saying.

Like about not believing in love in first sight. My friends wouldn't agree with me; it's mostly what they go on about. Charlize has been my friend since we were five: we used to tell each other *everything*. We were closer than I have ever been to anyone outside of my own family. But things changed when she discovered boys: she's in love with someone new every other week, and that is mostly all she ever wants to talk about now. So of course I haven't said anything like that to her.

And that stuff I said about not believing there can be one person out there we are somehow fated to be with. No one I've ever met has even come close.

Ava is somehow different from all of my friends. I was

really trying to draw her, just as she is, but I couldn't get her eyes how I wanted them. I want her to pose again; I *need* her to.

Please be OK, Ava.

I barely know her. If *any* girl in my school was in danger, hurt, I'd care, but this feels so far beyond that. I don't understand.

12

Ava

The temperature is dropping and I pull my coat closer around myself as I walk.

The road I would usually turn down now to catch the bus is closed. I walk around further and further and there are more roads with orange and white barriers – police – and they look alert, nervous. I'm not sure which way to try next.

Dad would know the best way to go – taxi drivers always do – and I hesitate, think of calling him, but if I do he'll worry and it's not like he can come and get me with all the closures. I head for a corner shop I go to sometimes to ask if they know, but when I get there it's closed. It's never closed. I look around me and it really hits home then, how empty the area is just now – and so quiet, too, like the street, buildings and empty pavements are holding their breath. Where is everyone?

More police cars go past now at speed and then sound replaces the silence: yelling and crashing, and then there is banging, even louder, that reverberates in my ears – and screaming. Was that gunfire?

At least the way to go is clear now – away from the

sound. I hurry in the other direction, wanting to run, but not sure if I should: police in London don't like it when you run, these days. I walk and walk until the sounds are distant and I'm exhausted, far from where I should be and completely lost. At last there are people around again – though not as many as you'd expect on a clear evening – but I start to breathe easier.

My phone vibrates with a call; it's Dad.

I answer. 'Hi.'

'Where are you?'

'I'm not sure. I was heading for the bus, but had to walk the wrong way.'

'I'd guessed that might be the case. Work out where you are, and I'll come and get you.'

I should say no. I'm seventeen; I'm away from whatever was happening; I should be able to find the tube or a bus and get myself home.

Instead I walk to the corner, and read out the names on the street signs to him so he can find me.

13

Sam

I can't sleep, and finally get up again. Dad would be able to find out if Ava is OK, I'm sure of it. The police must know if anything happened to her; they'd tell Dad if he asked them. It's been years since he left Scotland Yard but he has connections enough to get quick answers. I go to the front of the house and watch for him through a window that overlooks the main entrance.

It's gone midnight when his car finally appears. I wait for him at the top of the stairs.

'Hi, Dad.'

'Sam? You're still up?'

'Yes, I want to ask you something.' But in the middle of saying that my phone vibrates in my hand. I glance down.

This is Ava, I was given your number as your tutor. Didn't want you to worry: I'm safe home. Goodnight.

'What's that?' Dad says.

I shake my head. 'I was worried about someone — never mind, they've said they're all right now.' Did she only just get home, after all this time? Or maybe she only just thought to text. Huh.

He leans forward, puts an arm around my shoulders. 'As you're up you might as well have a celebratory drink with me. Mine'll be whisky. How about a hot chocolate?'

'What are we celebrating?'

'Things have gone very well tonight. Come on.'

I follow him to the small kitchen off his offices, surprised he's saying *celebrate* instead of *sleep* on a school night. Unless he knows there's no school tomorrow?

'Does this have anything to do with my school or what was happening around there?'

'Yes. The power outages were a ploy. There were attacks planned around the area: we stopped them.'

'Near my *school*?' I'm shocked. I've been going there since I was eleven. I've often felt bored there; trapped, too, with all the fences and gates and security – but I've always felt safe.

'I was monitoring the situation. And things were under control – or I'd have been there in a helicopter to pick you up. It's a promise.'

He's poured the whisky; the kettle whistles and he pours water into a cup and stirs in instant hot chocolate. I haven't had it here in months; it's probably out of date. 'There you go,' he says.

'How close to my school were these things happening?'

'Close.'

'And what will be going on around there tomorrow?'

'The entire neighbourhood is being checked and searched; your school will be closed for at least a day.'

I clink my cup against his glass. 'Yay! For sure?'

He nods. 'Don't get used to it.'

'Who was behind it all? What were they going to do?'

'This is all being released soon so I guess I can tell you. Say nothing until tomorrow.'

'Of course I generally have a conference call with the press after midnight, but I'll cancel it just this once.'

'See that you do. Have you heard of A4A? Anarchy for All?'

'A4A? I saw some graffiti of that the other day from the car; that was the first I'd heard of them, though.'

'They are one of those fringe groups, wanting chaos, destruction. They sabotaged the power grid as a first step in staging a number of attacks through bypassing vulnerable security systems – at homes, businesses. Their targets seemed random. But we knew about it in advance, let them get into place and then rounded them up. It was a resounding success for our police and security forces.' His glass clinks my cup again.

But I feel cold now and holding on to a mug of hot chocolate isn't helping. Attacks were planned near my school? '*Why* would they want to do these things?' But even as I'm saying the words I'm remembering snatches of half-heard conversations, bleak graffiti, and the woman by our car pleading for help to feed her children. Anarchists don't recognise authority that have made their lives this way: that's it, isn't it? They want to destroy order, break things down.

'*Why* they want these things is beyond the imagination of any rational person,' Dad says. 'But don't worry about it: we stopped them. We're rounding up the rest of their contacts now; they won't get another chance to cause trouble.'

One of those fringe groups, he said: even if they manage

to track them all down this time, what about the next one?

'Stop looking so serious and head off to sleep. Even without school being open I'm sure you've got work you can do on your own tomorrow. How are things going with that tutor?'

'Fine. I mean, she's all right.'

'See if you can get her to come around tomorrow.'

Not much later I'm walking, fast, back to my room – almost running, as if by going fast enough I could leave it all behind. There are too many things crowding in that I don't want to think about, and none of the usual things to distract me, either, with no school tomorrow. I don't want to be on my own all day, but I don't want to be where I'd usually go, either: if I go to Charlize's she'll be endlessly planning her birthday party, probably make me give detailed opinions on every possible combination of outfit and shoes. She'll never just accept I like one better than another, she wants to know exactly why, and while I've done this before many times it seems so unimportant just now.

Dad said to get Ava around, and I'm half-horrified to think a day off school could be ruined with studying – but only half. Does Dad or one of his aides have her number to contact her themselves? Even if so I'm guessing they've got other things on their minds just now. If I don't remind him he'll probably forget.

I close my bedroom door and get out the drawing of Ava I started: it's getting there, but it's still not right. Something is missing.

And Ava texted me: *I've* got her number.

Is it too late to answer her? Before I can change my mind I tap at the screen: *glad 2 hear u r ok, i was worried! I've got inside info school is closed 2moro: come around?*

I don't expect an answer – it's after one a.m. now – but it beeps a moment later when I'm brushing my teeth.

Sounds good.

I get into bed, pull up the covers. My night light is on but its thin light isn't enough to stop the shadows creeping closer tonight. The fear is coming back. I get up and put the desk lamp on, too.

Blankets snuggled in close around me. Extra pillows both sides to make a nest. Bumble the lion guarding my back.

But it's still not enough. I fight to keep my tired eyes open: when they're closed, everything disappears.

It's dark.

I can't see anything. I open my eyes wide and then wider and I still can't see. Every monster in the world could be there next to me and I wouldn't know it. And I'm crying and scared, more scared than I could imagine ever being.

Still nobody comes.

I won't be bad any more, I promise: just take me home. Please.

My eyes are fixed wide open and now there are spots in the darkness that come and go – I swat at them but nothing is there. My hearts thuds faster and louder.

Please take me home ...

14
Ava

'A house the size of the Coliseum,' Dad says, and he's only exaggerating a little. From what I can see of it through the high fences and gates, it's huge and sprawling: three storeys, or maybe four? Landscaped grounds stretch around it as well. This whole neighbourhood is gated – contained, controlled. I bet security here has emergency generator backups, instant police response, the lot.

It's so different from most of the streets we passed on our way.

I'm feeling sick deep in my stomach. I don't belong here; I knew it would be like this. Why did I say I'd come? I could just about deal with tutoring Sam at school – even though it was her – in my home away from home, I felt, I don't know, like I was still in charge. I won't feel that way here.

But it's too late. Dad is pulling up to the security gates; he pushes the button.

'Yes?' A disembodied voice.

'Taxi here with Ava Nicholls.'

There's a pause, and then the gate swings slowly open. There are two guards in front of a small guardhouse, and they are armed. Do all these big houses have these measures now, or is it because her dad is a politician?

One of them gestures us forwards and we pull in between gates. He taps on my window, holds out a hand for my identity card and I give it to him. He studies it, looks at me, then nods and hands it back. Speaks into a microphone on his headset.

We wait but the next gates to the driveway don't open. Instead a woman comes out through a narrow door next to them.

'Looks like I'm not allowed through to the inner sanctum,' Dad says, an annoyed note in his voice. 'Away you go, then.'

I take a deep breath and open the door, getting out as she approaches.

'Hello, Ava? I'm Penny.' She smiles. 'I'll take you through.' She has money in her hand to pay for the taxi and I can see Dad is about to wave it away, but it's a big fare.

I turn back to the car to gather up my coat and books. 'You might as well take it,' I say in a low voice. 'If I'd come in a different taxi they'd get paid.'

He takes it but I can tell he hates it. Places like this – moments like this, when he remembers how much we need the money – sharpen his bitterness, remind him what he lost when his university department closed. Classics wasn't high enough priority for the cost of it; his PhD became useless overnight.

'Call when you're done,' he says, and waves with a set look on his face.

I turn and follow Penny through the next gate.

Penny seems oblivious to any atmosphere; she's probably in the category that doesn't notice the existence of taxi drivers unless it is to argue that they're not taking the best route. Going by her dismissive glance at my jeans and long-sleeved T-shirt, I don't think she's that sure about me, either. We walk up the footpath to a side door, not the big grand front one, and go in.

'Just a moment,' Penny says, and uses an intercom near the door.

'Samantha, Ava is here.'

'Bring her up, please,' Sam's voice says.

'This way,' Penny says. I follow her through a door that leads to a hall, a staircase. At the landing at the top I can see the ornate curved staircase in the middle that must lead down to the main doors. We go up another set of stairs, down another hall, and I lose count of the rooms we go past. This place is even bigger than it looks from the front. The ceilings are high; there are paintings on the walls that look like the real deal. I feel like I'm in a museum. What a place to live: could it ever feel like home?

We round a corner and then Sam is there, walking towards us.

'Hi,' she says. 'Thanks, Penny. I'll show Ava the rest of the way. Could you have tea sent to my studio, please?'

'Of course.'

Sam is in jeans, too, but even though they're faded they sit exactly as they should; they cling to her without being tight and have that designer look. A casual red shirt sits off her shoulder on one side like she just threw it on in a hurry. I was one of the few starting sixth form who was sad to say goodbye to school uniforms; as a scholarship student mine were supplied, and made me look more like everybody else. But Sam? Even in uniform at school she always looks effortlessly *right*, and this in a school where most go to a lot of effort. And today, too, without a trace of makeup or jewellery. It's somehow even more intimidating that she doesn't seem to try, that she's just … amazing, as she is.

'What?' she says, and straightens her shirt.

Was I staring? 'Sorry.' I look around us. 'I'm just a bit stunned by this house you live in.'

'It's big. Most of it completely soulless, though,' she says. 'I can give you a tour if you want.' I can tell she doesn't want, so I shake my head even though I'm curious.

'I'll take you to my corner of it,' she says, and we go to a door. She holds it open and then her eyes focus on what I'm carrying. 'That's rather a lot of books.'

'According to your teachers you're behind in most subjects.'

'All the joy!' We go down a hall and then she stops at another door. 'This is me.'

She opens it. Inside is a huge bedroom – bed, desk, bookshelves, wardrobes, even a sofa; a door at the far end – en suite, maybe? – and another door she leads me to now. Is this what she called her studio? There's a *keep out* sign painted on the door, with a gruesomely accurate skull.

Through it is a bright mess. One wall is all huge windows, and even on a greyish day like today natural light fills the room. The other walls have been painted with scenes from what looks like *Lord of the Rings* on one wall, *Harry Potter* on another, and every spare inch has other paintings or drawings pinned up. There are tables covered in drawing materials, paints, brushes. One table in the middle is almost clear and she moves some things away from that one; when she gestures I put my stuff down there.

'Did you do all of these? And the walls, too?'

She's shifting from one foot to another: is she embarrassed? 'Yes. I went through a phase when paper or canvas weren't big enough. I mean to paint over it but never get around to it.'

'But it's amazing!' My books are forgotten on the table now as I go around and look at first one painting or sketch, then another.

There's a knock on the door and Sam goes through, comes back with a tray. 'They're not allowed in here. I don't usually use this space to study, but I like the light for drawing. That's why you're here, you know. I didn't get to finish my drawing yesterday, and a deal's a deal. Not sure why you've brought all *that*.' She grimaces at my books as she puts the tray on the table next to them.

She's kidding – I think. Isn't she? I don't take the bait. '*I* finished my drawing; it's not my fault you're slow.'

'Did you bring it?'

'Yes. But I'm not showing it until you show me yours.'

'That's fair, once it's done. Tea first?'

There are biscuits, cakes, scones. 'This is all for us?'

'Our cook thinks I need fattening up. Mum isn't here today; *she* thinks I need to go on a diet.' She rolls her eyes.

'What? No, you don't – either way.'

Sam shrugs. 'I eat what I want, unless one of them is

[67]

watching. So please have loads and then when the tray goes back, they'll be happy in the kitchen.'

I tuck into a scone with cream and jam – it's perfect.

'What happened after you left last night?' Sam says, between bites of a biscuit. 'You should have come with us.'

'Probably,' I admit. 'Dad wasn't happy with me either. It was OK, though. He ended up coming to pick me up.'

'But we heard gunshots behind us, not long after we left. Were you near that?'

'Not far, I think. I went in the other direction so didn't see much: just police going past in a big rush. It's been all over the news today – that they stopped these attacks that were planned.'

Sam nods. 'Dad told me last night. He was in a good mood about it when he got in, said they were rounding them up. According to the news this morning it's all over.' She looks down when she says that, as if something about it is on her mind still.

'According to the news, you said: is there more that isn't in the news?'

'Isn't there always?' She shrugs. 'Nothing I know about. Dad would never tell me anything that isn't going to be headlines in five minutes. Speaking of dads, was that yours who brought you?'

I nod.

'You should have told me it was him! I'd have got him to come in. Though Penny's eyebrows might have got stuck in the up position on seeing that your dad is ...' She stops, looks embarrassed.

'What – that my dad is a taxi driver?'

'I'm sorry. I didn't mean anything by that.'

'It's OK, it doesn't matter,' I say, but it does. Is it that he does what he does, or that Sam knows how people would view it? Maybe she is the same. I'm not even sure what part of that bothers me the most. I change the subject. 'Who is Penny?'

'Like an assistant housekeeper or something? She's OK really, but nosy.'

'So doing a head count, you have two guards out front, a cook, an assistant housekeeper – which suggests a housekeeper, too – and you, your mum and dad?'

'Yep. And a team of gardeners. Maids. Drivers and more security that come and go, depending what is happening. Sneaking out of here is almost impossible.'

'Almost?'

She grins, but doesn't say more on that one. 'Have you had enough?'

I nod, she takes the tray out, returns. 'All right.' She looks around, pulls a chair nearer the window. 'Sit here.'

I get up, sit on the chair. She sets up a small easel nearby.

'I'm only going along with this if we do another subject afterwards,' I say.

'Sure. Of course. But then after that it'll be my turn to choose what we do next.'

'I'm not sure your parents, who are paying me, would think we should do anything but schoolwork.'

'Tough. Mum is oblivious in this area – and she's at her spa. And Dad is at Westminster for the day. No one else comes in here; they won't know. Now stop talking.'

She's intent, her face tilted to an angle. 'Turn a little

to your left; no, too much.' I move back to the right a little but she shakes her head, comes over.

Her hand is warm and light on my cheek. She turns my face slightly, stands back. Now she lightly touches my chin, tilts my face up just a fraction more to the light.

She stands back. 'There. Now try not to move.'

She sits on a stool by her easel, pencils in hand, eyes on me again, considering, but it's almost like she's not seeing me. Does she instead see a line here, shading there – just marks on a page?

I stay still, so still I'm almost not breathing. I feel light-headed – held in place by a spell, cast to stone. Frozen so still inside myself I may never come out.

15

Sam

She's a good subject: once I told her to be quiet and still, she was – her face stayed at the best angle to the light.

But I *still* can't get her eyes the way I want – I can't read them, not at all.

Finally I sigh, and unclip my sketchbook from the easel. It makes a snapping sound and Ava jumps, then breathes in deeply. She rolls her shoulders, looks at her watch. Her eyes open wider.

'Look at the time! We should get to work.'

I glance at the clock on the wall behind her and I'm surprised too: it's been almost two hours since Ava arrived. When I'm obsessing over a drawing I stop noticing time.

'I'm sorry for making you stay still for so long,' I say. 'You should have said if you needed a break.'

She shrugs. 'I didn't realise. I think I was asleep with my eyes open. I didn't get much sleep last night.'

'Me neither. Did you dream?'

'Last night, or just now?'

'Now.'

A half-smile. 'If I did, I forget,' she says, and I'm not sure I believe her. 'Can I see?'

'I guess so. But I'm not happy with it.' She comes around, and when she sees what I've done her mouth drops open.

'Oh! That is so good! It's exactly me.'

And I look between my drawing, and Ava in the flesh, and I can see why she says that. The detail focus is there, but at the same time it is not the version of her I was searching for when I drew her.

'Why aren't you happy with it?'

'It's hard to explain. It looks like you, how you are in the world. But at the same time it isn't *you*.'

'You've lost me. I think it's brilliant.' She turns to her book, pulls out a sheet of paper. Waggles it. 'Now you'll see how bad I am at this.' She hands it to me.

It's my eyes, but drawn separately. One looks up to the right, the other down, so the lid across it obscures most of the eye. And OK, the proportions are wonky and they're not a copy of something in the way that mine is – but it's interesting.

'Why did you choose eyes?'

She shrugs. 'I don't know. When you said to pick something, some part of the face, it was what interested me.'

'It's more abstract than representative – which is fine if that is what you wanted. But if you want it more like the real thing, look at it like maths: fractions. I know you like maths.'

'How do you mean?'

'If you look at my eye, what fraction of the iris is the

pupil? What fraction of the white is the iris? It's about studying the detail and getting the proportions correct.'

'Or I could just say I meant to be abstract.'

I laugh. 'Exactly. Do you want to trade them?'

'Really? Do you mean I can have this one of me?'

'Of course. I'll try again another time – take it.'

'I'll give it to my dad. Thank you.'

'Here – sign yours and I'll sign mine. It's what artists do – apparently!' I initial it at the bottom, and she does likewise.

She holds the one of herself, examining it again. 'You're so talented.'

I shrug. 'Drawing is just what I do. What I've always done. But it's all fantasy, isn't it? It doesn't seem' – I pause – 'real enough any more.' I wave at the walls around us. 'Of course a lot of this was fantasy on purpose, but now that I want real, I can't seem to get things how I want them on the page.'

'If you're as bored as you seem with academic subjects, why don't you push to study art? Learn as much as you can; make it as real as you can. You could be great.'

I draw my arms in around myself, uneasy. 'Maybe I don't want to be.'

'Why not?'

'Not everyone is driven like you are. Why do you work so hard at school?'

'I want to go to a good university, get a good job. No one is going to give me anything if I don't work for it.' Then she bites her lip. 'Sorry, I didn't mean that the way it sounded.'

'It's OK,' I say, even though it stung – if only because

it's true. 'But just because you are driven like that doesn't mean everyone is.'

'But I look around this room and on every wall I see how talented you are. And I see how you love it, too: I saw you drawing, so lost in what you were doing that you didn't notice hours going past. You are an artist, whether you want to be one or not. Why not strive to be a great one?'

As she's talking I see something flash in her eyes that wasn't there before; it is that *something* that was missing from my drawing, that I'm itching to try to capture — though if it is anything like the other times, as soon as I take out a sketchbook what I thought I saw will disappear.

Instead I shake my head. 'Look, I can't explain it in a way that makes sense, but I've just never seen myself much beyond *now*. Especially lately.'

'Is now enough for you?'

'Sometimes,' I say, but it isn't, and I'm annoyed. She's pushing me to think about things I don't want to.

Before I can say anything else, though, her phone rings. She starts to reach for it, and then mine rings, too.

16

Ava

'Hi, Dad. What's up?'

'Something's going on. I was going to say I'll come and get you right away, but too many roads are closed. I can't get there.'

'What's happening? Are you all right?'

'You know me: always fine. And I don't know what it is: they've closed a network of roads to cut off some areas, like where you are.'

I glance at Sam; she's off her phone now. 'Wait, I'll see if they know anything here. Sam?'

'That was an aide of Dad's. He said there's been some incident, but he didn't know what. People are spilling out on to the streets all over the place, stopping traffic. You can't leave; connecting roads to key areas have been closed as a precaution, and Dad said you must stay with us until things calm down.'

'Did you hear that?' I say to my dad on the phone.

'Yes.'

'Sounds like I'm stuck here.'

'Promise me you won't try to get yourself home. *Don't* leave without talking to me first.'

'I promise,' I say, and I mean it: what happened after I left school last night – well, it shook me. I don't want to repeat it.

We say goodbye, and I look at Sam, the implications sinking in: I'm *staying* here? 'Sorry. Looks like I'll have to stay until the roads are open again. What do you think is happening?'

'I don't know. It sounds like something different.'

'Maybe your dad set it up to imprison a tutor in your house until you pass all your exams.'

'Huh! I wouldn't put it past him. But you can ask him yourself: his aide said he's coming home later, so he'll be here for dinner. Mum is out.'

'He can get home?'

'You can still get from Westminster to here if you really want to, apparently – just not much beyond either. There's some meeting he's having here before dinner so he has to come back.'

'Oh. All right.' I feel uncomfortable. Dinner? In this house? With the deputy prime minister. And Sam.

'Let's catch the news and see what they're saying,' Sam says. She gets up and I follow her back into her bedroom. She picks up a remote and points it; a door that I thought was part of her wardrobe opens to reveal a TV. She sits on the side of her bed, gestures at a desk chair for me.

'Ready?' Without waiting for an answer she points the remote again, turns the TV on. It's already on the twenty-four-hour BBC news channel.

'... just in. There will be a press conference with the Mayor of London and security forces at four p.m., followed by the prime minister live at Downing Street.'

I glance at the clock on her desk: it's 3:45.

In the meantime they shuffle through the same reports about last night that were on earlier: the blackout, the police response. The security forces' raids on houses in London, Birmingham, Manchester, Glasgow. Swift and decisive action against A4A. But now they add that there are rumours of unrest in London in connection with the raids, and widespread road closures.

The press conference begins: the mayor summarises the news reports we've just watched, with emphasis on the events in London – the locations of raids, number of arrests. Then they take questions.

'How did the security forces know what A4A were planning?'

'I know you understand that we can't reveal sensitive security information. This success shows we can trust in those who protect the people of London.'

'There are reports of heavy-handed police action in the raids. Can you comment?'

'Regrettably, tough measures were required to make the city safe for all of us. We can't risk any of these terrorists getting away.'

Someone whispers something in the mayor's ear, and they wind things up before anyone can ask anything else.

'They're hiding something,' Sam says. 'I wonder what it is?'

'Politicians are always hiding something,' I say, then realise she might think I mean her father. 'I'm sorry, I didn't mean—'

'It's all right. It's true enough,' she says, but she looks

uncomfortable as she says it – like how I felt when she said Penny would raise her eyebrows at my dad being a taxi driver.

'It may sometimes be valid to keep things back.'

'Or not.'

The screen has changed to 10 Downing Street; Prime Minister Powell walks out. She smiles tiredly in a rumpled suit.

'Our fearless leader,' Sam says. Sarcasm. 'I've had enough, do you mind?'

I shake my head and she hits the off button on the remote. The prime minister disappears without a word.

'Doesn't your father like Powell?' I say, curious. 'He put her into power.'

'I am actually allowed to have my own opinions occasionally.'

'Sorry, I didn't mean that you didn't—'

'Chill; I know. It's just a sore point, having to maintain a united front all the time in public. But I don't say stuff for my dad; you can ask him about the PM if you want to. And whatever the PM may think she wants to do, she never seems to actually *do* anything, does she? I mean, I don't think she's a bad person – she's just a crap leader.'

'The election last year was … shocking, wasn't it? Were you following it?'

'Whether I wanted to or not. But it was kind of exciting. And everyone was so freaked out when the usual parties were voted out, and that Armstrong's Law and Order Party got the most seats but no clear majority. And of course then everything got turned on its head again when Dad's Freedom UK Party made a deal with the Reform Party instead of with Armstrong to form the government.'

'No one knew what would happen until it did. Did you?'

'No. But there was something Dad said the day before – you won't tell anyone, will you?'

'Of course not,' I say.

'I remember him saying, would you prefer the company of rats, or the sinking ship?'

'Which did he think was which?'

'He never said. But either way it was a decision he didn't want to have to make. With all the uncertainty and trouble already in the country he said that it'd be worse for everyone to have another election, and so he had to choose – and that he had to do what he felt was right for the most people, no matter what he thought personally.'

I'm fascinated, watching Sam: the emotions that flit across her face as she talks – about things I've discussed many times before, but she has been inside all of it.

'You and your dad must be close: your eyes shine when you speak about him.'

'Do they?' She's embarrassed. 'Yes, I guess we've always been close. Though I see less of him than I used to.'

'Now that you've seen how things are going with the government, which would you choose? Would you prefer the company of rats, or the sinking ship?'

Sam grins. 'Rats, of course. Who wants to sink? But what if it is all a trick and they are *all* rats, both on and off the ship, and no choice is the right choice: what then?' The darkness in her eyes goes against her smile. 'Enough politics,' she says. 'I might even rather do some homework.'

'Excellent. Let's get that science assignment done.'

'If and only if we can do what *I* want tonight.'

'What?'

'Not telling.'

'Hmm. I might regret this, but all right.'

17

Sam

Ava looks so different in some borrowed stuff of Mum's. She refused until I showed her that it was from the lot pulled out to send to charity. Besides, nothing I have will fit her, and they're about the same height.

I chose black trousers for her – they're maybe slightly short, but otherwise fit her well – and a long purple jumper that seems to somehow make the shine in her dark hair come out more.

Ava seems unsure as she inspects herself in a mirror. 'I don't feel like me,' she says.

'Welcome to my life. Come on: Mum isn't home, so dinner will be amazing.'

'Not that I'll be able to eat much of it in these trousers.'

'The top is long enough to cover: unbutton the trousers if necessary. Come *on*.'

She follows me down the halls and stairs and then to the main stairs.

'What a banister,' Ava says, her hand stroking the carved wood.

'Want to slide down?' I say, but then hear voices

[81]

below us. 'Maybe later.' We descend to the main entrance the conventional way.

'Hi, Dad,' I say. Next to him is Astrid Connor: what on earth is she doing here? She's in the opposition.

'Ah, Samantha,' he says. 'And this must be your tutor, Ava?'

I nod, and they shake hands.

Astrid gives me the London double-cheek air kiss, then Dad introduces her to Ava. Ava looks relieved to get another handshake instead of the kisses. Then Astrid says goodbye.

The front door shuts behind her. 'Was *she* your meeting?' I say.

'She just popped by for a neighbourly chat. She lives nearby,' he adds, for Ava; and she does, but she's never been particularly neighbourly before.

What were they talking about? There's something about her, something I've never been sure of. Because her daughter Stella goes to my school we've bumped into her at school things now and then; and Astrid was the one who bailed me out when I was dumped at Westminster the other day. Why was she *really* here today? I can't ask Dad about that directly in front of Ava – and he probably wouldn't answer me, anyway.

We follow him to the small dining room. I say small, but it can seat ten; our places are set at one end of the table. Dad takes the seat at the end and Ava and I are opposite each other.

'And what have you two been getting up to today?' Dad says.

'Science: I finished my assignment.'

'And when was it due?'

I roll my eyes when he says *was*. 'Today. But we weren't there, so everyone's will be late.'

'Did that take all afternoon?'

'Well, no, but—'

'We were also checking the state of things on the news, and talking about the election last year,' Ava says, and I'm glad she interrupted. I'm not sure he'd be thrilled to know I spent hours drawing, and I've never been any good at lying.

'Excellent! A political debate. Were you following the election, Ava?'

'Of course. There was so much at stake.'

'Not many young people take that much interest.'

Ava's eyes narrow; she sits up straighter, shakes her head. 'You're wrong there. We can't vote but we're stuck with the results.'

'What are you stuck with that you'd change?'

'Leaving Europe. Closing the borders. United Ireland leaving the UK. Economic decisions that have led to the current collapse. Cutbacks on healthcare and libraries and universities and social care.'

'Ouch,' he says. 'Do you want to add the abolition of the monarchy, too?'

She shrugs. 'That one I'm not so bothered about.'

'As for the rest of it, if you were following the election you'll know my party's stance on these issues is much the same as yours.'

I feel like I'm at a tennis match: serve, volley, next point?

'So perhaps you're stuck with things you'd change if you could, too.'

Now he laughs, and I can see: he's enjoying this, sparring with Ava, and something like jealousy stirs inside of me. He never wants to know my views on these things.

But why would he? I'm always on his side.

'Would you change them if you could?' she says.

'Perhaps, but I have to consider the situation as it is, not as I want it to be. That is the difference between being sixteen—'

'Seventeen.'

'All right, seventeen – and being in a position where decisions you make will affect people's lives, and you can't control the situation that made the decisions necessary in the first place. I have to deal with the hand as played.'

'Such as choosing to form a coalition with the Reform Party, despite your political differences?'

'Indeed.'

'What do you think of our prime minister?'

'On that one I'll keep my own counsel.' Which says it all, really.

'Do you ever wonder how things would be if you'd made the opposite choice, and made a deal with Armstrong and the Law and Order Party instead?'

There's a quirk of amusement to his lips, and I'm connecting dots: is that why Astrid was here? Were they talking about this? 'It's human nature to question your decisions,' he says, at last. 'I may be a politician, but I'm still human.'

My fork clunks against my plate when I put it down and he turns as if he's just remembered I'm there. 'So, what are you two planning to do tonight? More studying?'

'Dad! I've already done maths AND English AND

science this week. Is school definitely shut again tomorrow?'

'I should think so, yes.'

'Then we can take tonight off,' I say. Charlize has been texting, asking me to come over, and I hadn't decided. But now, all at once, I have. 'We're going to Charlize's.'

'I don't know if you should go out.'

'She says it's a matter of life and death!'

'I see. Well, in that case ...'

'It's only just around the corner. We can go in a car if you want us to.'

'Yes, do. I'll arrange it. For eight p.m.?'

'OK, fine.'

18

Ava

Sam's dad says he has some work to do, that he'll leave us before pudding arrives. As I watch him walk across the room I'm struck by how genuinely likeable he is in person. From seeing him on TV I wouldn't have guessed that.

'Your dad is all right,' I say.

'He has his moments.'

'He didn't seem to mind me asking him so many questions – I hope I didn't push it too far,' I say, suddenly worried. 'But when he made that comment about young people, I couldn't help myself. Was it all right?'

'Believe me, Ava, he loves a good debate – why do you think he is a politician?' There's some spark of annoyance behind her words, and I realise now that she didn't take part. Did she feel excluded?

'You should say what you think, too; when we were talking earlier you did, so why not tonight?'

'Sure, that'd go down well. It's OK, Ava. I'm not the brainy kid he wanted; you are.'

'Sam! Don't be—'

The door opens and I cut off my words, shake my

head at Sam. There's a tray being brought in – of cake. Huge slices of chocolate cake.

'My favourite! Thank you,' Sam says. 'Can you send Dad's up to his office with his tea? And check if he's ordered a car for us for eight p.m.?'

'Of course, miss.'

The door closes and Sam takes a bite of cake. 'YUM.'

'Are we really going to Charlize's house?'

'Yes.'

'As in, Charlize Leighton.' The *it* girl: the only one who might outrank her in general popularity is Sam herself. But Sam is, well, nicer than Charlize. Nice isn't a word I'd use to describe Charlize at all.

'The one and only.'

'Look, she's your friend; why don't you go without me? I'm happy on my own with a book. You don't have to take me with you.'

'Yes, I do: I did my science assignment, and that was the deal: now we do what I want.'

'Does she know I'm coming?'

'Yes, I told her.'

'She doesn't mind?'

'Of course not!'

'What's this stuff about life and death?'

'With Charlize it's hard to say. It'll probably involve angst over a boy, or a tricky wardrobe choice. You can join the debate.' She winks and I wonder if she knows how uninterested I am in these things.

They tell us when the car is ready.

We get in, and one set of gates opens; then the second.

We pull out to the road and the driver soon takes the first left, and pulls in a few houses along – which considering the size of them is further away than that would usually be, but it still really is just around the corner – perhaps a five-minute walk at most?

There's a camera; the gate opens, we drive in and another one opens, and we're through.

This house is even bigger than Sam's. Bigger and newer – more modern. The driver opens our doors, and we get out.

'Return time, miss?' the driver says.

'We'll call,' Sam answers.

The front door opens. 'Sam!' It's Charlize; she gives Sam a hug. 'And this must be Ava?'

'Yes. Hi.'

'Come in.' She's almost bouncing with energy, excitement, something. A puzzled look crosses Sam's face as we step into the hall.

'So, what is the crisis?' Sam says.

'Not a crisis, exactly. I just needed to make sure you came.'

'Why?'

'Come *on*.' She links her arm in Sam's and pulls her across a long hall to another door. I follow behind. There are voices, laughter: we're not the only ones who managed to make it here through the roadblocks – or maybe her friends all live in this area.

Charlize opens the door to a huge room. There are sofas and nooks, tables and chairs, and a bar with a waiter at the back. There's a dozen or so people, girls and boys both – some of the girls I recognise as the in crowd at school. But Sam's eyes are fixed on one boy, draped across a sofa with a few girls in rapt attention.

'Lucas is here?' she says, and looks at Charlize, then shakes her head. 'What have you done?'

She laughs. 'Don't you mean, *Romeo*? Just say *thank you*.'

'Charlize!'

Lucas – it must be him – gets up, walks towards us. Tall, curly hair, somehow familiar though I know we haven't met. *Romeo*, Charlize said? Ah yes: that's why I recognise him. He must have been the model for Sam's drawing. But where that was an exaggerated caricature, Lucas is a flesh and blood not-quite-perfect-but-near-enough Romeo. Charlize must have seen the drawing Sam did in English and made the connection.

He's smiling, focused on Sam, and she's flushed and awkward. When he gets to us she looks up to his eyes.

Ah, I see. Is that the way things are?

They look good together: they're both so attractive, one dark, one fair.

Charlize takes my arm now, says she simply must introduce me to *everybody*, and draws me away – leaving Lucas and Sam on their own.

I go along, speak when spoken to, try to engage – but this place, these people, are so alien to me.

No, that isn't it, is it? It is more that *I* am the alien. The odd one out. Now in a room full of people, I feel more alone than I did before.

19

Sam

'I'm glad you could come,' Lucas says. 'I was hoping to see you again.'

I watch Charlize and Ava retreat behind him, not sure what to say.

'Charlize said she's your tutor? The girl you came with?'

'Ava? Well, yes, she's helping me; I'm not a great student, apart from art. But she's also a friend,' I say and realise the truth of it when I say the words. I'm regretting making her come tonight; she'll hate this. And maybe I will, too.

'Charlize has shown me some things you drew for her. You're really very talented.'

I'm racking my brain: what drawings does she have? I cringe inside when I realise: dresses, that was it, wasn't it? She described and I drew for her dressmaker.

I shake my head.

'You really are. Tell you what: did you get a chance to talk to my uncle at that charity dinner? Do you want to meet him? I could take you to his studio, you could see what he's doing with paint these days.'

Part of me is thinking, *Wow – go to a real actual artist's studio?* But then I sigh. 'It isn't that easy for me to go places without a big fuss of security and stuff. He might not like it.'

'Do you want a drink?'

'No. I'm definitely not having champagne ever again.' Though maybe it would help me stop feeling like a creature from the socially inept lagoon.

He grins. 'Understood. Soft drink?'

'OK, sure – ginger ale?'

He heads for the bar area and I look around to find Ava: she's sitting on one of the sofas, next to Anji. Not a bad option – Anji's likely to be friendlier to an outsider than some of the others. I head to them.

'He's *divine*,' Anji says.

I'm uncomfortable. 'He's all right. Not really my type, so away you go if you want to.'

'Charlize'd have my head after she went to all that effort to fix you up.'

'Who is he?' Ava asks, but Lucas has found us now with my drink before I can answer. Soon he's away again getting something for them as well.

'Why does Charlize keep trying to fix me up?' I say to Anji.

'She takes it as her duty as your friend to find you your prince; to finally melt the ice queen.'

'Huh,' I say, uncomfortable like I always am when this kind of thing comes up. I've just never met a boy I had that kind of interest in. I don't think I ever will, but if I said that they'd just see it as a challenge.

Anji looks towards the door. 'Ruth is here, at last,' she

says, and she's gone, leaving me and Ava, but before I can say anything Lucas is back with her mineral water.

I clink my glass against hers, and turn to Lucas. 'Sorry: we are the ultimate party animals. Feel free to seek more interesting pastures.'

'Not a chance.' He sits down.

'Ava was just asking who you are. There isn't much I can say, so perhaps you could fill in?'

'Who am I? Ooh. Existentially speaking, or more mundanely? I'm Lucas somebody.' He grins.

'Huh.'

'I met Sam at a charity dinner and plied her with champagne.'

'Is that the one where you had a headache the next day?' Ava says.

'The very same,' I reply.

'There's not much else to say,' Lucas goes on. 'I'm in the lower sixth at East London College.'

'That's quite a distance away,' Ava says. 'Do you live in that area?'

'Yes.'

'So how did you get here, then? I thought most of the roads were closed,' I ask.

'Took a bus as far as I could, then walked.'

'With all the road closures, that must have been quite a walk,' Ava says.

'Well, according to Charlize it was a matter of life and death that I come tonight.' He grins. 'Sam, I know you're not comfortable with feeling like you're being fixed up. Neither am I. Let's annoy her by being friends?'

I smile back at him, relieved. 'I think I can manage

[92]

that. But tell us: you've been out there tonight, do you know what is happening?'

'A light drizzle. A quarter moon. A swell of anger that is spreading. One of the raids was on the wrong house: a boy ran and was shot in the back. He's in hospital now.'

'What?' I'm shocked. 'Do you mean it was a mistake, that they shouldn't have been there?'

'Exactly. They were next door to where they should have been.'

'If this is true, why isn't it on the news?' Ava says.

'Why do you think? The authorities are denying it all – saying the family in the house they raided also had ties to A4A. It's a crock.'

'How do you know all of this?'

And his face is deadly serious now. 'Because I know him – the boy in hospital. He's my friend.'

20

Ava

We get back to Sam's just after midnight.

We go in the front door and start up the main staircase, but then more car lights shine on the windows below us.

Sam pauses, turns. 'I wonder which of my parents has been out late tonight?'

We go back down the stairs and a moment later the door opens. It's Sam's mother.

I'm curious to see her. She's always in the paper for some reason or another – her dress, her hair, attending an event – and she's even more beautiful in person. Stunning, in fact, in a long dress, hair swept up. What I'm guessing are real diamonds sparkle at her neck, in her ears and hair. She is very like Sam but taller – she doesn't look much older. They could be sisters.

'Samantha, darling,' she says, and holds out her hands for Sam's, sweeps her close for an almost-kiss on each cheek. 'And who is your friend?'

'This is Ava – remember, I texted you that she's staying? She's my tutor. She's here because she can't get home with all the road closures.'

'Of course. Lovely to meet you, Ava,' she says, and

smiles. A wave of perfume follows an air kiss of my own. 'What have you girls been getting up to today? Why are you still awake?'

'We've been waiting for you, of course,' Sam says. 'What time do you call this?' A mock stern look.

Her laugh tinkles. 'We were locked in, at the Royal Albert Hall! They wouldn't let us go until the road was cleared – such excitement. Go to bed, darling.' Her hand touches Sam's cheek and there is a feeling inside, of longing – for a mother's hand on my cheek.

We all go up the stairs but her mum stops at the first level and says goodbye while we go up to the next.

'Penny texted earlier to say she's put you in the guest room opposite mine,' Sam says. 'There should be some clothes, towels and so on. There's an en suite.' We walk along the hall. 'It's here,' she says, opens the door, switches on the lights.

It's as big as Sam's room but without any personal things – it's grand but looks hotel-like – and probably big enough to put all of our two-bed flat inside with some room to spare.

'Is this all right?' she says.

'It's more than all right. Thank you.'

Sam hesitates at the door. 'Are you tired?'

I shrug. 'I guess, but not sure I can sleep just yet.'

'Me neither. Let's talk.' She gestures and I follow her back to her room. There's a tray on the table by the sofa: popcorn; crisps; soft drinks. And more of the chocolate cake.

'Yum: a midnight feast!' Sam says. 'Our cook must have read our minds.'

She puts the popcorn in a bowl, motions me to sit next to her.

'What a day,' she says.

'Yes.'

'Do you think what Lucas said about his friend was true?'

'It wouldn't surprise me. Mistakes get made, but that sort of mistake?' I shudder. 'Whoever is responsible should be in the worst sort of trouble, not hidden behind lies.' I frown. 'Seems a bit odd, though.'

'What does?'

'If that boy who was shot is Lucas's friend, then why did he come to a party?'

Sam tilts her head to one side. 'I don't know,' she says, finally. 'He didn't seem upset at first. But maybe he was trying not to think about it.'

'Maybe,' I say, and that is something I can understand. The things that upset me the most are often the ones I keep the closest, inside. But if that were the case then why would he mention it at all? There's definitely something odd about it.

We munch in silence for a while, and despite what we've been talking about I'm warm and cosy here, with Sam, and in her mother's clothes.

'Your mother is so beautiful,' I say.

'Huh. She should be; looking good is her lifetime occupation.'

'Sam!'

'Seriously, it is. It's more important to her than anything else.'

'You shouldn't speak about your mother like that.'

'You don't know her at all – I do.'

'You're right, I don't. But I'm sure she cares for you. And at least you *have* a mother.'

There's a pause as what I said sinks in. 'I'm sorry,' Sam says. 'I didn't know. What happened to yours?'

'She left. Six years ago, when the borders were being closed. She was from Sweden: she decided to go back there and not risk being trapped here. She chose to leave us behind.'

'That's awful; I'm so sorry. Hasn't she been in touch since?'

'No. Nothing: not even an email.'

'Oh, Ava.' Sam's eyes are brimming with sympathy; her hand reaches out to mine, and my fingers close around hers.

'It's the not knowing that is the worst. Is she all right? Has something happened to her – is that why there's been no word? Anyway.' I shrug. 'Part of me almost wishes something has happened to her. At least that way there is a reason beyond her control that she hasn't been in contact. And then I feel terrible for thinking like that.'

'The day of decision, they called it: stay or leave, decide now. It must have hurt so many people.'

'It tore families like mine apart. But she didn't have to go; she wasn't forced to leave for not meeting the language requirement – she spoke perfect English. At the end she *chose* to leave my dad and me.'

'What was she like?'

'Lovely. That's what I don't understand. All my memories of her are of this warm, amazing woman who looked after me, sang to me, cared for me in all the ways a mother should. It never made sense to me that she left. I guess it still doesn't.' I tilt my head, looking at Sam next to me, her hand holding mine. 'I don't usually talk about my mum like this,' I say, and it's true. I never do, so why did I open up about this to Sam?

In so many ways Sam isn't what I expected – not at all. I'd been so uncomfortable to be around her to begin with, and now she's not just what I saw from the outside. She's more – she's funny, she's talented, she's kind.

Then she lets go of my hand. Pulls away just slightly as she reaches for a piece of chocolate cake. Doing so she puts more space between us that may be only inches but is somehow too far to cross.

And now I'm hoping she hasn't seen these things in me: how I wanted and didn't want to be near her at the same time; how I wanted her to be somebody I could despise. She isn't, and that just makes it harder.

She starts talking about Lucas now; admits he was the model for her drawing, as I'd thought.

'Is he *your* Romeo then?' I pretend to tease her, but I want to know. She shakes her head, but I can tell there is something more in her thoughts about him.

And I smile and I am both happy and sad. Happy for her confidences and her friendship; less alone than I was before I met her. But sad at the same time.

21

Sam

I watch Ava's taxi disappear from the front of our house the next afternoon. The police have calmed things down enough to open the roads; she's going home.

Last night: the stuff we talked about – for hours. We barely made it up in time for lunch.

We haven't known each other for long, but there is something about her; I trust her. And I was *myself* – I said what I thought and felt without thinking about what I should or shouldn't say. It felt so ... liberating, is that the word? And I want to know when we can talk like that again.

That story about her mum leaving was so sad. Maybe there is something I can do for her.

I knock on Dad's door that evening.

'Come,' he says.

I open the door, peer in.

'Hi, Samantha.' Hunched shoulders, a frown between his eyes: he's tired, stressed. Not a great time for a favour, maybe, and I hesitate, about to retreat.

'It's OK, come in,' he says. 'I need a break.'

'All right, if you're sure. Do you want some tea?'

'Good plan.'

'Have it sent up or make it?'

'Let's make it ourselves.' He gets up and we go to the small kitchen down the hall, and I fill the kettle.

'Is something wrong?' I ask him.

'There usually is. Don't worry, though.'

'You're always telling me that.'

'You've always been very good at worrying.'

'Huh.' I pour the tea, remembering now the other thing I'd wanted to ask him. 'Does it have anything to do with Astrid Connor being here yesterday?'

He hesitates, stirs milk into his cup. 'No comment.'

I roll my eyes. Usually I'd leave it there – but I really want to know. 'It's not every day the deputy prime minister meets with a significant member of the opposition. Is she planning to jump ship?'

'No comment.'

I study him. 'No, that's not it, is it? Hmm.'

'This is worse than *Question Time*. Has Ava been rubbing off on you? You seem to be developing an interest in politics.'

Now I'm annoyed. 'I don't know about developing it; it must be in the blood.'

'Stay out of it, Sam. It's a brutal business.'

'So I couldn't handle it, is that what you mean?'

'I'd rather protect you, that's all. Now, I've got to get back to work. Was there something you wanted?'

'I was wondering, actually, if you could do something for Ava.'

'What's that?'

'Her mother left for Sweden on the day of decision; she's never heard from her since.'

He shakes his head. 'That must be hard for her.'

'The thing is, from what she said her leaving didn't make sense. Almost like there was something behind it. And it wasn't the English-only law, either; Ava said she spoke perfect English.'

'And you're wondering if I can find out?'

'Yeah. Could you?'

He hesitates, reaches for his pocket, takes out his phone. 'What's Ava's full name again?'

'Ava Nicholls,' I say, and he makes a note on his phone. 'Thanks, Dad.'

'No promises; there may be nothing to find out. Now go to bed, get some sleep: school should be back on tomorrow.'

Before long I'm in bed, staring at the ceiling, willing sleep to come. Staying up late last night and then sleeping in today seems to have mucked up my body clock.

And something is bothering me, too. Why did I feel so annoyed at Dad earlier when I asked him about Astrid?

He doesn't listen – that's it. He doesn't accept I have an interest or anything to say – he was completely different with Ava at dinner last night. Maybe he was just humouring her as a guest and possible future voter, but I don't really think that's all it is. Somehow he's got this view of me, carefully slotted into a daughter-shaped box – one that can hold no other dimensions – and it stings. Have I always been so careful to stay there and be what he wants that it's too late now for him to see anything else in me?

Finally I'm in that just-drifting-off place between awake and asleep, random images of the last day floating in my mind – Ava, Lucas – when my phone vibrates on the desk next to me, again and again. Someone is calling?

Ignore it, I tell myself, but it's too late: I'm completely awake again. Might as well answer it. I reach for it, thinking it'll be about to go to voicemail, so I click *answer* straight away before registering that it's an unknown number. At midnight?

'Hello?' I say.

'Sam? It's Lucas.'

'Ah, hi.'

'Charlize gave me your number the other day. Sorry for calling so late.' There's a note in his voice, something out of key – of distress.

'Is something wrong?'

'Yes. But I – maybe I shouldn't have called you, I don't know why I did. You were asking all about things last night, and, well—'

'Just tell me. What is it?'

'My friend, the one I told you about …'

'The one who was shot by the police?'

'Yes. Kenzi is – was – his name. He's died in hospital.'

22

Ava

I read Sam's text again on the way to meeting her: *I need to talk – library, lunchtime? But only if you can keep more secrets*.

When I get there she's sitting on a chair, pretending to read. The book is upside down.

'What's wrong?' I say.

She pulls me by the arm to the back of the library. She looks around the stacks; no one is there.

'Lucas's friend, the one who was shot by the police? He died last night.'

I stare back at her; first shocked, then alarmed. What will this lead to?

'His friends and family are organising a protest – a vigil, really – tonight. Lucas is involved. He's asked me to go with him.'

'Are you going to go?'

'I don't know.'

'What are they going to do?'

'Join hands across part of London – they're aiming for a square mile, all around Bow, near where his friend lived. Different groups are involved: they are demanding peace, answers, an end to violence.' Her eyes are intent, her voice is passionate, alive, more than it has been before.

'You want to go.'

'Yes. I'm scared, though. I'll have to sneak away from security – that's easy enough to do from school. But my dad …' She shakes her head. 'What do you think I should do?'

I hesitate. The obvious answer is, don't go, stay safe. But is that what she needs right now?

'Think it through. The other day you said that you're entitled to your own opinions: you are. Saying what you think is one thing, but will it affect your dad if you get involved?'

'This really isn't about him for a change. I want to do this – to join them. I want to get involved, to be part of what is happening out there.'

She needs to go. I can see this, but there is a sinking feeling inside me: what if something happens to her?

'How about if I go with you?' The words are out before I even know I meant to say them. This could be serious: if the school thinks I'm involved in something I shouldn't be, I could lose my scholarship. I'm about to take it back.

'You'd really do that?'

Sam's eyes are shining, and my resolve is gone. 'Of course,' I say.

'Thank you.'

23

Sam

It's easy enough. As a sixth former, Ava has the side gate code. Halfway through our set tutor session after classes have ended we let ourselves out. I've already cancelled my car, saying I'm getting a lift with Charlize and going there after school. If anyone calls there she'll cover for me: I told her I was meeting Lucas. Which is true, but what we're doing today isn't at all what she thinks.

And I have thought more about how this could affect my dad, but today I'm doing something as *me*, not as his daughter – so no one needs to know who I am. With Ava's help I changed my appearance: she found some glasses from the theatre department with clear lenses in; my hair is pulled back tightly and covered by a scarf; I changed from uniform to jeans and borrowed an ugly thick black jumper from lost property. It's too big and is so different from anything I'd usually wear that I bet I could walk past Mum right now and she wouldn't even notice.

We walk up the road. It's dusk. There's a wild feeling inside me. Is this what it is like to be able to walk down any street by yourself whenever you feel like it? It's windy;

the last leaves, orange and red, swirl in the street lights and cover the path.

'Are you sure about this?' Ava says.

'Yes. Are you? I mean, you don't have to come. I'd be all right on my own,' I lie, but as I'm saying the words the street light just ahead of us suddenly flickers, goes out, and the automatic fear kicks in. I move closer to Ava, grab her arm. It's not completely dark; there's another street light further ahead, I tell myself, but I can't stop the fear. I walk faster towards it, pulling Ava along.

'Are you all right?' Ava says.

'No. Yes. I mean, it's just that I don't like the dark,' I say, something I don't usually admit out loud, and now I'm breathing easier as we're closer to the next light and I wish I hadn't said it.

'I wondered about that.'

'About what?'

'If you were scared of the dark. There was something about how you were that day of the blackout at school.'

I'm surprised. She picked up on that? I thought I was better at hiding how I feel – no one else seemed to notice. 'Well, I guess I am. A bit. But it's OK.' We've reached the corner now of a busier road; there are more lights from shops and restaurants, too, and the fear starts to lose its grip.

'Why? I mean, is there a reason, or is it just one of those things?'

I hesitate, and give the short answer. 'I got locked up in the dark for ages once when I was little. Can't stand it since then.'

'You got locked up? You don't mean that someone

[106]

did that to you on *purpose*, do you? It wasn't your parents, was it?'

'No, of course not.' I can see the questions in her eyes but don't want to go there, not now. 'Look, it's a long story for another time,' I say, not sure *another time* will ever come.

'OK. Here we are,' Ava says. We take the steps down to the tube, and push our bags through the metal detectors – step through the gates and collect them on the other side. She's got a pass like most people do, and has already got me a ticket. We touch them to the readers as we walk through. There are people all around us now.

I've been on the tube before, but the last time was a few years ago – before the election. Even then I'd never have gone on it on my own or with just one friend like this. And not at all since this airport-style security was brought in.

I'm looking at the people around us, curious, and Ava says low, close to my ear. 'Don't stare at people. Some won't like it.'

And then I'm staring at my shoes, at the walls, and can't work out where to look.

'Try to relax,' she says.

Five stops; we get off, change to another line. It's another six stops now and I count them down until it is time to get off. We start up the stairs to the exit.

'What time is it?' Ava says, and I peer at my watch.

'We've got twenty minutes.'

We walk out and down the road. Am I imagining this or is there something almost crackling in the air? There are people *everywhere*. Is it more than usual, or is this typical London around here? I don't know.

We find the left turn Lucas said to take. It's been worked out: the number of people for each street to connect to the next one, and the next – and we're going to be part of it: a chain of people all around the reach of the Bow bells.

I see Lucas before he sees us. He's tall, he stands out, and the light from a lamp catches his hair. We're almost up to him before he sees us.

'Sam? I didn't recognise you. You came!' He's pulling me into a hug but I don't mind; then Ava, too, and I see she's not comfortable with it but doesn't say anything.

'I said I would.'

'I know, but this must be a big deal for you. So thank you.'

There are people milling about all around us as if randomly, but then Lucas shows us our places. A row starts to form.

'This is my sister, Molly,' Lucas says, and he introduces us to a girl with dark hair like his, 'and my little brother, Nicky. He isn't supposed to be here, but he followed Molly so we're stuck with him.' A boy about four or five years old stares up at me and smiles. He's fair, not as fair as me but with streaks through his hair. 'And this is my uncle Gil – remember, the artist?'

It's time.

We join hands. Molly has Nicky's, Lucas has Nicky's and mine, I have Ava's, Ava has mine and Lucas's uncle's – and all along the road as far as you can see, people of London, all ages, all races, in almost-rags to posh and in heels, are hand in hand.

There are sounds of traffic, horns – the roads are being blocked now by people holding hands all around us.

'It's happening,' Lucas says. 'It's really happening!'

And it's growing. People walking past or in cars who want to know what is happening stop and some of them join in, or applaud.

And there is a swell of feeling inside me not quite like anything I've felt before. We're standing together – for peace, against violence – demanding the government provide answers, too.

There's a miked-up podium set up in an elevated position down the road from us.

'That's Kenzi's mother and father,' Lucas says. 'They're just waiting for – ah, here they are.'

The press. There are cameras. Lucas points out a woman with one of the cameras: it's his mother, he says. She's a journalist.

Kenzi's mother has tears on her face, but she's smiling. His father holds out his hands and a hush falls all around.

'This is our London,' he says. 'We want it back. We stand together – ordinary people – and all we want is peace, for our children to be safe. We were accused of anarchist connections. They were proven false, and we've been released. But our son, our baby boy...' His voice wavers, he has to pause. 'Kenzi was scared and he ran; he was shot in the back. He died yesterday. We want to mourn him in peace, not with violence.'

There are tears; everyone is still holding hands.

It's beautiful.

And then the riot police come.

24

Ava

Weapons appear in hands – some from the crowd around us, others that were in our chain, too. Were they waiting for this moment – for the riot police to get here? There are cries of anger, and they rush at the police.

Kenzi's parents were calling for peace on the podium moments ago; now they cry out for calm, tell everyone to stop, but no one is listening. Then the podium is knocked over and I lose sight of them both.

'Run!' Lucas says and we're running – me, Sam, Molly, Lucas with his little brother in his arms. We are part of a whole wave of people who don't want to fight, who want to get away – but we're caught between police with batons and shields and those who hid their weapons and waited for them to come.

Molly is hit on the side of the head and falls. I help her up – her head is bleeding. Where is Sam?

Sam? And I'm screaming out her name. Lucas and Sam aren't in sight now.

Someone I don't know grabs my hand and Molly's and pulls us along and it's all noise and shouting, screaming; sounds like breaking bones as truncheons rain down on arms, heads, and then somehow we're in an alley, away from the noise – me, Molly, the boy who pulled us both away from it all.

'Where are my brothers?' Molly is crying; he is holding her.

'We'll get you out of here, then I'll come back and look for them. All right? All right?' he says, and she protests but lets him lead us both away, to a door. He knocks twice; it opens.

'In, get in,' a woman's voice says – a kind-looking woman, sixty or so years old. 'Tch,' she says when she sees Molly, and pushes her into a chair, touching a cloth to the blood that runs down her face with her tears, and the boy starts for the door as the woman protests for him to stay.

I follow him out the door.

I have to find Sam. I can't do anything else.

We go back out into the night.

25

Sam

Bodies. Shouting, screaming. A stick swings at my head but Lucas blocks it somehow and then I trip and fall to the ground. The crowd surges and I lose sight of Lucas. I can't get to my feet; I try and get knocked down again. I try again and then a hand grips my shoulder, yanks me to my feet, and half carries, half drags me along.

It's a man, twenty-something, short hair, dressed plainly in a dark suit. I don't know who he is and I'm struggling uselessly; his grip on my shoulder is painful. The police let him through their line and he keeps dragging me along. Then we're on the other side of it all.

'Stop struggling, Samantha Gregory,' he says. He knows who I am? And the shock is enough to make me stop.

'Who are you?'

He doesn't answer. We've reached a car and he opens the door. 'Get in, and I'll take you home.'

I stare at him, not moving. Then he reaches into a pocket, holds out his ID.

Government ID. Agent Coulson?

I get in the back of the car.

I'm shaking. Where is Lucas? Ava? Nicky? Molly? Are they OK? What about Kenzi's parents?

What happened?

The unknowns are too many, too frightening. My phone is still in my pocket and I take it out: the screen is cracked and it's dead. Must have broken it when I fell.

How did this Agent Coulson even find me?

And now he's taking me home.

To Dad.

26

Ava

We're just heading up to the end of the alley, closer to the noise, when the boy motions to wait. His phone is out, he's answering it.

'Yes? Lucas? Thank God.'

'Ask if Sam is with him,' I say.

'And Nicky and Sam? ... Yes. OK. Can you get to my aunt's? Molly's in a state ... OK. Bye.' He ends the call, puts his phone back in a pocket.

'You're Ava, aren't you?' he says now. 'Sam's friend?'

'Yes?'

'I'm Juro – Molly's boyfriend.'

I nod, impatient; why isn't he telling me about Sam? And then I'm scared, fearing the worst.

'Lucas saw Sam being bundled off through the police line – he reckons she's been bailed by someone who recognised her. She's all right. Nicky is fine, he's with Lucas. They got away down a side street but in the other direction so aren't going to make it back here tonight.'

And the relief is so strong I almost sag against him. He takes my arm. There's noise – running, shouting –

and it's getting louder, coming closer.

'Uh-oh. Best get out of here,' he says.

We run.

27

Sam

Dad shakes Agent Coulson's hand. 'Thank you. I owe you one, and I always pay my debts.'

'Not necessary, sir.'

The door closes behind him.

'Come,' Dad says. One word, one only – full of barely contained fury. I follow him to his study; he closes the door.

'Samantha, *what* were you thinking?'

I stare back at him, mute – there are so many things I want to say, I don't know where to begin.

'If that agent hadn't realised who you were – my God. If anything had happened to you …' And then his arms are around me, he's pulling me close, and the fear and drama and the night are all there in my mind and now I'm crying. He strokes my hair. Is he … is he crying, too?

And I try to tell him why I went, what it meant to me to be there, but he won't listen. He says he understands, that I'm young, that he knows I know I've made a mistake. That I won't do it again. That because of Agent Coulson's quick action it looks like no one realised who I was.

And we will never mention it again.

He takes me to my room, tells me to go to sleep – that I'll have to be as I always am tomorrow, not let anyone see, anyone guess, that something is wrong.

And then the door is shut, and I'm standing there, shaking.

Ava? Lucas? Are they all right? It all looked so far from all right when I was pulled to my feet and from the crowd by Coulson, and now the fear floods back: I could have been crushed, trampled.

How can I just be at home now and pretend nothing has happened after what I saw tonight?

I stand there, not moving, for so long – a statue. My thoughts are frozen and I try to make myself think.

Without my phone I haven't got Ava or Lucas's numbers and I don't know their email addresses. I could try searching for them online – no, wait. What about school email?

Now I move, fast – log on to my tablet and then the school system.

And there, in my inbox – I almost collapse with relief. There's a message from Ava: sent about an hour ago.

Hi Sam, can we make our next tutoring session begin a quarter of an hour later? I've got something to take care of. And don't worry about getting your English back tomorrow; I'm sure you'll get a good grade. Romeo came to life on your page – he's fine.

She's OK. Lucas – she must have realised he was the model for Romeo – he's fine, too. They're both all right; I can breathe easier again.

I answer so she'll know I'm OK, too: *Sure, no problem. See you tomorrow.*

Somehow I get myself into pyjamas, under the covers. Lights on – not just night light or desk lamp but overhead tonight as well.

There was something so beautiful, so pure, in what we did – holding hands for peace. I've never felt connected like that to so many other people before.

But then the riot police came. Why? We weren't doing anything but holding hands. And as soon as they got there, those others appeared as if from nowhere – the violence began.

We were caught in the middle, but it wasn't what we wanted. There were so many people crying out, hurt. What happened after I was dragged away by Coulson?

Is it on the news?

I find the remote, click it on. I sit up and watch, hour after hour, horror growing inside me with each update. Violence is everywhere, not just London: it's taking place in Manchester, Birmingham, Glasgow, other places, too. It spread from here to there so fast. Streets are overrun – there's looting, beatings. Buildings and cars set on fire.

Because of who I am, I was brought home. I'm warm and safe. But for people who live in these places there is no safety.

What is happening is beyond what I can understand. Kenzi's parents were stricken with grief, yet what they started was about peace: demanding a stop to the cycle of violence. But all around the country people are using his death to react with violence of their own.

And Dad? I'd expected fury, demands for explanations and the names of who I was with. I'd expected that maybe, for once, I would be able to tell him what I really think – that maybe he'd even listen.

But there was none of that.

Until today, in all the major ways I've always done what is expected of me.

He didn't take what I did seriously, did he? He doesn't understand how I feel; he doesn't want to know. He wants me to be safe; he wants me to keep quiet; he wants me to stay out of the press. He wants never to speak of any of this again.

But you can't always get what you want.

28

Ava

The next morning my head is heavy, as if it had been hit like Molly's. I struggle to wake when my alarm goes.

There's a knock on my door. Dad is home? It opens and he peers in. 'I'll take you in this morning; I don't want you on the bus.'

So I get up, go through the motions – getting ready for school as if this is any other day, but the sense of unreality is strong.

The news is on in the kitchen while we have breakfast. Areas of London are still in chaos, but not where I need to go; we check an online list of school closures. Mine isn't on it.

The reports blame the riots on the initial protest, on Kenzi's family, but it wasn't like that, it wasn't – some other group used it and made it into something else. Anarchy for All is named in the reports.

Dad is quiet, worried; more so than I can remember seeing him before.

'Things will settle down soon, won't they?' I say.

'This city – this country – is a tinderbox. It has been for a while. People are hungry, desperate, fed up.

That boy's death has thrown a match. I honestly don't know.'

'Should we stay at home today?'

He looks at me properly then. 'You, my little Ava brainbox, wanting to stay home from school? That isn't like you.'

'No. I don't feel myself, not with what has happened – is happening.'

'Keep calm and carry on: words from another time, but what else is there to do?' He gets up, leans over, kisses my forehead. 'But I won't make you go if you want to stay at home.'

And then I'm remembering Sam's email answer: *see you tomorrow*, she said.

'No, you're right. Let's go.'

'That's my Ava.'

When we get in his taxi he spends a while on the radio before we set off, working out the best route to take. And we don't see anything wrong, at first – I mean, the streets are as they always are around us. Maybe there is something different in how people walk, the looks on their faces – the hurried whispering.

Then I start to notice the graffiti. There's always some around but there is fresh red paint in odd corners, walls, even on pavements, and it all says the same thing: *A4A here to stay*. None of it was there yesterday. There is a cold twisting feeling inside me: was it A4A who crashed the demonstration last night?

There is more police presence than usual; there seems to be a police car going past on almost every street. Smoke hangs on the horizon, too – they said on the news that there are some fires.

We're barely moving in slow traffic: a few metres forward, stop, a few more. The light ahead is red.

'I could get out and take the tube?' I say. There's a station on the corner ahead of us.

'No. I'll take you. Not sure you'll be on time, but—'

He stops speaking; his head turns to the left and I look over too. People are running – from the tube station? Some are screaming.

Then the ground beneath us rumbles and shakes.

'Get out!' Dad says. We open the doors, and run.

29

Sam

Part of me wants to grab Dad, shake him, *scream* at him to listen to me. But more of me is numb.

We're playing a game, one where we say good morning, and pass the toast, and then get into the car together. I'm being taken to school on the way to Westminster with Dad: maybe he's making sure I don't make any more *mistakes* on the way.

We pull out of the gates in front of our house.

'There is something I forgot to tell you last night,' Dad says. He forgot or was distracted by me being hauled home from a riot by a government agent? 'I found out something about your friend Ava's mother. There was a story there.'

Now I'm looking at him with full attention. 'What is it?'

'Not a happy one, I'm afraid. It was in her healthcare records that she had cancer, a very malignant sort: she was dying. That is likely why she left.'

My breath catches inside: her mother – cancer? Poor Ava. 'But what does her being sick have to do with leaving?'

'It was the day of decision – Euros could decide to stay or go before the borders were closed. But with the changes those who stayed had to go through an involved citizenship process before they could have any of the usual rights or benefits they used to have as residents. So no free medical care until it was completed. I imagine she left because of that.'

'Ava didn't know, I'm sure of it. Why didn't her parents tell her?'

'Sometimes parents keep things from their children, to protect them.' And he's looking at me like there is something behind what he is saying, but I'm not concentrating on that now.

What am I going to say to Ava? Should I even say anything at all? She said the worst thing was not knowing, but would she want to know this?

I stare out of the window. Traffic slows, stops.

There's a red light ahead.

The pavements are busy, people rushing to work or to school and I watch them, wondering if any of them were holding hands where I was last night.

Then there's a ripple in the crowd. Heads turning. Eyes widening.

People screaming and running.

Dad asks the driver what's happening and I'm straining to look. People are scattering – there's a blur of red on the ground between their feet.

As they disperse it becomes clear. It's graffiti: *A4A here to stay*.

'Get us out of here!' Dad says to the driver, but how can he? We're hemmed in by cars on all sides. And then we see her: the crowd has parted around a girl. She's in a school uniform and smiling widely, but that isn't a coat she's wearing – it's big, bulky, all wires and technical stuff, and I can't believe what I'm seeing, but what else could it be but a suicide vest?

Her hand: there is something in her hand.

'Everybody down!' a voice screams. At almost the same second a gunshot rings out – I see the policewoman now, the gun in her hand – the girl's head jerks back; it's red – *red*, like the paint—

And then – then –

A blaze of LIGHT

SOUND

FURY

Part 2: Control

Like most abstract concepts, the relative importance of freedom and security varies with how hungry and afraid you are. Before freedom we need safety, economic stability, equality. It is only when these needs are met that freedom can truly be sought and valued.
Leader of the Opposition William Armstrong,
coalition debates

Nothing is more dangerous than a man convinced he is doing right.
Nothing is more useful than the man you have convinced.
Opposition MP Astrid Connor,
private diary

1

Ava

I hold my dad.

He's coughing, trying to speak.

I'm sorry – is that what he said?

'Don't try to talk,' I say. 'Whatever it is; it doesn't matter.'

'I think I – I – was wrong. Forgive me,' he says through gasps, and then he is coughing more – gurgling – and there is blood coming out of his mouth, and I think he's trying to say, *I love you*.

'I love you too, Dad,' I say. And now he's stopped struggling to speak, he's stopped doing anything. He's completely still, and I'm crying.

There are paramedics after a while; they try to pry me away from him but soon realise they're too late. There are cries of pain, of anguish, all around us; other people can still be helped, and they leave us alone.

We were running – everyone was – from the blast underground, the smoke and flames coming up from the tube. When we reached the corner, there he was. A boy, one wearing a vest: a suicide vest.

Dad threw me to the ground, covered me with his

body – saved me.

He's gone, but I hold him tight. There is nothing else I can do.

2

Sam

Why do things seem to slow down when they go wrong? Is it so you can take every detail in and remember it and be forced to live through it in your mind, again and again?

I couldn't close my eyes. I tried, but I couldn't. But it wasn't just what I could see.

The first sounds – the gunshot, the deafening blast – weren't the worst. It was the screaming.

And the smells, too: burning cars and buildings and *people*, leaving a singed path down my throat that tastes of destruction, death.

The feel of my father's hands – sure and strong – undoing my seat belt, pulling me out through the bent back door of the car.

The front of our car – and the security car that was ahead of us – I try not to look. One flipped and landed on the other. Our driver's blood – is that the metallic zing I can taste and smell? Or maybe it's my tongue: there's blood in my mouth. I bit my tongue. The security detail that was behind us are here now to take us away, but Dad pushes me to them; he says *no*. And he goes back to help the injured. He was trained in emergency first aid years ago, when he was in the police; he says he has to help.

I'm proud of him then. I often have been, but I feel it so strongly just then that it swells inside me; it even helps take the horror away.

For now.

The nightmares will come later.

3

Ava

'Name?'

'Ava Nicholls.'

'Of the deceased.'

Deceased floats around in my brain before it makes the connection.

Daddy.

'He's my father. Ethan Nicholls.'

'Date of birth? Address? Next of kin?'

I'm answering questions as if by rote, but all I see is this bag they're zipping him up in. One of many around us. Ambulances are taken up by the living, so the dead have to wait.

Date of birth, to today – date of death. He was fifty-two years old.

'Is there someone who can pick you up?'

I focus on her then. 'I'm staying here with him.'

'Love, it's cold, you need a change of clothes. Go home.'

'Home?' I stare back at her: *home* was where I lived with my dad. How can I go there now?

'Public transport is shut down tonight. If no one can pick you up there are some free taxis being organised.'

'A taxi?'

'Are you all right?'

How can I be? But she's trying, and there are other people who need her help. I lie to her, say my uncle is coming to get me, and can see she's relieved to move on.

But I stay. Wait. Eventually ambulances return, and finally one of them takes Dad.

It's late. I'm numb – with what has happened, with cold. I start towards home-that-isn't-home-any-more. It's too far to walk but I don't know what else to do.

After a while I see a café with lights on; I stumble in. Everyone looks at me and I see the horror in their eyes. I look down, see I'm covered in blood. Dad's blood.

Someone pushes me into a chair, someone else brings me the English answer to all moments of crisis or inability to cope: a cup of tea. At least it's warm, and I wrap my hands around it.

There's a TV on the wall: they are hanging on every word. But no one really knows what has happened, or why – there are reports from places all around London. Death, destruction – more bombs. Suicide bombs. This wasn't the only one.

What do I do now?

My phone is still in my pocket. I take it out; it's almost out of charge but there is a signal. One of the advantages of a phone as old as time: it'll survive anything.

Who can I call? We've always been self-contained, my dad and me; he liked it that way, he said, though in truth most of his university friends seemed to lose interest when he started driving a taxi – we saw less and less of them over time. His parents are both dead and he wasn't close to his only sibling, a brother. I don't even know where he lives.

I call Sam. I don't know why. We hardly know each other, really, but somehow it is her voice I want to hear right now.

It rings several times; she's not going to answer, is she? Then it clicks and a voice says *hello* but it's not Sam, and now I panic that something has happened to her.

'Is Sam there? Is she all right?'

'Who is this?'

'It's her friend, Ava.'

'Hi, Ava, it's Penny. Sam is fine, her number is diverted to home as her phone is broken. Is there any message?'

'I – I don't know...'

'Ava? Are you all right?'

I don't know what to say. I almost end the call.

'Ava? Are you still there?'

I find the words. 'My dad. He's d-d-died. In one of the bombs.'

'Oh, Ava, I'm so sorry. Where are you, is anybody with you?'

'No. I don't know where I am; some café.'

'Just a moment.' She goes quiet, comes back. 'Ask someone where you are and we'll send a car for you.'

4

Sam

'Really, I'm fine,' I insist. I'm lying – sort of – but after what has happened to so many people, being a bit bruised from being thrown around the car seems not worth complaining about.

'Hold your arms out like this and bend over.'

I sigh, do so and gasp with pain.

I'm poked, prodded, pulled in different directions.

'Nothing serious,' she finally says.

'Told you so.'

'Some painkillers will help. Maybe sleeping pills?' She's sending a prescription through on her computer and then Dad walks in. I go straight into his arms for a hug. He holds me for a moment, then lets go.

'How's my girl?' he says, and the doctor gives him the same spiel.

'Really, I'm fine,' I say again. 'Can we go home now?'

'Best idea I've heard all day.'

It's late, and I've got a weird, forced-awake feeling, as if my brain has been pried open like an oyster and will never close again.

We get into a car soon after. It looks just like the car

we were in before, but that one was wrecked. Now I'm remembering the driver we had earlier, his blood. It's a different driver now, too, of course; do I know this one? They change so often and now it seems wrong that I can't even remember who was driving our car before. He won't be going home like we are.

Dad is on his phone. 'Change of plan,' he says. 'We'll take you home, then I've got to go in. Emergency meeting.'

'At this time?'

'It started a while ago; I'm already late. And there's something I have to tell you,' he says and fear rushes through me.

'Is Mum OK? Nan? Auntie Mo?' I say and go through a hurried list of everyone I can think of.

'Hold on. Our family are all accounted for. It's your friend, Ava. She's all right – it's her dad.'

'What's happened?'

'They were caught up in one of the bombings. Sadly, he's died.'

I'm struggling to take this in. Her dad? The one who drove her to our house? I never met him.

'Ava called for you, and Penny answered. She and your mum arranged to send her a car. She should be there soon.'

5

Ava

'Ava Nicholls?'

I turn my head slowly. There's a man there in the dark suit government drivers wear.

'Yes?'

'Your car is here.'

He knows about my dad. I can see it in his eyes, and the way he helps me up from the café chair. 'Here,' he says, takes his jacket off and tucks it around me.

Some of the others in the café are looking at us, wondering who I am now, why a driver like that is here for me and giving me his jacket. But most of them are too deep in their own fear and worry to care.

The drive to Sam's is short in miles but there is such chaos on the roads and so many diversions that it takes much longer than it should. I see through the glass that separates the front and back of the car that the driver's on the car radio a lot of the time, but can't hear what he says.

When we finally arrive at Sam's house and go through the double gates Penny is already standing there, with a blanket to wrap around me, and no sign of the snooty face I thought she had when I first met her.

'Thank you,' I say.

She takes me to the room I stayed in before. She says Sam will be home soon, that she'll come and see me then. She fusses, runs a bath.

When she finally leaves me alone I sit there, on the edge of a chair, looking around.

Where would I be now if I didn't have Sam as my friend? I don't know. And I don't know how long they'll let me stay here, either, or where else I could go, but these thoughts – the ones about myself – are fleeting, because I can't believe what's happened. Even though I can't deny it, nothing feels real.

It's a mistake, some nightmare. I'll wake up from this—

It can't be true. Dad would never leave me—

This morning: why didn't I insist we stay at home? He would have, I know it, if I'd said I needed him to be there. I wanted to, I should have. Why didn't I?

I didn't, and he was taking me to school.

And then—

I try to push it away, what I saw, heard – the blast, the screaming – and ... and ...

But I can't *not* go back; I have to remember. Dad saved me. Didn't he?

And yet the last thing he was trying to say was *sorry*, as if there could be anything he needed to say sorry for.

And then ... and then. He died. He really died. Didn't he?

They took him away from me. A body bag – that's what they put him in. Where did they take him?

Daddy?

But he doesn't answer. He can't, and he never will again.

I wrap my arms around myself, and cry.

6

Sam

I knock lightly on Ava's door, but there's no answer. What should I do?

I hesitate, then open the door. The overhead lights are off and my eyes take a moment to adjust with just the small bedside lamp on. She's on the sofa wrapped in a dressing gown, sitting upright. Her skin is pale and her cheeks look hollow, as if in hours she's lost weight or something's been knocked out of her, and I try to put myself in her place: what if it had been my dad who died? It so easily could have been. We were just metres away from dying – both of us.

Her eyes turn towards me though she stays still, and I close the door behind me.

I stand there in silence. 'I'm so sorry. I don't know what else to say,' I finally manage.

She shakes her head, a slight movement I can only just see in the dim light. 'Me neither,' she says. A whisper.

I go to her, sit next to her, take her cold hand in mine. She leans towards me as if she's wilting against me. And we just sit there, not moving, for so long. Eventually I sense her breathing evening out: is she falling asleep?

The curtains are open. The sun is starting to rise outside, and it is a sunrise of glory – streaks of vibrant colour soon light up the sky.

Red skies cover a bloodied London that will never be the same again.

7

Ava

I wake slowly. I'm stiff, uncomfortable, warm down one side and cold on the other – someone is next to me? My eyes open: it's Sam, asleep – on the sofa, the one in their guest room – and at first I'm confused but then everything comes back in a rush of pain.

Daddy.

There's a knock on the door. I ease Sam away, but the door opens before I can get up. Penny peeks in as Sam stirs, yawns and stretches.

'I didn't like to disturb you, but you both need to eat something. You can come down in half an hour, or I'll have something sent up if you'd rather?'

'Is Dad home?' Sam says.

'He got back in a short time ago. He said he'd be at breakfast.'

'Give us a minute,' Sam says, and Penny retreats back through the door. 'Would you rather have breakfast here or down there?' she says.

I stare at her mutely. Breakfast – with her and her dad? In that dining room, at that long table? Maybe her mother will be there, too. I shake my head. 'I'll stay here.'

'Of course.' She hesitates. 'Do you mind if I go? I want to find out what is happening.'

'You go. Report back,' I manage to say.

'Are you sure?'

'Yes. Go.'

'I think I need a shower, too,' Sam says. She stands; she's moving awkwardly and I focus on her now, see the bruises on the side of her face.

'Have you been hurt?'

'No. Well, not seriously. It's a long story – one for later?'

'All right. Go and have your shower.'

She starts to go, then turns back and swiftly kisses me on the cheek. 'I'll tell Penny to have your breakfast sent up.'

The door opens, closes, and she's gone before the feel of her lips leaves my skin.

She wants to find out what's happening from her dad? My brain doesn't seem to be working properly. Around London – that must be what she means.

I get up, go to the bathroom. Wash my hands and then notice that my old clothes that I'd left on the floor when I finally had a bath last night, the water almost cold by then, are gone. Back in the room there are clean clothes folded on a chair.

There's a TV on the wall. I find the remote. Get into bed still in the dressing gown I put on last night. I need to sleep, I know it, and there is a part of me that still can't believe any of this, that thinks when I wake up it will all have disappeared, like a dream – or a nightmare. But when I woke up this morning nothing had changed. Somehow I'm not ready to let go of consciousness just yet.

I turn the TV on and go to the BBC.

Scene after scene of yesterday's violence fills the screen. I flinch with each report. There were seven suicide bombers in total around London. All young, like the one we saw – teenagers – younger than me, by the looks of some of their faces. Why would they choose to do this to themselves, to everyone else? To my *father*.

Images of red paint – A4A, Anarchy for All – at each location. This was the organisation the government – the prime minister herself – claimed to have eliminated. They've been proven wrong in the most shocking way. Everyone is calling for her resignation.

The details are washing over me and not taking hold: the places, the numbers of confirmed dead, injured. Then I hear them say something about Sam's father and I rewind a bit to watch and listen.

There's CCTV footage: a girl in a suicide vest; people running, screaming. A gunshot – and then light and sound rip through the girl and everything around her. A car flies through the air and lands on another. Sam and her father somehow climb out of the back of the one underneath, and I shudder to see how close they were to dying – she never said.

Much is made of the deputy prime minister staying to help the wounded. He was in the police, they say, before he went into politics; I vaguely remember knowing this before the election, that he'd been some sort of hero, but I didn't realise how frontline he'd been – a counterterrorism expert, they say, and also trained in emergency first aid.

So he knew this world of terror back then – one he knows now, so personally. His daughter's life and his own were at risk.

I remember the man I met, the public man, too, and the things he and his party stood for: having to deal with the hand as dealt, he said.

Maybe if the election had gone differently – if his party had won – none of this would have happened.

The turnout was very low: so many people didn't vote. Were they lazy? Apathetic? Or disillusioned: convinced that whoever they voted for, nothing would change. And many of those who did vote seemed to throw their votes away: the protest vote, they called it. And now who are the ones who complain the loudest about the government, the prime minister?

I was sixteen during the election: not allowed to vote even though it was *my* future being decided in so many ways. It wasn't just that election, it was also the tumultuous ones that came before it – the ones that led to the split from Europe, then the day of decision – my mum leaving for Sweden – the closed borders.

I don't want to deal with the fallout, not any more. Without my dad, what is left for me in this country?

School, grades, university – they seemed so important before, but who knows when school will even be open again.

I can't lie to myself any longer. No matter what she did, or why she did it: the only person I want right now is my mum.

8

Sam

'How is Ava doing?' Dad says.

'I don't know,' I answer truthfully. He holds out his hand to me and I take it. As much as I felt I shouldn't leave Ava alone right now I had to see him, to see he was OK with my own eyes. Mum is here already; she looks tired, too. But then she doesn't usually make it to breakfast, even a late one like this.

'Does Ava have any other family?' Mum asks, and that's when it hits me: with everything that has happened it's been driven from my mind. Ava doesn't know about her mum; why she left, what was wrong with her. Do we have to tell her? Should we?

'I don't think so,' I say, and if that is true she really has nowhere else to go. 'Can she stay with us? I mean, not just for now?'

Mum and Dad exchange a glance. 'We'll have to think about what is best for Ava,' Dad finally says.

Before I can say anything else the door opens and breakfast is brought in.

'I don't know about you, but I'm starving,' Dad says. It's always been a family rule with serious stuff: eat first, talk after. Better for the digestion, he used to say, but it seems to me that putting things off makes them less likely to be said.

He tucks into his like he hasn't eaten for a day but Mum is like me and is picking, and I don't think it's her usual watching-her-waistline thing. She's not even looking to see what I eat. There is worry around her eyes that the morning light shows.

Finally, Dad puts down his fork.

'What can you tell us?' I ask.

'Most I expect you've heard already,' he says, with a tired half-smile. 'Anarchy for All – A4A – have reincarnated, garnered wider support. Mostly amongst disaffected young people. And they planned those suicide attacks.'

'Why? I mean, what do they want?'

'That's not entirely clear, apart from chaos. But don't worry: we'll contain them again.'

'But you didn't know. I mean, you stopped them in London the last time, but nobody knew what was going to happen this time.'

'No.'

'So how can you stop them if you don't know what they may be planning next?'

'Samantha,' Mum says, with a warning look.

'It's OK,' Dad says. 'She's easier going than the press will be later. All I can do is promise you, we're doing the best we can.'

Then he is explaining how they plan to increase security for us, but I'm having trouble listening. If the government can't stop things like this from happening, then who can?

No matter how many security measures they come up with, is anywhere – anyone – safe?

It's a weird day – weird isn't the right word. Surreal, maybe? Nothing feels like it is actually happening. I check on Ava but she says she wants to be alone; I go back later and she's either good at faking it or she's genuinely asleep.

I try to paint in my studio – things I saw last night and can't stop seeing, as if painting them will make the images in my mind go away. But somehow holding a paintbrush in my hand strengthens the sense of unreality.

My camera: where is it? I've barely used it. It's a clever little one, smaller than a phone – a Christmas present from some relative or another. I hunt around in my room and finally find it in the back of a drawer.

I'm going to take it everywhere I go. If I take photographs myself, when I look at them later, I'll know that what they show is real.

If I'm ever allowed out of the house again, that is.

I go online. I feel cut off without my phone. There are messages from half the school wanting to know how I am but I can't bring myself to get in touch over and over to answer the same questions.

I message Charlize: explain about the phone so she can let people know why I'm not in touch.

She answers; says everyone at school is fine. With Charlize 'everyone' probably means her particular friends and not the unnoticed or unpopular, but I check on the school website, too; nothing is reported there.

Charlize tells me that Lucas has been trying to call

me. She gives me his message details but I ask her to tell him I'm OK, that I'll be in touch later.

I put my tablet aside. As the sun goes down there is a faint smoky glow on the horizon: fires?

I'm restless, uneasy. Dad went back to Westminster and hasn't come back yet; I stand in shadows by the window in my darkened room, watching for his car. Ava's father died; one moment he was with her, then he was gone. No amount of security can make anyone completely safe, can it?

Finally three cars pull in. When I see Dad get out of one of them and go through the front door, I close my curtains and put the lights and TV on.

There's a pale newsreader with frightened eyes. Widespread rioting? Looting? Property damage? It's not clear any more who or what is responsible. It can't all be A4A. It's almost like everyone who is unhappy about anything has joined in the destruction.

I go across the hall, put my ear against the door: Ava has the news on, too. I knock and open the door.

'Is it OK if I come in?'

She nods. We sit and watch the news together, hour after hour. Unrest in London, the home counties, too. Other cities, towns and villages around England, Wales and Scotland.

The army has been called in. Roadblocks are being put into place.

'It's like a war zone,' Ava whispers, and we'd both been silent for so long that I jump.

'Yeah. I don't understand how this has happened here.'

'My dad,' she says, and flinches, 'said the city was like

a tinderbox. That anything could set it off.'

'Looks like the rest of the country was, too.'

'Yeah.' There's silence again while we watch the same bits of footage we've seen already, then she takes the remote and mutes it.

'Sam, there's something I want to ask you,' she says.

'What's that?'

'I know there's a lot going on right now, but when you feel you can, could you ask your dad something for me?'

'Of course. What is it?'

'I want to leave. There's nothing for me here now. I know the borders are closed, but could he help me get out of the country? I want to go to Sweden, and try to find my mum.'

9

Ava

Sam's eyes: they're full of emotion, pain. She swallows.
'Ava – I don't ... I mean, I can't ...' Her words trail
away, and now I'm scared.

'What is it? What's wrong?'

She shakes her head. 'I wanted to leave this; for a
while, at least. It's too much.'

'You don't have to ask him. I'll do it.'

'That's not what I mean. It's just that I kind of
already did.'

'What do you mean?'

'Days ago. Before – well, before everything that's
happened. Not about going to Sweden, I mean. But I
asked him if he could find out anything about your
mother. And, well, he did.'

And it's not good: it's all over Sam's face. Inside I'm
sinking, as if I'm in the sea, the water is closing over my
head and I can't reach the light and sky above it. I see
rather than feel Sam move closer, take my hand.

'Go on. Tell me,' I say. My voice is faint.

'All right. I'm so sorry, Ava. Your mum was sick – she
had cancer. You know what happened on the day of

decision, when Europeans had to decide to stay or go before the borders closed. If they stayed they had to apply for citizenship, and they didn't have medical or other benefits until it went through. Dad said she probably left to get healthcare back home in Sweden.'

My mother – she was sick? I try to remember back to the time just before she left. Did I know, were there signs? I can't think of anything, but I was a child. Mum fixed my skinned knees, soothed my fevers, not the other way around: if there was anything wrong, I didn't see it.

'But maybe she was treated, and she's all right now?'

Sam shakes her head. 'I'm so sorry, Ava. Dad said she was terminal. She was dying when she left.'

I close my eyes, lean back on the sofa. I'm numb, I can't take this in, I can't understand. She left because she was sick? She should have been with us: the family that loved her.

To watch her die: suffering, without any medical help. She couldn't do that to us. That's it, isn't it?

For so long I was angry with her for leaving me, for leaving Dad – but she was sick, and I didn't know?

Did Dad?

10

Sam

Ava asked to be alone again but it felt wrong to leave her. She was so calm and quiet. I thought she'd be in pieces; maybe that will come later. I told her to come and get me no matter what time it is if she wants to talk.

Back in my room, I pace. It's late, very — after two a.m. now, but how can I sleep?

I open my laptop; hesitate. I don't want all the superficial chat with Charlize or anyone else, but what about Lucas? Charlize said he was trying to get in touch. After what we went through together at that demonstration, maybe he is one of the few people I know who feels real.

Me: *Hi Lucas, hope you and all your family are all right. Crazy few days, and some terrible news to add to it: Ava's dad has died in one of the bombs. She's staying here.*

He answers almost immediately: is he another insomniac? *Oh no, poor Ava. And what about you? I saw on the news how close to it you and your dad were. Are you all right?*

Me: *Not physically hurt other than some bruises. Not very all right. Why are you awake at this time anyway?*

Lucas: *Bit noisy around these parts. Sirens etc.*

Me: *Etc? What's happening?*

Lucas: *From my window it looks rather like I'd imagine Armageddon. Don't worry: we're locked up tight and not going anywhere.*

I'm horrified. Most people I know are in secure gated communities, like this one; it didn't occur to me to think he could be in danger just because of where he lives.

Me: *Promise me you'll check in now and then so I know you're OK.*

Lucas: *Aw, you DO care! Honestly, we're fine; nothing to steal here except for books – that doesn't seem to interest looters much.*

Me: *Promise!*

Lucas: *I do solemnly swear to check in again in the morning. I'm going to stuff a pillow or two over my head now and try to sleep. You should do the same.*

Me: *I will.*

Lucas: *Take care.*

Me: *You too.*

I get into PJs and bed, but put the TV back on. Live footage – from a helicopter; on the ground – what's happening on the streets of London and other places has gone beyond anything riot police can control. That glow I could see in the distant sky? Buildings are burning. People with their faces covered are taking what they can from shops; there is fighting on the streets. And it's spreading, too; a map shows the areas affected, and they're growing with each update.

I feel sick inside.

Despite the bright flames, all is darkness.

*

Shopping with Mummy is boring! I play hide and seek by myself around and behind racks of clothing, giggling while she and then the shop girls try to find me. But their voices go further away and when I peek out someone else is there, someone I don't know.

Hi Sam, *she says, and smiles.* I'll take you to your mummy and daddy.

She takes my hand. But when we leave the shops and Mummy still isn't there I'm scared, try to pull away from her. She holds me tighter.

I'm bundled into a car, then into a house I don't know, and Mummy and Daddy still aren't there.

I'm locked in a room. I'm cold and hungry, and it's dark.

It's so dark — I can't see anything. The darkness is like a monster inside me, one that only comes out when I'm alone.

I'm crying, but still nobody comes.

I'll be good, I promise: just take me home. Please.

Please take me home ...

11

Ava

I close our front door, turn the locks, lean against it for a moment with my eyes shut.

It's a relief to be alone – I'd insisted on it, and anyway I doubt Sam's father would have allowed her to come here, to this neighbourhood, even though it is clear of the trouble so far. Sam's dad had wanted the driver and security he sent with me to come up and help me pack, but I insisted that I needed time and space to do this by myself.

But I breathe and count and breathe some more before I can make myself open my eyes.

So few days have passed since I stepped out through this door with Dad for the last time. Everything is as we left it; why wouldn't it be? Everything is so ordinary.

Our chess game: it was my turn. I leave it that way so the last move will always be Dad's.

My room, first. It's easier.

I run my hands over my bookshelves. As I grew up, my books were my friends, most of them gifts from Mum or Dad. I stroke the covers and gather them up into the boxes I've brought.

I know I can't take too long. They'll check on me in an hour or two, come up and help me carry things, they said.

Dad's room. It used to be Mum and Dad's, of course, and there are still things of hers in here. Dad wouldn't get rid of them. Even though she left us he hung on to her in so many ways, or so I used to think.

But maybe things were different for Dad than they were for me.

Is that the real reason I'd insisted on coming here so soon? There must be something within these walls that will give me the answers I so desperately need.

I go carefully through Mum's things first. I find her locket hidden away in a drawer, and I'm shocked she left it behind. She always wore it; it had my baby photo and a lock of my hair from my first haircut inside. I open it, but it's empty. Did she take the contents with her, but leave the locket here for me to find one day? I slip it around my neck and the silver is soon warm against my skin.

I find a jumper I remember her wearing, and pull it on over my T-shirt; a book of poetry she liked – it's in Swedish so I can't read it, but I take it anyway.

Now Dad's things.

He had little that was personal, apart from books: he studied and later taught classics before his university department closed. I pack some of his favourites, ones I remember him reading again and again. I touch pages he would have touched.

There is a lumpy scarf I knitted for him years ago that he insisted on wearing. I hold it; it smells like him, like mint and coffee and something else. I breathe in and out again, trying not to lose it.

His desk.

Financial information. Bank details; not much in his account. There's some cash in a bottom drawer that I take. I find the rent receipts: it's paid quarterly in advance. He'd only just paid it three weeks ago, so there is some time before I have to work out what to do with everything. Papers, loose photos: I find one of the three of us I don't remember seeing before. And underneath the photos is a box, an old chocolate box. I take off the lid.

Inside? Letters. From Mum – postmarked from Sweden. There's a stack of them, in date order, from many years ago – before me, before they got married, when she was going back and forth until she finally moved here to be with Dad.

But as I look through them, the dates jump – to years on. Goosebumps rise on my arms, my neck. Some of these letters are from after she left us.

And interspersed within them are some – unopened – that are addressed to me. My hands are shaking. I've never seen them before. I stare at the letters in my hands from a mother who I thought left me with never a backward glance. She wrote to me?

I can't deal with this now, I can't. I tuck them into my bag with the other letters, to look at later.

At the bottom of them all is one letter that doesn't match the others. It's in a corporate sort of envelope, with a printed label instead of handwriting on it. It's addressed to Dad and is the most recent one, postmarked a few months after Mum left.

This one I open.

The words swim before my eyes.

... instructed to inform you as next of kin ... died last night.

Dad knew. He had letters she wrote he never gave me. He knew all this time what happened to her, and he never told me.

12

Sam

Ava stands in front of the window in her room, her back towards me. Boxes – not many, if that is all she's brought from the life she had before – are stacked neatly against one wall.

'Ava?'

She turns. Her face is even paler than it was before, and there are shadows and darkness under her eyes. She clutches a shoulder bag tight against her chest.

'You look like you've seen a ghost.'

'I think I kind of have.'

'Are you all right? Sorry, stupid question. '

'It's OK. I feel more ... numb than anything else.'

There's a thick knitted scarf around her neck. Like she's just noticed it is there she unwinds it quickly, throws it to the floor.

'Ava?'

'He knew, Sam. My dad. He knew about my mum.'

'He did? Are you sure?'

'Yes. I found letters she wrote to him. And also, the ...' She shudders. 'The notification of her death, a few months after she left.'

'I'm so sorry, Ava.'

'I guess we knew as much, but still, seeing it written – it's a shock. But that's not all.' She looks up at me. Her eyes are full of bewilderment, pain, anger. 'Mum wrote letters to me, too. He never gave them to me: they were in a box in his room.'

'Have you read them?'

'Not yet. They're here.' She looks down at the bag she holds tightly against her, then up again. 'I'd guessed he probably knew. Just before he died he was trying to tell me something. He said *sorry*.' She shakes her head. 'How could he do this? Not tell me anything – leave me thinking she just chose to abandon me, like I was nothing to her?'

It's my turn to shake my head, helpless. 'I don't know.'

'I can never ask him now. I can never get angry with him, hear his side, finally forgive him. It will always be there.'

'Oh, Ava.' I don't know what else to do, so even though she looks wild, furious, I go to her. Take her hand, pull her to sit down next to me on the sofa. She sits there, her back bolt upright.

'Now that I know for sure that … that my mum has died, I have nowhere to go. I can't just stay in your guest room for ever.'

'Why not? It's not like we're short a few rooms. You could get lost in this place.'

'That's not the point. And what about your parents?'

'What about them? Please stay. Anyway, I can't see Dad turfing you out: think of the bad press he'd get for that. First he says they've crushed A4A, that they're no

[162]

longer a threat, and then he chucks a girl orphaned by A4A out on to the streets. It'll *so* never happen.'

She looks at me, head tilted to one side, then almost laughs. 'You're probably right. But that's still not the point.'

'What is?'

She shakes her head. 'I don't even know any more.'

'Stay. Trust me on this one.'

She gives a half-smile. 'Thank you for listening. But now I need to do some reading.' She touches the bag she still holds. 'And for that I need to be alone.'

'Are you sure?'

'Yes. I'm sure.'

'You'll let me know if you want company, or to talk? Anything?'

'I will. I promise.'

I lean towards her, give her a hug. Her body is rigid but then she relaxes a little, touches her cheek against mine. Pulls away and looks at me. There is something that wasn't there before, unreadable, in her eyes.

She looks down. 'Now, go,' she says.

13

Ava

I watch Sam walk across the room. She hesitates at the door, looks back, then goes through. It shuts behind her.

I sigh, lean back against the sofa. The anger is starting to leave me: Sam, saying what she did about her dad, she did that. I do smile this time, but it soon fades away.

She still has no idea the real reason I can't stay here like this, as her friend. I don't know how much longer I can hide how I feel about her.

But where else can I go?

I shake my head. I'm just trying to distract myself from what must be done. I'm both desperate to read these letters, and afraid.

I open the bag. The ones to Dad are here too; those I'll leave for another day – or maybe not read at all.

I take out the ones addressed to me, keeping them in date order.

The first one in my hands, I touch the writing on the envelope – trace the letters she wrote to send this to me.

I break the seal, open the envelope. Draw out the sheet of paper inside. Unfold it, and begin.

My dearest Ava,

First of all — I'm so sorry I didn't say goodbye. I agreed it was the right thing to do, but I'd barely left you before I saw how wrong this was. Forgive me.

I've gone back to Sweden. I miss you so much: more than all the stars in the sky, all the waves in the sea. I didn't leave because I wanted to.

I'm sick: a bad sort of sickness. I need doctors to help me, and we couldn't pay them in London. So Daddy and I agreed that I should go home to Sweden.

I know Daddy loves you. He'll do everything he can to look after you and make you happy. Forgive him, too.

Love Mummy.

The tears come now, so many my vision is blurred. I can't read any more for a while.

Later, I open the others, one after another. She tells me in every one how much she loves me. Also stories of the flowers in the hospice garden, the things she sees in the clouds in the sky, the kind nurses and doctors who try to make her well.

In the last one she must know what is coming. She tells me I must be brave, that I have the strength and will to be anything I want to be in this world.

And then she says goodbye.

14

Sam

I'm barely back in my room when there's a knock on the door, and it opens. It's Mum.

'Dad's back,' she says. 'He wants to talk to both of us in his study. Now.'

'What about?'

'I don't know,' she says, but she's troubled: I can see it.

We walk there together, go through the open door and Mum shuts it behind us.

'There you are: my two girls,' Dad says.

'What's happening?' she says.

'Come, sit down.' We exchange a glance, go to the sofa when he gestures. He pulls his chair across so he's facing us both. 'It's time for a family conference,' he says.

'What is it, Merton?' Mum asks.

'Before I say anything else, this is confidential.'

He never tells me anything that is confidential. 'You're freaking me out,' I say.

'Prime Minister Powell is resigning over recent events in London and elsewhere.'

'When?' I ask.

'There will be a press conference early this evening.'

'Does that mean you'll be the prime minister now?' Mum says.

'Unlikely,' he says. She's disappointed; I'm relieved.

'Does that mean the Reform Party are out, or are they going to appoint another leader?' I ask, my mind racing. 'What about the coalition? Is there going to be an election?'

He raises an eyebrow. 'Final details are still being worked out. I've got to go back now.'

'Have you been awake all night?' Mum says.

'Most of it. I had a nap on the sofa in my office for a few hours.'

'Can't you tell us anything else?' I say.

'Patience.' He hesitates. 'Things need to change: this country needs a firmer hand,' he says, and as he does so he takes my hand in his left, Mum's in his right. 'Team Gregory on board?' he says, like he used to do before a big political appearance or event, the sort with Mum and me in the background smiling and waving. It means us against the world, no cracks that anyone can see.

It doesn't mean they're not there.

'Of course,' Mum says.

He kisses her cheek, then tugs on my hand.

'Samantha?' he says.

He wants me to agree when I don't know what's coming, what I'm agreeing to or supporting. But that's what I do. Isn't it? I nod; he kisses my cheek.

'I've got to shower, change, go,' he says. 'Watch the news and stay off the phone. The switchboard has been instructed to block calls for now.'

He gets up and goes through the door.

Mum looks at me and I look at her. She shakes her head. 'Whatever next?' And she reaches out, hugs me – properly – without worrying about creasing her outfit or smudging her makeup.

It's so rare that it makes all this seem somehow scarier.

I wait at the top of the stairs for Dad. There's a sick feeling inside me, that something is about to go very wrong: not just with the country, but with us, too.

Soon he's hurrying down the hall towards me, fresh suit on, and I walk to the door with him.

'Dad? Is it rats or the sinking ship time again? How about neither: let somebody else sort things out.'

But he's not really listening. He never has, so why would I think he'd start now?

15

Ava

I hesitate in the doorway, not wanting to be around people. But once Sam texted to tell me what was happening I couldn't not come, and I'm hoping no one will see me standing here – that I can just observe, leave if I want to, with no one noticing.

But Sam must have been watching for me. She turns to the door a moment later, waves me in and, caught, I go. She's saved me a spot next to her on the sofa. Her mum on the other side of her nods. Penny is here, too, standing behind the sofa, and there are a dozen or so other people I don't know on other chairs and sofas. There is a woman who looks like a rounder, softer version of Sam's mother – her sister? – and others that I guess are relatives, friends, senior staff. Penny touches my shoulder with her hand briefly but says nothing, and no one else says anything, either. There is a sense of them all holding their breath, which makes it easier to release mine: everyone is focused on the large TV screen on the wall, not on me.

There are BBC updates on what they're now calling the *A4A Atrocities*: the way it is said you know it must be capitalised. London, Birmingham, Manchester and

Glasgow were the four targets of the suicide bombers. I start to get more of a sense of all the other people who have been touched by this, and feel less alone than I did before. But it has spread so far beyond that beginning: the unrest and violence can't all be from A4A, can it? It's almost like they've unleashed something that has been lying in wait.

And it's not just in this room that people are waiting, holding their breath; you can see it, too, in the faces of the newsreaders and the experts they go to for speculation: something is about to happen that could change everything.

Finally the words come: *Now we're going live to the press conference at Westminster*. Someone here finds a remote and turns up the volume.

All three party leaders – Gregory, Armstrong and Powell – are standing together. Is it really a press conference, though? It's within the gates of Westminster, so the only media there must have been specially invited.

Prime Minister Powell approaches the microphone. She clears her throat. She has a piece of paper in her hand; it's shaking.

'Thank you for coming on this day, one after a week of the darkest days I've ever known. First and foremost, on behalf of everyone in government across all the parties, my deepest and heartfelt condolences to all the innocent victims of these terrorist atrocities – the dead, the injured, their friends and family. We'll do all we can to help them in the aftermath.

'We've talked through the night and reached an historic three-party agreement. Effective immediately,

I am resigning as prime minister. Parliament is dissolved and a national state of emergency is declared. This situation is without precedent in our country. There are agreed amendments to the relevant legislation, again by three-party agreement; more details on this will follow. An interim government with a new coalition will take the country forward until the emergency is resolved, at which time elections will be held.' She pauses. 'Thank you for the honour and privilege of leading this great country.'

She steps back, and then ... Armstrong and Gregory step forward together. Armstrong takes the mike.

'This is a desperate time for all of us. Our country needs order; a firm, fair hand; and for these despicable A4A terrorists to be brought to swift justice. This isn't a time for party politics; this is the moment to step forward and be counted. Together.'

He goes on and on; much of what he says is the sort of thing people will cheer, but without much content. His words start to fade away. Despite everything that has happened in my own life, my mind is spinning with what I've heard.

What are the implications? They've dissolved Parliament, and agreed Armstrong will lead with Gregory as deputy PM until ... things are resolved? What does that even mean? And how can they lead without Parliament to legislate?

They *can't*. Not as a democracy.

Excited chatter starts to break out around us as I turn to Sam. There is shock on her face, too, but then her mother says something low in her ear and it is replaced by a plastic smile.

16

Sam

My face feels frozen, the muscles aching from holding an acceptable expression when it is all I can do not to jump on a table and scream: don't any of these people see what has just happened?

Team Gregory: I remind myself before Mum can. Ava, the only one whose face held the shock I felt, slipped away soon after the news conference; her hand squeezed mine quickly before she went. I wasn't sure she'd come after hiding away to read her mother's letters, but now I'm desperate to get out of this room and go to talk to her. I can't breathe.

No chance.

It's mostly family Mum invited, a few close friends, but there are some sharp eyes amongst them, too: ones that we can't count as part of the *team* who would be gleeful if there were anything to leak to the press.

A three-party agreement. Does that mean Dad actually *chose* to go along with this? I'm desperate to talk to him, too, to find out what happened behind the scenes.

Not that he would tell me much.

*

It's hours before Dad gets home. Hands are shaken, he's congratulated on his political nine lives: still in power, still deputy prime minister – he didn't fall on the prime minister's sword.

There's a dinner.

Dad is jovial: he is his public self. Mum is sparkling: she is her actual self, happy to still be in the centre of things. But how long can this last?

How long *should* it?

The eye of a hurricane may be the only calm place in the centre of violence, but you can't stay there, not for ever – sooner or later the storm will catch you out.

My smile is in place but my eyes are pleading with Dad: tell me something, anything, that will make this all make sense. But if he sees my silent plea he says nothing.

Maybe Dad has more wine than usual; maybe his hand shakes slightly as he toasts the health of the new prime minister. There are no other clues to what he really thinks.

When I'm finally released I rush back to my room, wanting to knock on Ava's door, not sure if I should – but then it opens. She must have been listening for my steps.

'Hi,' she says. 'I wasn't expecting all that.'

'Me neither.'

'Want to binge-watch the news all night?'

'Not really, but you know.' I half smile.

'Yours or mine?'

'Mine? I've got snacks. I mean, if you are sure you want to. Are you OK? I mean, about your mum's letters?'

'Not really. But I don't want to talk about them – at least, not yet.'

'OK. Come on.'

We settle ourselves under a blanket on the sofa in my room, TV on. My emergency box of dark chocolates is open. Ava's arm is warm against mine and just having her there I breathe more easily, my headache starts to ease.

The news conference we watched live earlier is shown over and over again. Reporters go to experts, members of the public, various politicians; they speculate on what it all means. But their reactions seem strangely muted.

And in the background the violence continues.

17

Ava

There is a knock on my door the next morning; I assume it is Sam but when I open the door, it's Penny.

'Hi, Ava.'

'Good morning.'

'How are you? Is there anything you need?'

'No, thank you.'

'Are you free? Mrs Gregory was hoping to have a chat with you.'

Sam's mother wants to have a chat with *me*? Now – with everything else that is going on? 'Of course. Give me a moment?'

'I'll wait,' she says, and closes the door.

If this is what I think it may be, I was kind of part expecting it, part not: which makes no sense. My ability to think rationally seems to have diminished. Instead of thinking I brush my hair, straighten my shirt – it was one of the things that was left in the room for me to wear when I first got here; probably it belonged to Sam's mother. And then I take a few deep breaths and step into the hall.

Penny takes me down a hall, a flight of stairs, another

hall, then shows me to a sitting room. She ushers me in and leaves.

'Ava, darling,' Mrs Gregory says, and gets out of her seat and air-kisses my cheeks. We both sit down. 'How are you?'

Is that a real question, or a social nicety? I decide the latter. 'I'm fine, thank you, and yourself?'

'Well, a bit tired from all the excitement yesterday! I thought we should have a chat.'

I try to make myself look relaxed and then give up.

'We've loved having you here, Ava.'

'Thank you. It was very kind of you.'

'Moving forwards now, we need to think about what would be best for you. Do you have any other family or close friends you'd prefer to stay with?'

'My dad has a brother, but they didn't get along. I don't know where he lives. And my mother was from Sweden. There may be family there but I don't know them.'

'Oh yes, Merton mentioned about your mother. Such sad news for you with everything else. I'm so sorry you had to deal with that at the same time as your father.' She reaches out, touches my hand. 'You are welcome to stay with us if you'd like to, but there is another option. Your head teacher has been in touch, and she said they can extend your scholarship to full boarding until you finish school. How does that sound?'

I'm surprised. 'I thought scholarships like mine only covered school fees?'

'That may be the usual case. But it seems they have some room in the budget, in the circumstances, for board as well. What do you think?' It's obvious what she thinks

I should say and there is little choice, really.

I can't stay here. This is the perfect solution. 'That'd be great. Thank you,' I say, but I feel a reluctance, or sadness, or something – to be leaving here, and Sam. It's been a refuge, hasn't it?

The boarding girls are about as warm and friendly to me as Charlize and her friends. That's fine at school when I can leave at the end of the day, but what will actually living with them be like?

'They're hoping school will be open again soon, probably some time next week. We'll arrange a car to move you and your things. But now there is something else we need to discuss.'

'Of course. What is it?'

'I'm sorry to have to raise this, Ava; it must be so hard for you. The coroner's office has been in touch regarding your father's body.'

His *body*: the words take me back to that last moment, watching Dad being zipped inside a body bag. Taken away by an ambulance, and to where? I flinch, fight for control. I should have thought of this, but I hadn't.

'Do you know if he had any funeral plans, a family burial plot or the like?'

I shake my head, not sure I can trust my voice.

'Merton and I have discussed it, and would like to help. Penny has the information and can discuss some options with you.'

'I ... thank you.'

As if she reads minds Penny appears almost instantly through the door, armed with a folder.

Sam's mum says goodbye, says she has to get on, and

I get the feeling that thinking about death or talking about arrangements is too far outside the nice world she lives in, that she can barely make herself think about it, let alone talk about it.

We go back to my room. Penny talks about things like burial, cremation, what to do with ashes, whether I want some sort of funeral. I try to listen but now I'm thinking of something that hadn't occurred to me before. Where is my mother? Was she buried, was she cremated? The borders are closed. If she is buried I can never visit her grave.

I'm not sure if I want to be able to visit my dad's, either.

Cremation. Nothing religious – Dad was an atheist. A very simple ceremony. Penny will find out when and where it can be scheduled, and let me know. Ashes to be scattered by me later – I don't know where.

'Are you OK?' Penny says, and her question feels real.

'Of course not. But thanks for asking.'

She nods, sympathy in her eyes, and touches my hand. Says to let her know if there is anything she can do.

We say goodbye at my door, and I glance at Sam's across the hall. I so want to talk to her about all of this. But maybe she's still asleep: we were up late.

It can wait. I shut my door, go back to bed. It's my bed for now, but how much longer? I wonder when things will have settled enough for me to move into school?

I switch on the news, and conclude: not any time soon.

18

Sam

That morning when I wake up, just for a moment, my mind is that half-asleep confusion of forgetfulness. Part of me is thinking, *Shouldn't the alarm for school have gone by now?* And part of me doesn't care, and wants to go back to sleep.

Then it all comes flooding back in a rush. There's no school again today, and I'm even wistful for that boring part of normal life.

I fumble around for my phone: it's still early, anyway – the alarm would have only just gone. Maybe my internal clock is puzzled at the irregular hours and so prodded me awake to see what is going on.

There's a message: from Lucas, sent a few minutes ago.

Lucas: *Guess what I saw out of my window this morning?*

Me: *I don't know, what did you see?*

Lucas: *Guess.*

Me: *A flying saucer. A giant white fluffy talking bunny. Um ... your identical twin that you never knew existed.*

Lucas: *Wrong, wrong and wrong! I saw this:*

There's a pause, then a photo pings in.

I stare at the image on my screen in shock. It's huge,

it's metal, and it looks completely out of place on a typical London street. At least a street that *was* typical: now there are burnt-out shops across the road, debris, wrecked cars. I have to blink and look again to be sure I'm actually seeing what I think I am.

It's a tank. An actual military army-type tank, and it's on the street below Lucas's window.

Me: *Is that what I think it is?*

Lucas: *Do you think it is a tank?*

Me: *Yes.*

Lucas: *Unless we're both suffering from the same delusion, that must be it: it's a tank.*

Me: *What's it doing?*

Lucas: *Right now? Hang on, I'll just check … OK, it's doing nothing. Just sitting around out there looking intimidating, I think. And there are some army types wandering about in the vicinity of the tank, too – they seem to be occupying a shop down the street and now are just generally hanging about the place. Last night when it turned up the mob on the street just got up and ran. It's been pretty quiet since then.*

I shake my head. I'm guessing Lucas's tank can't be the only one. So, there are army tanks – on the streets. In London?

I start to answer him but then my phone rings in my hand and I jump. It's Mum. Before eight a.m.? *No way.*

I hit *answer call*. 'Hello? What's wrong?'

'Sorry, I know it's early, darling. We need to get ourselves ready for a press thing: we've got to leave in a few hours. A joint statement by the PM and your dad, Team Gregory in attendance, and Armstrong's family, too. Get yourself up and Penny will be there with a new dress soon – *assuming* the delivery makes it through. I'll try to come up with a plan B in case it doesn't.' There's panic all through her voice. 'Go, go, Samantha.'

'All right. Bye.'

There's another message from Lucas: *Still there, or have you fainted with shock at the size of my tank?*

Me: *I don't faint. But duty calls, have to go and get ready for some press thing. Keep an eye on that tank.*

Lucas: *Will do. You get all the fun. Enjoy.*

19

Ava

'I'm guessing you're going somewhere.'

'I'd never be bored enough to get done up like this just for fun,' Sam says, and pulls at the skirt of her dress – it's pale blue, made of something shimmery, and goes with her eyes. She looks perfect and oh-so-uncomfortable at the same time. She looks at me more closely. 'Is something wrong?'

'Penny has been talking to me about organising a funeral and stuff for Dad.'

She touches my hand. 'That must be so hard to have to deal with right now.'

'Has to be done. Your parents are helping with it, by the way, which is generous of them.'

'Take it from one who knows. Throwing money around is easy for them; actual sympathy or being there is much harder. They're taking the easy way.'

'Sam!' I say, shocked.

'All I meant was, don't be too grateful. I'm glad they're helping but the money isn't a big deal to them.'

'Anyway, you didn't say: where are you going?'

'The new government' – and her eyes widen then

narrow when she says the word – 'is making a statement. Families to be in adoring attendance at the back of the shot.'

'I wonder what they have to say?'

'No idea. I've been practising not reacting no matter what. Try me.' Her look of unease vanishes. She pats her hair down, stands straight, hands clasped in front, leaning forward slightly as if in rapt attention; her plastic smile is in place.

'Very good. Hmm, OK, let's see ... National service will be brought in for all.' Her composure doesn't waver. 'How about national service starting at age fifteen?' Still no reaction. 'OK, you've got that nailed. Hope it's not too dire for you.'

Her smile fades; she leans against the doorframe. 'Oh, it will be dire, as far as I'm concerned. But I'm more worried about what they will say.'

I nod. 'Me too.'

She looks up at me. Even though she is in heels I'm still taller. Her head tilts to one side. 'Thank you, Ava.'

'For what?'

'Despite all that you've had to go through, being here; listening. You have no idea how much it helps to be able to say what I think once in a while.' She leans in and gives me a quick hug; her soft hair brushes against my cheek. There is something pricking at the back of my eyes.

She doesn't know, does she, that I'm leaving – she'd say if she did. But with what she just said it doesn't seem the time to tell her.

After she's gone I think I should have done so: what if her mother mentions it now? But it's too late.

20
Sam

Mum casts an eye over me. Tugs one sleeve a fraction down, adjusts my necklace. Links her arm in mine and we turn a little so we're facing the big, ornate mirror in the upper hall together.

She looks so serious as she studies our reflection that I say what she likes to hear. 'We look like sisters.' And we do: she doesn't look anywhere near old enough to be my mother, and we are so alike, apart from her being taller, especially dressed as we are: me in a dress, her in a suit that is a darker shade of the same material and a similar style. She must have had someone working through the night to get these ready in time.

She smiles. 'We'll do, I suppose.'

Dad has already gone. We head down the stairs to the main entrance below, where we're to be met by a new security detail. I'm nervous, and not about what will happen when we arrive – at least, not yet: it's the getting there. But like a talisman my camera is held close. It has a tiny ring and I attached it to my bracelet: it can be tucked into my sleeve or used in my hand, and is small and thin enough to have been missed during Mum's outfit scrutiny.

Downstairs is a group of half a dozen men and women. One of them is an assistant of Dad's that I've met before; he hurries towards us.

'Lleyton, it's lovely to see you again,' Mum says.

'I'm honoured to accompany two such beautiful young ladies,' he says, and I suppress the urge to roll my eyes. 'If I may introduce you to your new security detail?'

Names are given and I nod and smile along with Mum as we're introduced to each of them, until we get to one that I recognise: it's Agent Coulson, the one who yanked me to safety at that protest for Lucas's friend after everything went so horribly wrong. I was angry at the time that he hauled me back to Dad but, if he hadn't, I might have been hurt in that riot. Or worse. Is this a promotion, Dad's way of repaying him for what he did?

I glance at Mum – do I admit we've met before? No. There's no way Dad would have told her about that. There's a quick wink from Coulson to me once she's turned her head, as if he realised the same thing.

Mum and I are ushered to a new car: it's limo-sized, with two rows of seats facing each other in the back. We're told it has double-reinforced bulletproof glass and hidden armour that will withstand pretty much anything, but instead of making me feel more secure, I feel nervous: what are they expecting, exactly, that it needs to withstand?

We head out through our gates. Before long we reach our community gates, and there, outside them, is a tank. I'd be more shocked if I hadn't seen one in Lucas's photo already, but it still seems unbelievable to see one here.

Mum's eyes widen. 'Is that really necessary, in this neighbourhood?'

'It acts as a deterrent and protects your community,' Lleyton answers.

I take quick photos of the tank, the newly reinforced gates. The extra guards at Westminster when we arrive.

The doors are held open; it's time.

21

Ava

'And now from Westminster: a statement from our new prime minister, William Adam Armstrong, and our deputy prime minister, Merton Gregory.'

The camera pans across the assembled group. Armstrong's wife, son and daughters, and Sam and her mum are on the right; advisors on the left; Armstrong and Gregory in the centre. Armstrong steps forward.

'The challenges we face as a nation will test us. We are stronger if we stand together: the divisive forces within our communities must be overcome. But that is not all we must achieve. For too long the wealth and resources of our country have been concentrated in the hands of the few at the expense of the many. This must change. It *will* change.'

He outlines bold plans: redistribution of wealth. Seizure of vacant private property to house the homeless. A jobs-for-all policy supported by government works. Even strict anti-discrimination laws on the grounds of disability, sex, sexual preference, country of origin, language. Does that mean the English-only laws are out?

Can they really do these things? Would it bring the

disaffected who have begun to rally around A4A back to the mainstream of society?

I watch and listen to this man who has somehow wrested power from the others, and done it in such a way that he answers to no one. He has charisma, but there is also a steel you can feel inside him. Would he really stand up to the bankers and old money, take their property away? What about people like Sam's family, who have money from her mother's side, and others that back Armstrong? Would they be made exempt to keep their support?

Sam's rapt listening pose and smile stay in place. But then Armstrong pauses. 'Of course, that's not all we need to do. Right now, we need to make the streets safe for your children, and ours.' He glances back at the families standing to his left. 'With his law enforcement, security and anti-terrorism background, there is no one better suited to implement the firm measures needed than Merton Gregory.'

Now Sam's father steps forward to speak.

'These last days and weeks have tried us all. This is not a time for a weak response; those who teach violence to our children have respect for nothing we value in our society. The rule of law must be re-established; order must be returned to our streets.

'Emergency measures will include the following:

'Our armed forces will be deployed as necessary to quell unrest, rioting and unauthorised assemblies: this began as of last night.

'A nine p.m. curfew will be imposed country-wide, effective immediately. Breach of the curfew will lead to automatic arrest.

'A new, elite security force is being established to detect and eliminate terrorist organisations within our society: this has already begun. A recruitment programme for this force and to expand the existing police and army will be implemented immediately.

'Finally, the death penalty is reinstated for perpetrators of crimes of terror and treason.'

My eyes widen. The death penalty? That hasn't been used in the UK for, I don't know, decades?

Armstrong speaks again, summing up what both of them have said. There is smiling and hand-shaking and back-slapping, and all the time I'm staring at the screen, mind spinning.

Property and wealth to be redistributed: whose property, and who decides?

The death penalty for crimes broadly titled terror and treason, but what does that cover? Again, who decides?

An elite security force: with what powers?

And a curfew: breach leads to arrest, but with what punishment?

Sam maintains her poise throughout, but is it just because I'm beginning to know her so well that I can see the strain by her eyes? Do her hands still clasped in front of her look rigid? Maybe I imagine these things.

Well done, Armstrong. You've arranged it all so you are the champion of the people, and Gregory is the enforcer. If things go too far it'll all be his fault.

22

Sam

When the red lights on the news cameras finally all go off I feel ready to collapse. My eyes search for Dad's, but he is talking with Armstrong, and then one of their aides ushers me and the Armstrong kids away.

'Are you all right, Sam?' Sandy, the oldest of the three, whispers, and I remind myself to stay composed.

I shrug. 'My feet hurt.' The truth, but only a small part of it.

'My face hurts. Too much smiling,' Sandy says, and grimaces. She must be eleven – she's in the first year at my school – and already a champion at standing and smiling at the same time. Which is much harder than it sounds, especially today.

We're brought soft drinks and cupcakes but I'd kill for a cup of tea.

'It's annoying being put in here with the children,' Sandy says, and I almost laugh: exactly what I was thinking, not that I wasn't happy to escape the public eye of that pressure cooker. Her brother and sister are twins, and what – eight years old? – and are soon arguing over who gets the last chocolate cupcake. Their lives have changed now. It's going to be all armoured limos and special agents; Team Armstrong and Team Gregory, and not enough chocolate cupcakes to go around.

My tiny camera was between my clasped hands throughout that press conference. I don't think anyone noticed; I didn't take any photos during the live filming, but did before and after. I tried to catch unaware faces; who stood with whom when the whole country wasn't looking; even how they stood – their body language – whether at ease, or alarmed. Now I take a bunch of selfies of Sandy and me with the twins fighting in the background.

They're getting tired and cranky, Sandy is yawning and my stomach is wanting food of a non-iced variety, when someone finally comes: it's Lleyton? And with him is Coulson and another agent.

'I've got some exciting news!' Lleyton says.

I raise an eyebrow. *It was all a dream?*

'You're all going home by helicopter! And these gentlemen will escort you.'

'By helicopter?' The twins and Sandy are cheering, getting their coats, but I'm looking at Coulson and see an edge of tension. I go to where he waits by the door, not wanting to freak out the kids.

'What's happened?' I say, voice low.

He turns, glances at me and I see a moment of indecision on his face – between the truth and a fob-off-the-child answer? – but the former wins. 'There are large numbers of protestors converging on the area,' he says. 'We're getting you out.'

'Thank you for telling me the truth.'

'You can handle it.'

Mum and Mrs Armstrong join us now and we're all hurried down the hall. Sandy starts to look uncertain, as if she's caught the vibe that something isn't right. Then when we get to the doors we can all hear it: the sound of the mob. It's indistinct and distant, groans and growls that hang in the air.

Coulson and other agents surround us, walk us quickly across to an empty parking area that they've somehow cleared to make room for our waiting ride.

It's a big military-style helicopter, with enough room for all of us. The blades are going around over our heads and the twins have to be urged forwards to go underneath them. We're helped aboard.

'Where's Dad?' I ask Mum as we get into seats next to each other.

Coulson is helping to strap us in; he overhears. 'He and the prime minister went in another helicopter already,' he says.

'Nothing like women and children first,' Mrs Armstrong says.

'They aren't given the choice in matters of security,' one of the other agents says – the one who seems to be in charge of them all. 'That's what we do.'

'Excellent,' Mrs Armstrong says, with layers of something like sarcasm in her voice. My eyes focus on her. I think I could like her. She used to be some sort of civil rights activist, didn't she? What does she think of what is going on now, and her husband's role in it all? I'm intrigued.

Up we go and my stomach drops. It's a weird feeling, going straight up, hearing the blades above us. I'd made sure to be by a window and stare out of it now as we sweep across the sky.

I'm pressed against the window with my camera in my hand, zoomed all the way. Hopefully it is at the right angle to capture what is happening on the ground below us, but I don't dare hold it to my eye to check in case someone notices, and takes exception and my camera away with it.

Below us is Westminster; the Thames. The mob that growls and grows and surrounded us until we flew above it. Another ring is moving in from beyond and will soon tighten around them: soldiers. Police.

What will happen then? Can they arrest this many people?

The death penalty is being reinstated, Dad said: without debate or a referendum or a vote of any sort.

Could all these people be guilty of crimes of terror or treason?

23

Ava

'Was that a helicopter I saw in the garden?' I say.

'Oh, you know; we just fancied a scenic flight.'

'What did you see?'

'Same old. Mobs. Riot police. Soldiers. A few tanks.'

'Are you OK, Sam?'

She shrugs, but bit by bit the plastic smile and bravado are fading, and she looks haggard. She glances up at me. 'I just can't – I mean—'

There's a knock on the door, and Penny peers in. 'Sorry to interrupt, girls. Samantha, your parents want you in ten minutes: a family dinner, just you three tonight. Ava, something is being sent up for you.'

Sam starts to protest at my exclusion, but I shake my head. 'I'm sure you need to talk. It's fine.' And it is from my point of view, but I can see Sam's slumped shoulders, and know it isn't what she needs right now.

'Thank you, Penny,' she says. 'I'll be there: I do know the way.' And we both look at Penny until she finally retreats, back out the door.

'Oh my God,' Sam says. 'More Team Gregory?'

'Team Gregory?'

She shakes her head. 'Just something Dad used to say that he seems to have brought back now. Sorry about leaving you up here on your own.'

'Honestly, it doesn't matter.'

'I'd better go and change. These shoes are killing me.'

'Before you go, there's something I need to tell you.'

She turns towards me again, giving me her full attention. 'Is something wrong?'

'No, not this time. I've had some good luck, actually.' I'm fidgeting a bit now. 'Well, school have offered to increase my scholarship. So I'm going to board there now, too.'

Her eyebrows move towards each other, a slight frown. She shakes her head. 'You don't really want to board at school – live there, and be there all the time – do you?'

'I think it's for the best.'

'Oh.'

'So when school opens again, I'll be moving there.'

She looks down. Then up to meet my eyes. 'Are you sure that's what you want?'

'Well, no. What I *want* is to be living with my dad still. What the hell – with my mum, too.'

Now Sam's eyes are brimming with sympathy, and that isn't what I wanted. I shake my head. 'This is just the way things have to be now. You're going to be late for dinner if you don't go and get changed.'

'Right. OK then.' She's still standing there.

'Go, Sam.'

Her eyes drop; she leaves my room. I hear her door across the hall open and then close.

I lean against the wall. That felt wrong, and I don't know why.

Would it be better if we'd had longer to talk about it? I don't know. I had to tell her, in case her mum said anything about it – I should have done already.

Why the rush to have dinner, anyway? They only just got back; you'd think they'd all want to take a deep breath first.

I frown, an uneasy feeling inside me. Do they want to keep anyone not part of *Team Gregory* away from Sam?

Maybe that is what this unexpected good fortune of an extra scholarship is actually about: getting me away from her, out of the house.

But surely if Sam's parents were behind the scholarship they'd have said so? Unless they don't want Sam to know.

I shake my head at myself, at the nonsense I come up with sometimes. After all they've done for me, why would they be trying to get rid of me now?

24

Sam

I should be rushing, I'm late, but my feet don't seem inclined to go over a certain speed. Yet as I head down the first flight of stairs Mum is just coming out of her dressing room. She pauses, waits for me.

'Well, that was quite a day,' she says.

'Yeah.'

We go through the dining-room door. 'There are my two beautiful girls,' Dad says, and stands.

We sit down; dinner is brought in. The usual house rule of talking of nothing important while we eat seems to still be applying. Mum and Dad discuss inconsequential things: the weather, the menu, but I'm not in the mood for this game tonight.

'You're quiet,' Dad says, noticing after a while

'I'm tired.' True. I was hungry before but don't seem to want anything now. But I seem to still be, I don't know, *processing* all that I've seen and heard in the last day. The sense that this is all a dream, that I'll wake up and laugh about it tomorrow, is still there.

Then I remember my camera, my photos – the ones I haven't had a chance to examine yet. I'd slipped it in my jeans' pocket when I came down, and touching it there is strangely reassuring. What it shows will make me see what is real, that I'm not losing my mind.

'Sam?' Dad says.

'Sorry?'

'I was just saying, we need to get you back into your schoolwork. We're hoping school will be back on again soon; you need to be prepared.'

'Really? We're talking about *that*, now?'

'I don't imagine Ava is up to tutoring you at the moment. We'll see if the school can suggest someone else.'

'No! I mean, I'm sure she'll still want to do it. Though she's told me she's moving out; going to board at school. They've extended her scholarship.'

'You'll miss her,' he says.

'Yes. I will. More than I knew I would. I've got used to having her around.'

Tea is being brought in now. The door closes again and we're alone.

'I wanted it to be just the three of us together tonight: a moment to take stock,' Dad says. 'I'm going to be very busy now for a while, but I think things went well today.'

'As always,' Mum says, and she's smiling up at him and I'm struggling with this weird happy families moment while London and the rest of the country is in the total mess it's in right now.

'Dad? What about needing a helicopter ride, and the mobs below?'

'As you can see we were perfectly safe and looked after. Nothing for you to worry about.'

'That's not what I meant. There were so many people

there: how did that happen just after your speeches like that? I mean, were they ready and waiting, or was it kind of like they didn't like what they heard and it was all spontaneous?'

'Investigations are continuing. We'll sort these elements out and get order back in this city and elsewhere very soon.'

'I was surprised about the death penalty,' Mum says, and *I'm* surprised she's said it.

'That is just one measure for the most extreme crimes,' Dad says.

'I thought you've been on the record as being against it,' I say.

'Times have changed, Samantha. Now listen up: we're going to have a security briefing tomorrow. Additional cameras are being installed, and there will be more guards and layers of security. Agent Coulson has been assigned to us to liaise with those implementing these measures. Also, we've been invited to Chequers for a few days.'

'Lovely!' Mum says.

'It's important to keep that under wraps for security,' Dad says. 'Don't tell anybody we'll be there.'

'Of course,' Mum says, looking a touch disappointed.

'Samantha?'

'Yes? I won't tell anyone. Is that what I'm supposed to say?'

'Don't just say it; do it.'

'All you all right, darling?' Mum says to me.

'Headache. And I'm really tired.'

'It's been a long day,' Dad says. 'Straight to bed for you.'

I agree, say goodnight. Unnoticed, I take a photo of them smiling at each other *that way*: ICK. You could look at my parents and wonder why they are together. He's older than her; she was and is gorgeous, and kind of had it all. I mean, my dad was all right back then, though it's weird to think of him like that. Mum says he was dashing in uniform: he was still in the police when they got married. But he's always working and thinking and she's always working out and going to parties. What have they even got in common?

I don't understand how or why, but even though in so many ways they seem a mismatch, somehow they belong together.

Team Gregory looks good in photographs: the politician, the socialite and me. But lately I'm feeling less and less comfortable being posed for camera.

Straight to bed? I don't think so.

I knock on Ava's door.

25

Ava

The BBC is pretty much on a loop: the recordings of the speeches. The areas of London affected by riots and how the army have stopped them from spreading, and are now pinning them in. The commentary. The pans to Mr and Mrs Public for comments about how amazing it all is that the army is crushing the extremists to make the streets safe for their children. We're deep into Sam's second box of emergency chocolates, but there isn't enough chocolate in the world for all of this.

'I don't understand,' Sam says.

'Which part?'

'Where to start?' She rolls her eyes. 'Why does everyone seem to think having the army involved and all the other measures, like the death penalty and the curfew, are good things? I mean, I get that what the BBC is showing doesn't seem very balanced. I'm sure they could find people who would say the opposite if they tried. But you can see it in the eyes of the ones they're talking to: they've really bought into it.'

'I know. It's as if the government has said, "You'll do what we say when we say it, and if you don't – if you dare wander across the road at ten past nine, for example – you'll be arrested. If we *really* don't like you there is always the death penalty. And, oh, you didn't vote for any of this, no MPs did either, but there's nothing you can do about it until we decide things are under control again. Maybe then we'll have an election but, in the meantime, that is just how things are." And everyone is getting up and applauding them.'

'Exactly. Let's try online, see if anyone is saying anything different,' Sam says, and gets her tablet. We look at some of the more sensationalist papers first, but they're either strangely silent or following the government line, too.

'This feels wrong,' Sam says.

'Let me try?' I say, and she hands over the tablet. 'Instead of going to recognised news sources let's go more general.' I think a moment, and enter 'UK undemocratic', then 'UK Armstrong Gregory democracy', 'UK journalists protest'...

There's some ranting here and there, the usual crazy internet stuff, and then...

'Try that one,' Sam says, and points to a link to a blog by Giana Economos. I click on it and when it loads there's a photo across the top. 'She's Lucas's mother. She was at that protest for his friend – he pointed her out, only from a distance, but I'm sure it's her.'

'Economos: their surname sounds Greek,' I say. Straight away you know she's someone who won't toe the line. So few names haven't been anglicised in recent years, to avoid the Euro label.

I click the *about* link for the blog:

I'm a freelance journalist with almost twenty years' experience. Recently all of the papers I write for have told me they can no longer print any of my work, and no reason was given. It was the same day I wept as I handed in an article on the three-party agreement to end the proud history of democracy in the UK. Make no mistake: that is what is happening.

I'll continue to report on this website on the situation as it evolves. Please share: tell everyone. Get in touch with your stories and images through my contact page.

We exchange a look, and read the only article. The title is *The Death of Democracy*.

'She's really angry,' Sam says, her voice quiet.

'Yes. And at last: someone is saying what I've been thinking, that they've just agreed to do this to us. And what about this new elite force in their bid for law and order? The ones that she calls *Lorders*?'

'She makes them sound like the SS, or the Gestapo. But nobody knows who they'll be or what they'll do. Isn't that unfair at this point?'

'Is it? There are no checks and balances in this system they've created.'

'Ava, is it really as bad as all that? All that stuff they said about making jobs and finding the homeless places to live are good. As for the rest of it, aren't they just trying to get things under control? That's why they've brought in the army and the curfew, isn't it? Though the thought of the death penalty freaks me out. What if they get it wrong? You can't release someone if they're dead.'

I want to comfort her, to make her feel better, but I just can't.

'I'm sorry, Sam. I know it's your dad. But things really *are* that bad. The way it's been set up they could do anything. And what about the press? Lucas's mum just happened to lose all her work the day she turned in an article telling it like it is? No. The coverage has been one-sided because they are controlling what is in print and on the news. There's no other explanation.'

'You mean they're controlling the BBC? And the newspapers?'

'They must be.'

'I just can't believe my dad is involved in stuff like that.' She tilts her head to one side. 'Maybe he doesn't know?'

'He may not be involved directly in making it happen, but he's got to be part of it at some level. If nothing else, he must be aware of it. He's a politician; he knows the flak they usually get whenever they announce anything. Its absence is striking.'

'If we can see this, won't everybody else?'

'Maybe. Maybe when things calm down a little people will wake up to what has happened, and do something about it.'

'But at the moment, they're scared. That's it, isn't it?'

'I think so. They've seen people dying on the news, or they know somebody or know somebody who knows somebody who has died or been injured and will never be the same again; and, on top of that, these out of control mobs have been on the streets. They want it to stop. And I'm scared, too: but more of what the government is doing than anything else.'

We start to search for more news, blogs, comments on the web. There's a knock on the door. We look at each other; it's after midnight.

There's panic on Sam's face as she jumps up to see who it is.

It's Penny.

'Is something wrong?' Sam says.

'Not at all. But I've been asked by your mother to make sure you don't stay up late, Samantha; she says tomorrow will be a busy day. And she also said you've got a headache? She's sent some tablets.' She holds out her hands: a glass of water in one, a small dish with tablets in the other.

Sam hesitates, then takes two of them, swallows them with the water and gives the glass back to Penny.

'Sorry, Ava. I am actually really tired.'

'That's not surprising after the day you've had. Speak tomorrow?'

'Of course.'

I follow Penny out of Sam's room and go across the hall to mine. I put the news on, then think to ask if I can borrow her tablet.

I go back across, knock once.

'Come in,' she says.

I open the door. Sam is already in her pyjamas, just getting into bed.

'Can I borrow your tablet?'

'Of course, take it. It's charging on the desk.'

'Thanks,' I say, and gather it up with the charger. 'Sleep well.'

I switch the lights off at the door.

'No!' Sam says. 'I mean, leave them on, please.'

I switch them back on. 'You sleep with the lights on?'

'Weird, I know.'

'Goodnight, Sam.'

Back in my room I'm uneasy, restless. I pull aside the curtains. Below, I can see the front of the house, the guards. There are more of them now than when I first came here. Beyond the gates there is a further group of sentries. Hard to tell in distant street lights but I think they're soldiers.

Every move Sam makes is watched. Did they know she hadn't gone straight to sleep – is that why Penny was sent up? Do they listen?

It is fair to say that Sam is someone many would envy, but I'm getting more of a feeling of what it would be like to be her and to live like this all the time. It makes me feel like I can't quite breathe, that everything is tightening around me.

She's been coping with it all for years, but now things are getting worse. And just when she needs friends around her, I'm leaving.

26

Sam

Hand-delivered headache tablets at midnight: that's a first.

I make a warm nest with my blankets. I've always felt safe here, in this room, the rest of the world held away. I've also always felt safe with my dad, like if he's there he can protect me from anything. That certainty has been shaken, both when our car was rocked in that riot and when we could so easily have died in that suicide bomb. There are things he can't predict, can't stop.

Is that why he and Armstrong are doing the things they've set in motion? Curfews, the army, the death penalty, even this force Lucas's mum called Lorders: it all seems unbelievable, over the top, harsh. But is that what they have to do to make their children and everyone else's children safe? If that is what they are trying to do, then that's OK, isn't it?

My headache is easing; sleep is there, waiting for me – I just have to let go. But somehow I don't want to, not yet ...

I'm trapped in the dark, quiet and still.

The blackness is thick, syrupy. I can't cry any more, I can't even breathe—

BANG. Shouting voices. More bangs. I'm so scared, I wrap my arms round my head and stop my ears with my hands. My eyes are shut so tight I see stars.

Samantha? Samantha!

Someone touches my arms and I find enough air to scream.

Samantha, it's me, it's Daddy. It's all right, you're safe now.

But I'm still afraid to open my eyes, afraid that this is a trick; it's what I hoped for and it's a trick.

But then he starts to sing how he sings me to sleep, and to rock me.

Is it really him? I open my eyes and can hardly see — the lights are too bright after being in the dark so long, and my eyes are full of tears — but it is *him: he's in uniform for work, but it's him.*

He picks me up, wraps his arms tight around me, and I'm telling him that I'm sorry, that I'll never be bad again, not ever — I promise.

Daddy's good girl, always and for ever.

27

Ava

'I've got to go for some fittings,' Sam says and pulls a face. 'Mum wants us to wait while alterations are made, and then Dad is meeting us and we're all going away to visit friends for a few days.'

'You're going away?' I say, surprised her dad would be going anywhere at the moment, with everything that has been happening. 'Are the roads OK?'

'It's not far, and apparently so,' she says, but I can tell she's nervous about something – whether it is the roads or where they are going – but she didn't say where, which seems odd. Odd enough that I don't ask.

'I'm sure it's fine or you wouldn't be going.'

'Will you be bored? Have you got stuff to do?'

'Bored? No, not at all. I've got reading to do for school, though I'm not sure I will today. I think I've caught your headache.'

'Do you want me to ask Penny for some tablets?' Sam says, then frowns. 'Though they must have been strong: did I ever sleep after I took them. You might end up having a long nap.'

'No, don't worry, I'm fine. Go on.'

Through the window, now that it's daylight I can tell that I was right last night: there are soldiers posted outside the gates. Sam, her mum and a security agent get into one of those big, new cars. The gates open; close after they're gone.

I put the TV back on to the BBC. They're showing the damage done by looters. Some fires are being put out. Arrests have been made; how many, they don't say. There's a list given of areas to avoid, but it seems like things *are* getting under control quicker than I'd have thought possible.

Almost like the protestors are capitulating.

I do have a headache, but that's probably from too many hours staring at Sam's tablet, looking for other traces of news that haven't been filtered out. Somehow I can't stop.

I don't know that much about Armstrong, and do searches on him now. The usual biography kind of stuff comes up. He's always been hardline; his wife, though, was a civil rights activist before they got together. They must have some interesting conversations.

On impulse I search for information on Sam's dad. Wasn't there something I've heard about him, something about how he got into politics in the first place?

To begin with he was the policeman who was only known for who he married, the beautiful, rich socialite that she was and still is.

And then, their daughter was kidnapped: *Sam was kidnapped*. She was only three years old. Ransom was demanded. But he cracked the case, found where she was being hidden. Got her home safe. Was that how he started to make a name for himself? It wasn't long after that that he got into politics.

I read what I can about the case. There's some sensationalistic stuff about the poor little rich girl held alone in darkness. Is that why she still sleeps with the lights on?

Another story says her father refused to allow the ransom to be paid, because he could never make a deal with criminals. That he said kidnappers rarely return victims even if a ransom is paid.

That's harsh. It all turned out for the best – but still: imagine if it hadn't ... if not paying the ransom had left Sam alone in the dark, for ever.

Is this story true? If it is, does she know?

28

Sam

I've been to Chequers once before, when the last Prime Minister invited us for the weekend. It's a lovely country place and I remember we went tromping in the mud with their dogs. Then it had all seemed exciting: Dad had just become deputy prime minister, and there we were.

Now it feels very different, especially as getting there is like being in a Bond film. Instead of hours in a car, we're packed away, driven a short distance to another location, and picked up in a helicopter. They really don't want anyone to know where we're going and that, in itself, is freaky.

I also feel weird that I didn't tell Ava – that I told her we were going away to visit friends. I felt like I had to say something, but was it a lie? Are the Armstrongs in the *friends* category? I don't know them very well; I doubt the word can stretch that far.

Before long we approach Chequers and it looks different from above, this country house of the prime minister. The grounds are extensive and still green; it's early autumn. I wonder if they have dogs?

We're met and escorted across the grass by so many

agents that the sense of weirdness comes back.

'Welcome!' Armstrong says. He's shaking Dad's hand, kissing Mum.

And standing just behind them with his wife? Astrid Connor, and her daughter, Stella. They're here, too?

'Astrid. It's lovely to see you,' Dad says, with no trace of surprise, and more hand-shaking and air-cheek-kissing follows.

Why is Astrid here? Before there was any hint of all the political changes she met with Dad at our house. Was she involved somehow in setting things up – a go-between for Armstrong and Dad?

They wander off, leaving me, Mrs A and the kids. Now that the three Armstrong kids are here running around with Stella tagging behind, everything feels reassuringly normal.

Later, instead of a fancy dinner, we have a barbecue. When we're finished, me and the kids are told to go with Mrs A to ... the library.

Library? Really?

When we get there, Stella still trailing behind, in the centre of it is a huge, long open space ... and there are wickets being put in place by the twins under Mrs A's direction.

Cricket, in the library. At Chequers? It's hard not to laugh.

Soon I discover that Mrs A has a mean off spin. I'm not sure Dad would think much of this happening here, in this historic building, but running around and being silly has me laughing and more relaxed than I have been in a while.

After a while Sandy announces the lights must go out so we can use the telescope. I almost yell *no* before I can stop myself, but I don't want to embarrass myself in front of a bunch of kids. Besides, it's not quite dark yet.

Their telescope is set up by a window.

Each of the kids wants to look and I'm praying for them to be done, fast, so the lights can come back on. I'm concentrating on breathing, on not freaking out; counting silently as each of them has a go until finally they're finished.

'Sam, it's your turn!' Sandy says.

'I don't need a turn.'

'Yes, you do! Look at the moon.'

'Fine,' I say, thinking agreeing may be the fastest way to get this over with and the lights back on. My hands are shaking. I look through the eyepiece of the telescope but it's all a smudge of light and dark. 'I can't see anything much; it's all blurry.'

'Focus the eyepiece against something on the horizon across the grounds, then swing it back up to the sky,' Mrs A says.

I angle it down like she said and twiddle the eyepiece until the view becomes clearer, and I'm about to swing it up again to the moon when something moving catches my eye. I centre it, adjust the focus a little and look again. *Yes* – just there, inside the grounds, keeping low – figures in dark clothing. If they weren't moving I wouldn't have seen them.

'Help me?' I say to Mrs A and she comes closer. 'There are people creeping up along the grass,' I say quietly, just to her. She bends to have a look, then straightens and turns to the others.

'Come on, you lot! Race you to the main hall,' she says.

They screech and run and Mrs A and I follow behind. She has a phone in her hand; I hear her hurriedly tell somebody what we saw. By the time we get to the main hall we're met by security.

'Everyone, get up the stairs. Now,' Coulson says.

29

Ava

I look up from my book at Penny, framed in the doorway.

'Hi, Ava. Can I come in?'

'Of course.' I close my book.

She sits in the chair opposite the sofa where I am.

'I've got some details for you about your father's cremation. It's been scheduled for a week from Saturday.'

'Oh. OK. Thanks for organising things.'

'That's no problem at all, Ava. Now, who should I notify? Friends, work colleagues, relatives?'

'Dad wasn't that social. He had a brother, but I don't know him and don't have his address.'

'How about places he worked, that sort of thing?'

I give her details of Dad's black taxi company, and the university where he taught classics before. Then she explains what will happen: the ceremony, then the cremation. I'll be notified when the ashes are ready to be collected, but they can be stored there until I've decided what to do with them. And it all seems so surreal, to be talking about this.

'I've got some good news for you, Ava, too.' She smiles.

'At last. What is it?'

'They're planning to reopen school next week, probably Wednesday or Thursday. The deputy head has suggested you move in ahead of time to get settled in first.'

'Oh.'

'Is that all right? You want to go there, don't you?'

'Well, yes. I'm just surprised it's so soon, and while Sam and her parents are away. It seems somehow wrong to leave without thanking them.' And without making sure Sam is OK.

'I can pass that along. We've loved having you, despite the circumstances that brought you to us. Can I help you pack?'

'No. I mean, it's mostly packed already – the stuff from our flat.' The boxes are along the wall still. 'There isn't much else.'

'How about we arrange a car for tomorrow morning, then? I'll book it for ten a.m.'

30

Sam

Bright lights now illuminate the grounds from points along the perimeter of the fences and by the house. There's shouting; sharp, loud sounds. Is that *gunfire*?

I press up against the window, camera zoomed in my hand on rapid repeat. Whoever they are, it looks like they're being rounded up – easily, quickly. They don't look organised, or armed: as soon as shots were fired near them they dropped and put up their hands.

No one was supposed to know we were here, but there were helicopters coming and going; it wouldn't have been that hard to figure out something was up. But if they were planning to attack surely they'd be more, I don't know, organised and military in their approach?

Coulson has stayed with us; he's on his radio at the other end of the room. I strain to listen but can't really hear more than the tone of his voice.

Then he comes to us. 'Things appear to be under control now,' he says. 'We're just searching the grounds and the rest of the house to make sure no one was missed.'

Mrs A nods. She's remained very calm, considering. My mum seemed more alarmed than her to start with, and is visibly relieved now to hear Coulson's words.

I go back to the window. There are other figures now – soldiers, I guess – sweeping the grounds as Coulson said, and it isn't long before we're told the place is secure. Mrs A takes her children and Stella off to their rooms but I shake my head, say I'll stay.

Dad and Armstrong look angry. They're talking to another security agent, asking if those arrested knew we were here. And how did they get through all the fences and past the guards?

The agent is saying it appears the intruders didn't know we were here, that they were just vandals who would probably have kept away if they had known we were here with all the extra security. An investigation is promised.

But what if the agents are wrong? What would have happened if we hadn't been mucking about with that telescope and spotted the so-called vandals creeping up the lawn? I feel queasy. I don't want to think about it. I don't want to think about what they might have done if they'd got into the house.

Dad must see my face; he comes over and puts a hand on my shoulder. 'No one will ever hurt you as long as I'm around; you know that. Right?'

'Right.'

He gives me a hug, sends me and Mum up to our rooms.

He, Armstrong and Astrid stay behind.

My room overlooks where we were before, where I saw those people. I feel uneasy, check the window is locked. The door doesn't lock; I put a chair in front of it.

I don't think I'm going to be able to go to sleep any

time soon, so don't even try. Instead I transfer all the photos I've taken these last few days from my camera to my phone so I can see them on the screen.

The photos I took from the window tonight are surprisingly clear. The camera has a powerful zoom, and adjusted automatically to the light conditions. It took a photo every second while I was using it; flipping through them, it almost looks like a jerky video.

The intruders? Other than a few of them they all look like kids my age, or even younger. The soldiers made them lie on the ground on their stomachs, arms above their heads. One by one they were roughly dragged up and cuffed, hauled away. There are maybe twenty of them.

They look scared, not angry; they didn't seem to have any weapons.

What on earth were they doing here? Were they really just vandals, like I heard that agent say?

I think about calling Ava to see what she makes of it, but it's so late. She's probably asleep.

I'll talk to her when we get home tomorrow.

31

Ava

I'm met inside the gates by the deputy head.

'Ava, I'm so sorry about your father,' she says, with regret positively oozing from her.

'Thank you,' I say, because I have to say something. But *thank you for being sorry* seems as empty as someone saying they are sorry in the first place. A social nicety, like sorry I bumped into you in the hallway, or spilt my coffee on your book. She's always smiled widely at me, like I'm some sort of special social project that needs to be shown as much insincerity as possible.

When school is back on it will be like this, won't it? From everyone. *We're sorry, Ava.* Sympathy and smiles from girls who've never spoken to me before.

But I can't react the way I might like to – challenge, or ignore – as I must tread carefully. If this scholarship is pulled it isn't just my education at risk; I'd have nowhere to live.

'The caretakers will bring your boxes. Come and I'll show you the way.'

Does she really think I've been at this school since I was eleven and I don't know where to go?

I follow her through the school buildings to the boarding house at the back. I may have known where it is but I've never gone through its doors before, and now I'm nervous.

'Are there other girls here now?'

'They've gone home until the school is open again.'

'Do you know when that'll be?'

'They're saying Thursday now. We're waiting for confirmation from the authorities.'

She opens the door to the house. We're met by the housemistress, who she introduces as Mrs Morgan, and then she says goodbye.

'I'll show you to your room,' Mrs Morgan says. I follow her up three flights of stairs and I'm feeling sorry for the caretakers, with my boxes mostly full of books.

We walk down a hall and she opens a door at the end.

'Here you are. A single room as you're in the sixth form; luckily one was available.' It's a rectangular box, with a single bed, desk, some shelves. Bare walls.

'The bathrooms are down the hall on your right. Kitchens are closed but we'll come up with something together: come down at six. There's a common room with TV,' she says, and points down the hall to another door. 'I'll leave you to get settled.'

The door closes behind her and I put my bag on the bed, walk to the window: there is a view of the almost empty staff car park, the fence beyond it – barbed wire on top.

It's cold; the radiator is off and I turn it on but nothing happens. I wrap my arms around myself, but it's not just the physical cold that is getting to me, is it? This is where

I live from now on. Alone. Until the end of the sixth form, and what then?

I can hear my dad in my head: *Study hard, girl; get a scholarship. Go to university and take something more practical than I did.* But then he'd usually continue with *so you can support me in my dotage.* And that isn't going to happen, is it? There's the twist of pain and confusion in my gut that is always there with thoughts of him now, the pain of missing him and the anger at what he kept from me coiled tightly together in a hard knot.

It's warmer in the common room – there are no external walls – so I go there, and do what is my norm these days and put on the news.

There's a story breaking about Chequers.

'A group of dissidents have bypassed security at the prime minister's country house in Buckinghamshire. Prime Minister Armstrong and his family and Deputy Prime Minister Gregory and his family were all in residence at the time, as well as MP Astrid Connor and her daughter.

'This statement from the prime minister's office has just been issued,' the reporter continues, and she reads from a tablet in her hands. '*We take matters of security, the safety of our families and the protection of public property very seriously. The perpetrators will be dealt with according to the full extent of the law.*'

Sam is at Chequers? Is that why she didn't say where they were going? She was likely told not to. I try not to mind that she didn't tell me anyway. I hesitate, take out my phone and tap in a text:

Just saw the news: are you OK?

There's no answer.

32

Sam

The next morning we're packing in a hurry: plans have been changed. All of us – the Armstrongs included – are going home today, after one night instead of two. No one has told us why.

Mum is at my door. 'Samantha, are you ready?'

'Almost.' I snap my trolley case shut and turn to pick up my phone, but it's not on the side where I thought it was. I check my bag in case I put it in already; no. I frown.

'What is it?'

'I can't find my phone.'

'What have you done with it this time?'

'Nothing! I mean, I'm sure it was on the bedside table.' I was really tired when I was looking at those photos on my phone last night; instead of putting it where I thought I did maybe it was on the bed next to me and slipped down to the floor? I look around, then bend down to look under the bed.

'We've got to go now, they're waiting for us. They can send it if they find it.'

I'm uneasy. It's hard to see how I could have lost it

since last night, but what else could have happened to it? Did someone take it? There were all those photos I put on my phone last night – maybe somebody noticed I was taking them, and wanted them deleted.

But that makes no sense: I've still got them all on my camera.

Unless they didn't know about the camera, and checked my phone – bypassed needing my security code somehow – saw the photos, and took it.

I shake my head. *Don't be so paranoid, Sam*, I say to myself.

When we finally get home I go straight to Ava's room, expecting to open the door and see her reading, or watching the news – but she's not there. I look again and realise all her stuff is gone.

I call Penny on the intercom.

'Hi, where is Ava?'

'She moved into the boarding house at your school yesterday.'

'Already? I didn't know.'

'You'll see her at school in a few days – now they're saying you'll be back on Thursday.'

Great.

I find my tablet and charger on my desk in my room: there's a message from Ava from yesterday, and then another one this morning – both asking if I'm OK.

I send one back: *Sorry I didn't answer, lost my phone. I'm fine; not much happened*.

She answers straight away.

S'OK. BBC – put it on

I switch on the TV, and along the bottom of the screen it says *Live, from Chequers*. What's happening there now?

I stare at the screen, blink and blink again. Soldiers are building something on the lawn, three somethings, and there's no mistaking what they are even though I don't want to believe it. Each has a rope hanging down.

No. Seriously? *Gallows*. On the lawn at Chequers?

I pick up my tablet to message Ava. *What the hell?*

Ava: *I thought you said not much happened?*

Me: *Not much did. I overheard that they were vandals, that they didn't even know we were there. They were kids.*

Ava: *They're only hanging the three who are over eighteen.*

Live. On TV.

I can't believe — I can't take this in — no. What is happening? Can it be real?

Me: *Gotta go.*

I run all the way to Dad's office, and knock as I open the door — not waiting for an answer.

'Dad!'

'What's wrong?'

'They're …' I'm gasping for air. 'They're hanging people! At Chequers!'

He puts down his pen, nods. 'Yes. They are.'

'Why? And what about a trial? What did they even *do*?'

'There was a field trial. And keeping you safe — keeping everyone's children safe — is our priority. We have to send a strong message.'

'But, Dad!' The shock is so strong through me I can't even work out what to say or how to say it.

'This is not open for debate.'

'Dad?' I'm looking back at him, but I'm not sure who I'm seeing. My dad, who most of my life I was sure could never do anything wrong. Has he changed? Or maybe I never really knew him.

I'm not sure which scares me more.

'Goodbye, Samantha. I've got work to do.' He looks back to the papers on his desk. *Dismissed.*

I'm backing out of his office, slow steps to begin with then running all the way to my room. When I get there I take out my camera, Bluetooth the photos to my tablet. The photos that I took at Chequers – I look at them all, again and again.

All I see are scared kids.

I go back in time, go through all the photos I've taken these last few days, starting with the ones I took from the helicopter with the mobs below us, the people that came out on the streets after the announcements the new government made. And again, most of what I see are teenagers. They're upset – like I am, right now – but I don't see any weapons in their hands. Yet soldiers are knocking them to the ground.

Dad has done this; making that deal with Armstrong has made all of this happen.

But he said he just wants me to be safe – for everyone to be safe.

I force myself to put the TV back on, and I watch. Two men and one woman – though if they are over eighteen it isn't by much. The ropes; the trapdoors that disappear under their feet. They fall and jerk and finally are still.

Ava said there would be no checks on what the government could do now, but I never thought they'd do anything like *this*.

What was it Lucas's mother said? About the death of democracy? I search for her website on my tablet.

That's odd: it's not coming up.

I go back into history and find the link, but it doesn't work. I go back to look again, to see if there is another page in history, but no – that was the only one – it just won't work.

But hang on, what's this in the list of links? Ava had my tablet. She was searching for stuff about Armstrong? And about Dad.

And me.

Why?

She was looking up stuff about when I was kidnapped. Why would she do that?

I'm unable to stop myself from clicking the links that she did, to see what she saw. I can't clearly remember what happened, I was too young, but I still get nightmares and can't stand to think about it. I never talk about it; I've never looked at this stuff before.

Dad saved me. They said he was a hero: is he trying to be a hero again now?

And then I see something that makes me stop, almost not breathe. He refused to pay the ransom? They threatened to kill me, and still he wouldn't pay. He tracked them down, he saved me, but what if he'd been too late?

He wouldn't make a deal with criminals, not even for me.

I should go and ask him about it. I've been around politics long enough to know what is put in print can be far from the truth.

But somehow, I just know: it is true.

Not paying the ransom didn't have anything to do with making me safe back then; is what he is trying to do really about that now? He wants to get the criminals; he wants to make them pay – lock them up, like my kidnappers were, or even hang them. Does what I think – or what anyone else thinks – matter to him in any way?

All my life I've tried so hard to do what he wants, be what he wants. But how can I stand behind what he is doing now?

I can't. I just can't.

A message pings on the screen: it's Lucas, asking why I don't answer his calls. I shake my head, ready to ignore him.

Then I remember that his mum's website is down. Is something wrong?

Me: *Sorry, I've lost my phone. Are you all right?*

Lucas: No. *Call me on the landline? Please. I need your help.* He gives his number.

What now?

I get the phone, dial the number. It barely rings before he answers.

'It's me,' I say. 'What's wrong?'

'It's my mother. She's gone.'

'Gone? What do you mean – gone?'

'They came and took her.'

'They?'

'Lorders – who do you think? She's a journalist. She'd

been writing this story about all the lines the government has been crossing. She was getting into her car to take Nicky to my aunt's, and a government car pulled in front, another behind, and they grabbed her arms and forced her into one of their cars. I saw it all through the window upstairs. I ran down but by the time I got there she was gone. Nicky was left alone, howling in his car seat; she was gone.'

No. I shake my head, not something he can see on the other end of this phone line. 'No, it can't be that – maybe they're criminals, she's been kidnapped, you'll get a ransom demand or something,' I say, and flinch to be thinking about kidnappers and ransoms just now even as I say it.

'It's scary to think that sounds better than what has actually happened. Dad's been everywhere trying to get answers and all he gets is silence. Can you see if you can find out anything?'

'But I just can't believe—'

'If you can't believe what is happening out there, you're living in a dream world. Wake up, sleeping beauty.'

The phone cuts off.

I stare at the phone in my hand, reeling. Could he be right? Was Ava right, too? Could it really be that the government, something my father is part of, is preventing the truth from getting into print – silencing reporters and, if they won't be silenced, making them disappear?

And leaving little Nicky – what is he, four or five years old? – screaming for his mother, alone in her car. What if Lucas hadn't been there?

Poor Lucas, and the rest of his family, too: I can't imagine what they are going through. I try to call him back but there's no answer, and then I start to worry – to hope it's only because he's annoyed with me, that there isn't some other reason.

Surely if his mother has been arrested for something there have to be charges, a trial, all the usual stuff – she'll get her phone call, they'll find out where she is.

But now I'm seeing the gallows at Chequers in my mind. Dad said there was a field trial, whatever that is, but if those three had any sort of trial it was pretty damn quick: they were hanged the day after they were arrested. That must be why we were sent home early: so we wouldn't be there when it happened.

Lucas asked for my help, but what can I do? Dad won't tell me anything. He probably thinks Lucas's mum is a criminal, too.

I try to think of journalists who always pushed things in the past, the ones who asked the tough questions and caused problems – the sort my dad would hate to have interview him. I come up with a list of five. One by one I check for them online. And there's nothing: no articles, no blogs. Even their social networking accounts have been deleted.

How can people know what is real if things are being censored? If they're not able to hear the truth?

There are soldiers on the streets of London. There is no war, not in the usual sense – there isn't an invading force. It's British against British: the army against civilians. The riots are quickly quashed while we watch, warm and safe.

It's reported by the approved media like the tough measures are a good thing, and in some ways you could argue that they are. The streets will be safe again. Businesses will open and people will get back to work. Schools – including ours – are meant to be opening again the day after tomorrow.

There's a curfew of nine p.m., and anyone found on the streets in breach of the curfew will be taken into custody.

There won't be enough jails: more will have to be built.

There won't be enough armed forces: the unemployed could join up to get a job, one where they can carry a gun and threaten their neighbours.

And to keep them all in check? These law and order agents – Lorders – like the ones who took Lucas's mum.

I've always believed in my dad. I mean, I still get annoyed with him, upset at him, but I was part of Team Gregory whenever he wanted. And even if he wouldn't listen to what I thought, I had been completely sure he would do anything he could to protect me.

But ... he refused to make a deal with criminals to save me when I was three. He didn't tell me to stay home from school the day that he knew attacks were being planned nearby, either. Maybe that was in case it tipped A4A off that the authorities were on to them – but that just shows what is more important to him, doesn't it?

But this isn't about getting back at him, or some teenage rite-of-passage rebellion against my parents. This is so much more than that.

It's time for me to stand on my own, and do what I think is right. Not what my dad wants me to do.

I message Lucas again on my tablet.

I'm sorry. I'm awake; I believe you. Dad would never tell me anything about your mum if I asked, but is there anything else I can do?

Part 3: Rebellion

To truly unify society, find someone to blame. Once the public embraces an us-versus-them mentality, advancing the regime's goals and ideals will readily follow.

MP Astrid Connor,
private diary

History shows us: disenfranchise and silence any segment of society, and there will be trouble.

Linea Armstrong,
wife of Prime Minister Armstrong;
former civil rights activist

1

Ava

The bell rings. First lesson: chemistry, and a lecture on the laws of thermodynamics. One part of me is taking notes, another is wandering. Entropy – the disorder in a closed system – must always increase, yet order is being forced on all of us. How long will it be before entropy throws off the yoke, as it must?

Another bell. A free period.

Word has somehow got around about my dad, and I negotiate my way through the halls and sympathy.

Sorry about your father is said again and again. But what about my mother? No one knows I just found out she died, too. I don't want to tell them, either: it is a wound I hold tight to stop it from bleeding.

Except Sam – she knows.

She never messaged back after that brief exchange the day before yesterday, when I told her to turn on the BBC. I hope she's all right, or as all right as she can be knowing what happened, and her father's role in it all. I know where she usually goes at lunch, or at least used to – in the hall of the art block. But Charlize and her friends would be there, too, and that's a gauntlet I don't want to face.

I feel raw, exposed. My mother's death might have happened a long time ago, but I only found out days ago. Now that the shock has worn off, the pain of losing her and missing her for so long — a pain that I'd held away, not let myself completely feel — have combined together into a well of loss and hurt.

I feel more alone than I ever have before, and I yearn for Sam. For us to be alone together. To be able to say what we think to each other in a way I've rarely, if ever, been able to do with anyone else. Though is that truly the same for her? She didn't tell me they were going to Chequers: maybe there are other things she holds back, too. But despite wondering this I still ache with missing her, and that somehow mixes in with the loss of my mum and dad, too.

Hidden away in my favourite corner of the library I'm surrounded by books. I used to be happy like this, alone, with the pages of my friends shelved neatly all around.

Not any more.

2

Sam

'Well, look who has decided to join us,' Charlize says, with a narrow-eyed look my way.

'Don't be an ass,' Anji says to her, and she and Ruth get up and give me hugs. But Charlize is looking annoyed still – hurt, even – and I'm struggling to work it out. When it hits me, I'm shocked: I can't believe it. I actually forgot her birthday? There's a pang of guilt inside me.

'Charlize, I'm really sorry I couldn't go to your party.'

'I'm sure an invitation to Chequers is higher up the scale.'

'That's not it; and anyway, it's completely untrue – I'd much rather have been at yours. It wasn't my choice, and I wasn't allowed to tell anyone where we were going, either. And I'm sorry I haven't been in touch much.'

'At *all*. Other than to get me to pass your messages around.'

'You're right. I've been a terrible friend. I'm sorry.' And I am, but in a remote kind of way – the way I'd feel if I upset anybody. I mean we've been friends for as long as I can remember, but is that mostly by habit now? I can't imagine talking to Charlize as openly as I have with Ava.

'Enough of this,' Anji says. 'Nearly getting blown up by a suicide bomber gives you some leeway. And then there was that attack on Chequers, too. Are you all right?'

I hesitate. The *attack* on Chequers – that's how it was reported. Should I tell them what really happened? Do they want to hear the truth – can they cope with it?

'What is it, Sam?' Anji says, and I hesitate, but Ruth's dad is high up in the police; Charlize's mum is in the BBC. It's not that I don't trust them, exactly; I just need to think some more about what I should or shouldn't say.

'Of course I'm all right. You know me. But there is something else I want to talk about. Two somethings, really.'

'What's that?'

'Tell me *all* about the party – every bit of it. And then I want to talk about Lucas.'

3

Ava

I'm keeping my eyes down – less eye contact, fewer *sorrys*
– as I leave the library and step out into the courtyard. I
almost walk past, don't see her, but something makes me
raise my eyes in time to meet hers.

The first smile of the day takes over my face. 'Sam?'

'Ava. Hi.'

She's on the bench where we sat that day under
darkening skies, drawing each other until she couldn't see
what she was doing any more. That seems like such a
long time ago now: is that because so much has happened,
both in my life and in the world around us?

'How are you?' I sit next to her.

'I don't know. You?'

'Much the same.'

'It's weird being back at school, with everyone acting
as if life were normal – like nothing has changed. It must
be much more so for you.'

She's saying exactly what I've been thinking all day,
and I'm nodding, about to say just that, when I take in
that she didn't smile back to see me, and is glancing at
her watch.

Her phone rings. She gets it out of her bag. 'Sorry, I've got to take this.' She gets up, walks away.

I'm unsettled, confused.

When I stayed at Sam's it was such an intense time for me, and for her and her family, too – she seemed to need someone to talk to as much as I did. But maybe either I imagined it, or that time has passed?

Or perhaps Sam is having trouble accepting the things her father has been involved in, and she's avoiding facing it – talking to me wouldn't help with that.

Or maybe something is wrong, and she needs help? I frown. If her phone hadn't rung I could have asked her.

Wait a minute: didn't she say she'd lost her phone?

I shake my head; I'm being ridiculous. She either found it again or got a new one. So what?

Still I feel uneasy.

4

Sam

'Lucas? Is that you?'

'The one and only. Was starting to think you weren't going to answer.'

'Sorry. I had to get away from someone first.'

'We need to meet up. Any luck sorting something out for this afternoon?'

'Yes. I'm going shopping with Charlize and Ruth at that new designer department store on Bond Street. There's a café there, fourth floor: I'll get away from them and meet you there, about five p.m. Is that OK?'

'Yes. I know where it is, I'll find the café. I'll see you there.'

'This is Anji's phone I've borrowed; I'll have to give it back to her. Any problems, contact Charlize.'

'Will do. Take care.'

'You too.'

We say goodbye and I click *end call* and just stay where I am, along the path behind the library block. My heart is thudding stupidly fast and my hands feel clammy. *Get a grip, Sam.* This is still a free country – in theory, at least – and arranging to meet a friend in a café during a shopping trip is hardly a crime.

Though maybe what we're going to talk about is.

I take deep breaths in, out, in, out, to compose myself, and start down the path towards the front of the library.

Wait. What if Ava is still there?

I was so distracted before, waiting for Lucas's call, that she caught me off guard. I'm not sure I want to go and talk to her; at least, not right now. There's something about her that seems to make me spill stuff I'd rather keep to myself. Meeting Lucas – and why we're meeting – are things she's better off not knowing, and if I don't tell her she's sure to know I'm hiding something.

But that isn't the only thing: I'm still weirded out by her doing searches on me and Dad.

I turn back and go the other way, around the backs of a few buildings, to avoid the front of the library.

The afternoon goes by slowly; minutes feel like hours. When the last bell finally rings I jump out of my seat.

'In a hurry?' Charlize says with a wink. I'd let them believe what they wanted to about why I'm meeting Lucas: they assume there's something going on between us. And I guess there is, but not what they think.

The car – one of the new limo-like ones – is waiting outside when we get there. I had to get Mum on the case to get this cleared with security: I spoke in her language, telling her I'd missed Charlize's party and I'd simply *die* if I didn't have something new to wear to Ruth's – something I could pick out myself. If she hadn't got involved there's no way it'd have been sorted without days of notice.

The driver gets out to open doors for us; Charlize is in

raptures over the interior before I even make my way in. Coulson is sitting next to the driver in the front and nods in the mirror, but says nothing.

The roads seem eerily calm after the way things have been. We go through checkpoints; there are numberplate recognition scans. Some cars are stopped and we are waved through, but everywhere there are fewer cars, fewer people, than you'd expect in London.

'It's quiet, isn't it?' Ruth says, breaking the matching silence inside the car.

There are guards on some of the corners we drive past – with guns, serious-looking ones. Who are they? They don't look quite right for either army or police; they're dressed in black in something a bit bulky, as if it's all Kevlar bulletproof stuff.

Are they Lorders? If they are, that was fast. The new law and order force was only just announced, but it must have been in the works for a while for them to be standing there kitted out like that. It feels longer because so much has happened, but it really has just been days.

I've become adept at taking sneaky photos with my little camera: arms crossed, it is in my hand between fingers against the window.

It's after four by the time we get there. Once we're through security and the big internal glass doors, Charlize takes charge. Ruth's sixteenth has a dress code: formal – tuxes and ballgowns. I have to come home with an acceptable outfit for Mum to check out; luckily Charlize's shopping skills match Mum's own.

I'm in a changing room with Ruth while Charlize brings one dress after another and I'm trying them on, peering at my watch, wishing I could wear a tux instead. Finally they've got it down to three.

'Ruth, it's your party, you choose,' I say.

'You *are* keen to get away and see Lucas, aren't you?' Ruth says. 'This one, maybe?' She holds up one of them, a black dress. It is simple but with some definite wow factor.

'Do you want your mum to like it?' Charlize says.

'Good point. Best to keep her on side.'

'Then the blue one,' Charlize says, and Ruth agrees.

Charlize insists on a quick swipe at my face with eye shadow, lipstick, before they let me go.

I go up two levels to the fourth floor. The café is at the back, but I'm a few minutes early and pause, pretending to look at bags. There's one that would go well with that dress – actually, I do rather like it. I model it in front of a mirror, holding it this way and that.

Movement catches my eye; a figure in the mirror. A man. He quickly steps back and turns away.

I only saw him for a second; did he move away because he realised I might have done? He was hanging well back, but I'm completely sure.

It was Coulson.

5

Ava

I'm in my room. I'm hiding, aren't I?

I can't be around other people who look at me the way that they do – sympathy mixed with a hesitant compulsion to say the right thing – before they back away, relieved it is over. There is fear in their eyes, too; as if what happened to me might be contagious, something their own family could catch, and they don't want to think about it.

But I can't think of anything else.

I read my mother's letters over and over again as if I can absorb her from these few pieces of paper, ones she held years ago. For so long I'd fought against thinking about her, convinced I'd been abandoned. Now that I know the truth it's as if I must go back and painfully remember everything about her that I possibly can, but so much is vague and uncertain with time and deliberate forgetting. I feel like I can't quite grasp who or what she was.

If I want all of her that I can have, there is another way to maybe find a side of her I didn't know: there are the other letters. The ones she wrote to Dad; the ones he wrote back to her.

I want to read them and can't bring myself to do it at the same time. I can't think of him too closely without pain and rage. I want to grieve for my mother, not the father who took her away from me.

Is that fair? I don't know. I can't go back and ask them why they did the things they did, but that is how I feel, right now, even though it seems so wrong to be angry with my dad when he's just died; when his body is still waiting to be burnt to ash. It makes me feel guilty, like I'm doing something wrong, when he is the one who should feel this way.

Something he can never feel, just like he can never feel anything else ever again.

I hold the letters she wrote to him. I can't open them, read them. Not yet. Maybe I'll never be able to do it.

Just like maybe I'll never be able to face what he's done.

I lie back on my bed, stare at the ceiling, the walls, of my small room. Me; this room: that is all there is. A box that is closing in around me, getting smaller, tighter. Holding me, pressing down.

I need to fight my way out, or curl up in a corner and scream.

6

Sam

I look down, pretend to examine the bag in my hands, my back to where I saw Coulson so he won't see the shock on my face. I can't believe it. He's actually tailing me around while I'm shopping?

What should I do now? I know Lucas; is there any reason not to meet up with him even if Coulson sees it?

What about Lucas's mother? If they don't already know who he is they'll find out, and what will they make of me meeting up with someone with that family connection? I can't risk messing things up before they've even begun. A sales assistant comes over now, starts telling me how amazing this bag is: it should be, for that much money. Even Mum would hesitate at that many zeros.

I smile, hand over a credit card and hope that Lucas doesn't come by, see me and say hello.

She's wrapping it in tissue paper and then carefully, reverently, even, slipping it into a matching drawstring bag – and I'm thinking *hurry* – when I see him. Lucas is at the front of the café ahead of me; he must have come up the other escalators across the floor. He's looking around at the tables.

Don't turn; don't.

He doesn't. He goes in, disappears from view, just as the sales assistant hands me a receipt. I step back towards the escalator.

'Miss! Your bag?' I turn and she holds out my purchase, left on the counter.

'Oh. Sorry – thanks.'

I take it and head back down to where I left Charlize and Ruth. I can't see Coulson anywhere now, but I bet he's following along, out of sight.

I find my friends still in the changing rooms, with armfuls of dresses of their own to try on. At least Coulson can't follow us in here.

'That was quick,' Charlize says.

I don't know what is best to say to them. I shake my head, and go for the truth. 'That agent who came in the car with us was following me. I didn't go.'

'What? Seriously?' Charlize says. They exchange a glance.

'That's ridiculous,' Ruth says. 'But why would you care if he saw you with Lucas?'

I roll my eyes and embellish. 'I can't see anyone without them having a full security clearance first, and that is kind of heavy when you haven't even worked out if you want to or not yet.'

'Flipping heck,' Charlize says. 'You two *are* like Romeo and Juliet.' She looks at Ruth. 'But he could come to your party, couldn't he?'

She grins. 'Of course he could.'

'Charlize, can you text Lucas, tell him I couldn't make it? Don't say why. And about Ruth's party. Don't forget to tell him it's formal.' At least I know he's got something to wear since he did at that charity dinner when we met him.

'Of course.' Charlize's expert thumbs fly across the screen, then she looks up. 'Now. Do you want to make sure you really like your dress? Since, you know, Romeo – I mean, Lucas – is going to see you in it.'

Afterwards we're driving back along still-quiet streets, and despite the armed presence – the menace I feel when I look at them as we go past each checkpoint – it's hard to argue with feeling safer than I did before the new measures were in place. We take Ruth and then Charlize home on the way, until it's just me, the driver and Coulson.

Why was he following me around like that? Is this a new thing, a general across-the-board guarding of the kids of prominent politicians?

Or maybe it is more specific to *me*: not so much guarding as keeping an eye on what I'm up to.

We pull in through our gates.

The driver opens my door, and I get out. He's gathering my bags of shopping; Coulson is already out of the car, standing there.

'Could I speak to you for a moment?' I say to Coulson.

'Of course.'

'Could you have those taken up to my room please?' I say to the driver. He nods, takes them inside. Coulson and I are alone.

'Why were you following me when we were shopping?'

He's surprised, then amused. 'You spotted me? I must be slipping.'

'Why?'

'It's my job to keep you safe.'

'From exorbitant prices? Pickpockets?'

'From all dangers.' His face is unreadable.

'That reminds me; since you've been keeping such a close eye on me – perhaps you could help with something else.'

'What's that?'

'My phone has gone missing.'

'Has it?'

'It went missing when we were at Chequers.'

'I see.'

'Do you know anything about that?'

'Sorry. I must have missed that particular pickpocket.'

Again – he's amused. He knows something about my phone. Did he take it? He must have. Why would he do that? Why wouldn't he say if he did?'

'I'll keep a closer eye on you next time,' he says. Is that a warning? 'Is there anything else?'

I shake my head, turn, walk up the steps. The driver is back now from lugging my shopping and holds the front door open. It closes behind me; I breathe in deeply.

What would have happened if Coulson had seen me meeting Lucas?

Maybe nothing. But we have to be careful, just in case.

7

Ava

She's singing, rocking me. I have a fever, spots: everything looks and feels wrong. My pyjamas are sandpaper on my skin, there are booming fireworks in my head, and I'm whimpering.

Mum kisses my forehead and her lips are warm and soft.

Lilla gumman, *she calls me; her sweetie, in Swedish. She says that I'll wake up tomorrow and this will all be a dream.*

She promises.

But when I open my eyes she was wrong.

There's a rumbling groan in the distance – the fireworks in my dream? I get up, pull my dressing gown around me in my cold room and cross to the window.

The almost empty car park is below, then the school walls and their barbed wire. And beyond? Light and sound.

Explosions? Fires? And now sirens scream in the night.

Curfew was hours ago, but all their curfews and rules couldn't stop this.

The sound echoes through the cold night, and I stand there, shivering, watching. I wish Sam were here with me.

8

Sam

I couldn't sleep so it didn't wake me: my eyes were staring at the ceiling when it began.

I'm standing at the window in my room; I even managed to make myself turn off my bedside lamp first so I'm not outlined in light.

But it's not dark like it should be in the middle of the night. Whatever is happening isn't far away.

I wish Ava were here. That I could go across the hall and we could talk and not be alone.

9

Ava

I slip out to the common room and its TV, even though it is still hours before breakfast. There are a few others there already, duvets brought along, wrapped around them on the sofas. The news is on.

There are scenes of unrest; fire. Sirens on the news bleed into the ones we can hear outside, but as the morning gets closer they die away.

It's said things are under control now, that roads are clear and guarded. London is business as usual and while schools will be closed today they will all be open again on Monday.

There's a collective groan in the room.

10

Sam

I knock on Charlize's front door on Saturday morning, stifling a yawn.

'Hi, Sam.' It's Charlize's dad. He looks a bit pale and tired, like I'm sure I do, too. 'Come in. They're set up in one of the suites in the guest wing; Anna can show you.' He gestures and Anna – one of the housekeeping staff – steps forwards.

'Thank you,' I say, and start to follow Anna, then one of the doors on the other side of the hall opens. I glance back: it's Charlize's mum, and she's not happy – the way she stands, rigid shoulders; the set look on her face.

She sees me, nods, as her husband goes through the door with her and it closes behind them.

Charlize has got a hairdresser, a makeup artist and a manicurist, too; they are all ready to make us look amazing for Ruth's party tonight – if it kills us. Well, more like this afternoon; because of the nine p.m. curfew it's going to start at two p.m. now, a weird time for a party.

After the lack of sleep the last few nights and *unrest* – as Dad calls it – only a mile away, I was so tempted to tell Charlize no, that'd I just see her there. But since I missed her party I'm not sure she'd have let it go if I hadn't turned up today, not even if the entire city of London fell into a giant sinkhole.

Upstairs, while my hair is being pulled and pinned, my face held in unnatural positions, my mind wanders back to what I saw below. Charlize's mum is big in the BBC – some sort of producer, heavily involved in various news and current affairs programmes: ones that have been strangely silent on the subject of politics lately. I'd expect her to be hard at work still, after what has been happening the last few nights. Why is she even at home?

They're finally done with our nails, faces and hair; we're sent to adjoining rooms to put on our dresses.

I knock on Charlize's door a moment later. 'Can you zip me?'

'Give me a sec. Yes, come in.'

She pulls up the zip at the back, one I could have reached myself.

'Is everything OK?' I say. 'Is there something going on with your mum?'

'Like what?' She turns to the mirror, adjusts her skirt.

'I don't know. She just seemed kind of stressed out; your dad, too.'

She gives me a sidelong glance. 'They've been talking about something they don't want me to hear.'

'And? Did you hear?'

'A bit. Mum's upset about some of her shows being pulled from the schedule. She's thinking about quitting.'

'No. Really?' I'm shocked. She's one of those extreme workaholic types; it's hard to imagine her giving it up.

'And Dad's angry with her. He said something about

how she should play the game.' She rolls her eyes. 'Anyway, it's not like we need the money; she should just quit if she wants to, don't you think?'

'Maybe. I don't know.'

Maybe if she doesn't play the game, she will end up disappearing like Lucas's mum.

11

Ava

Despite everything going on in the outside world, I still keep being drawn back to the same place, the same moment. In my room with the door shut. Holding a box of letters in my hands and daring myself to open them.

Well, I can open the box.

There are the first ones – the ones from Mum to me. I've read them so many times now that parts of them are locked in my memory.

Underneath those ones are the letters she wrote to Dad, and the ones he wrote to her, too. Someone at the hospice must have sent his letters back to him after she died.

There is one he wrote to her last of all; it's unopened. It's postmarked not long before the notice they sent about her death; perhaps it arrived after she died.

My hands are shaking.

Do it, Ava.

I carefully open the envelope.

A single sheet of paper and a photograph are tucked inside.

Photograph, first. It's me – I know this one! I'm in

front of the monkey enclosure at London Zoo: we went there for my birthday every year, the three of us. This was the first year it was just Dad and me. I was twelve.

I take out the letter. For a moment the words swim; I blink, refocus.

My dearest Brita,

I can only imagine what you are going through so alone, but I think of you every hour of every day. I hope you can feel my love stretching across the miles and wrapping around you.

You asked for news of Ms Mischief's birthday. A photo is enclosed. I wasn't sure it was the right thing to take her there without you being with us: I'd say she misses you even more than I do, but that isn't possible, so how about just as much? But once we started walking around she was back to asking all her endless questions about the animals.

Don't give the nurses trouble. Let the doctors make you well so you can come back home to us where you belong.

All my love,
Ethan
xxx

Ms Mischief: I'd forgotten he used to call me that.

Now I'm remembering how he was after Mum left. All the time he took off work. All the things he did for me, like the ribbons braided in my hair that I hated; I knew he was trying to be all things to me, so I went along with it for him.

I'd have sworn we were as close as a father and daughter could be, but he kept the one thing from me that I needed the most.

12

Sam

'It's good to see you.' Lucas's smile lights him up from the inside when I arrive, though I can tell: he's not been sleeping well, either. There are shadows under his eyes, his face is almost gaunt.

'This place — it's rather *wow*,' he says, but the look in his eyes isn't complimentary. It's a massive penthouse, overlooking the Thames and the lights of London. Did they sip champagne safe in their tower, watching the city burn last night? 'Does Ruth live here?'

I shake my head. 'It's her uncle's. He said she could use it for her party.'

'I've scoped it out. I think best bet for some privacy is the balcony.' He takes my hand in his; his fingers are warm. Is he playing the romance game like I was, to give them a reason to leave us on our own? Or maybe he's holding my hand because he wants to. Either way I'm not sure how I feel about it, but I leave my hand in his.

He leads me through the crowd. Charlize and Ruth's eyes are on us, others too; some colour climbs in my cheeks.

We step out on to the balcony. It wraps around; there's a large section just outside the doors where people are clustered, talking, and the music from inside spills out. He leads me past them to the narrow part that winds around the corner of the building.

'Here – it's cold.' He's taking off his jacket and I'm protesting but he slips it over my shoulders, and we sit down on a bench tucked away at the end of the balcony.

He's still holding my hand and now he takes my other hand, too. His dark-eyed gaze is intense. There's no one near us, and the background noise of the party should cover our voices if we talk quietly.

'I can't believe people live in places like this, when so many are hungry, cold, on the streets. It's just ...' He shakes his head.

'I'm sorry.'

'It's not your fault you're on one side of the great divide and I'm finding myself on the other.'

'Are you and your family OK?'

He shrugs. 'Yes and no. We've been evicted from our house.'

'*What?* Why?'

'No reasons were given. We've got help from extended family, or we'd have nowhere to go.'

'Oh, Lucas. I'm so sorry.'

'We carry on. Anyway, what happened to you the other day?'

'I was there, just about to go into the café to meet you when I spotted I was being tailed by one of the security agents who guard us. I wasn't sure we should be seen together.'

'That was probably wise, considering my family connections. We'll have to be careful – if you're in.'

'In *what*, exactly?'

'I'm completely committed to doing whatever I can, and not just because of my mum. But you don't have to be. Are you sure? Do you want to get involved? Have you really thought about it, what the implications might be?'

'I haven't been thinking of much else, to be honest, and I *can't* just stand by. I can't look the other way. But I also can't answer you without knowing what, exactly, it is that you're committed to doing.'

'That's fair. I've been getting in touch with other people, groups of teenagers mostly – we're just trying to work out what our course of action should be now. One of the things we think we need to focus on is *why* journalists have been disappearing. The government must want to stop everyone knowing what is really happening, so we think the key is getting information out as far and wide as we can.'

'That makes sense. Like on social media and stuff?'

'Exactly. We're setting up accounts with false names that can't be traced back to us, and plan to start with posts about people who've gone missing, like my mum. And how the government provokes violence instead of preventing it, like how that peaceful protest after Kenzi's death turned ugly when riot police attacked.'

I'm nodding, thinking. 'There was stuff said online about that at the time, but very little outcry, and what there was disappeared quickly. People will believe what they want, and they don't *want* to believe the government is getting things so wrong. And stuff gets twisted around in politics; they'll always have explanations for everything they do.'

'You're making it sound hopeless.'

'What I mean is that just saying stuff isn't ever going to be enough; you need to *show* what is really happening.'

'Show — how?'

'Use images as much as possible. Put the word out to everyone to get whatever photos or videos they can, and share them.'

He nods. 'Good idea.' And he starts talking about things they might be able to get images of, like that day at Kenzi's protest, but of course the real reason I thought of this is the photographs I've already got.

But how can they be used? If someone has my phone they'll know I'm the one who took them. And even if my phone is just lost and no one has seen my photos, how many people were in a helicopter over Westminster the day of the so-called riots, and then later also at Chequers? Someone would work out it was me.

'The next thing we need is a tag; something everyone can use,' Lucas says. 'One that will spread beyond us if this works. I keep thinking of that last article my mum put up online: *The Death of Democracy*.'

'D – O – D. Not so catchy, especially as it sounds like Department of Defence. How about instead: Democracy is Dead. D – I – D?'

'And *do* something! Democracy is Dead Do Something – DIDDSO,' he says.

'I like it. But does it sound, I don't know, a bit silly when you say it as a word?'

'The point is that it makes it easy to remember. And it sounds like something adults might think teenagers would say – if it's overheard no one will notice.'

'True,' I say. And that's not all. It feels *real* to me; it feels alive. I want this to work. I also want to tell him about my photos, but I'm scared.

Lucas is looking at my eyes, from one to the other as if searching for something. If he looks closely enough will he be able to see what I'm holding back?

Suddenly the music is turned off, voices are hushed. He pulls away, looks back down the balcony the way we came.

'What's going on?' I say.

'Let's find out.'

13

Ava

There's a knock on my door. It opens; it's a girl I half recognise from meals at the boarding house the last few days but haven't spoken to before.

'Hi. Mrs Morgan told us to tell everyone: come and watch.'

She's gone and is knocking on another door before I can say, 'Come and watch what?'

I close my book, get up and step into the hall; everyone is heading for the common room.

The BBC news is on the TV.

'It's starting,' someone says, and voices hush.

'And now, live from Westminster ...'

It's Sam's dad.

'We have security reports on the A4A Atrocities and the violence that followed, as well as preliminary reports on the unrest that took place the last few nights. What we have learned is both sobering and worrying. But we promise you: we, as a nation, can and will stop these violent incidents striking at our society.

'As has already been reported, the suicide bombers that caused so much pain and death in four of our brave cities were all very young, ranging in age from twelve to fifteen. The initial assessment was that our young people were being groomed for these acts with terrifying, violent results to themselves and those around them. But the closer we looked into the events leading to that bleak day, the more this initial view changed.

'The riots the day the government measures were announced were started by teenagers on social media rounding up their friends to come out on the streets. Likewise, this was the case with the countrywide violent unrest that has followed in recent days.

'The planners – the instigators – and the perpetrators; all those behind them and the ones standing there themselves, wearing suicide vests – *all* of them were young people. The problem we as a nation face is how to root out this evil that is flourishing still, in our own homes; it threatens all of us. No child is safe from this infection; they came from all segments of our society. Our young need our protection, both from themselves and from each other. We won't shirk in our duty to safeguard our children.'

I'm listening and staring at the screen. Sam's dad has this reasonable, calm look as he basically tells the nation that everything is *our* fault: us, the young. Outrage swells inside me. This country is in the mess it is because of people *his* age voting – or not voting – or wasting their votes in some sort of misguided protest, yet he is saying that everything is *our* fault? And at the same time he says we are the ones that need protecting. The twisted logic is unbelievable.

'Going forward, the following new measures will be implemented.

'Young people under the age of sixteen may not appear in public in groups larger than four without special permission for assembly from either their school or local authority. Guidelines will be provided to both. Any young people taking part in an assembly that breaches this rule will be subject to arrest. Those under sixteen will also be subject to an earlier curfew of six p.m. until further notice, unless accompanied by their parents or guardians. Anyone breaching curfew is subject to arrest.

'All young people aged twelve to seventeen must carry new official photo identification with them at all times, which is subject to inspection on demand by police or other authorised personnel. Those failing to carry ID or to present it on demand will be subject to arrest. ID will be issued over the next few days at schools throughout the UK and will replace the general identity cards in use for this age group.

'Finally, mobile phone ownership and use is banned for those under the age of sixteen. All such phone contracts will be suspended immediately. All mobile phones must be accounted for and handed in tomorrow through school collection points. All SIM contracts for tablets and other devices are likewise suspended. Anyone found in breach of these rules will be subject to arrest.'

I don't hear anything else he says because of the uproar in the common room, one that gets louder when those under sixteen realise that their phones have already stopped working. Somebody, somewhere, must have had their finger on a switch, ready and waiting for this moment.

It's a good day to be seventeen for a change, but I'm looking around at these girls, boarders at a prestigious, expensive school – hardly the kind of place you'd expect trouble. Yet the government pronouncements apply across the board – what was it he said, that no child is safe from this infection? So it must all apply to *everyone* of a certain age. Even their own children – like Sam.

Whatever happened to innocent until proven guilty?

They knew all along that the suicide bombers were young teenagers. Why all of a sudden do they want to take these measures? Before, they said that the country needed to protect the young from being targeted by anarchists like A4A – now they are saying *everyone* needs to be protected from *us*.

The group of girls in this school might not be the sort who would generally go against the system or cause trouble – they're wealthy, the system is there for their families and themselves to exploit. But now that may change. Measures like this, targeting young people everywhere, are going to make them *all* angry. It unites them in a common cause.

They're going to have a reason to protest, things they want to say.

Just not in groups of more than four, after six p.m., or on their phones.

14

Sam

'I'm feeling rather smug for having already turned sixteen,' Ruth says. 'Even though your dad has totally ruined my birthday.' A pointed look is directed at me. Around us the party atmosphere is completely gone. The music is still off, lights turned up. People are talking in small groups, and there are more looks in my direction. *Great.*

'Last time I checked they didn't consult me on government policy,' I say to Ruth. 'It's hardly my fault.'

'What do we do now?' Anji says. 'I mean, those of us who haven't passed the birthday milestone in question. It's after six p.m.'

'That couldn't apply tonight when they made the announcement *after* six p.m., could it? What do they expect people to do?' Ruth says.

'But the phone thing did,' Anji says, brandishing her now useless phone in her hand. Everyone under sixteen has already discovered their phones aren't working; if I knew where mine was I'm sure it wouldn't be working, either. And how am I going to hand it in?

'We should stage a mass slumber party in protest!' Anji says.

'In this outfit?' I shrug. I take Lucas's jacket off and hand it back to him.

'I'm up for it,' Lucas says, leans down and kisses my now bare shoulder: the shock of it, the feel of his lips on my skin and what he said combine and I don't know how to react. Was that real, or part of a game?

'More than four of us here are under sixteen,' Anji says. 'Do we need a permit?'

'Wasn't that only for public places?' Ruth says.

'Who knows? Who can keep up with all the new rules?' I say.

'What if we just *don't*?' Anji says. 'And by *we*, I mean everybody. If no one went along with their stupid rules, what could they do? They can't lock up every under-sixteen-year-old in the entire country, can they?'

'But your phone isn't working,' Ruth points out. 'So they've won on that one.'

One of the staff comes over to Ruth, says something in her ear.

'Well, Sam, you, at least, aren't stuck here overnight. Your driver has called up to say he's here to take you home now.'

Lucas comes to the door with me to say goodbye, and gives me a hug. He whispers in my ear: 'Think things through. Send me a message if you want to get involved: just a yes or a no. I'll know what it means.'

There is a hot streak of anger running through me when I get in the car. It makes me sit upright, fists clenched. I wasn't due to be collected for another hour, to get me home in plenty of time before the nine p.m. curfew. It's well after six already so there was no point in an early departure to beat the new curfew. Why am I being taken home now?

At least it'll let everybody still at the party talk about me more easily.

Once we're back I go straight up, put on some jeans. I check Dad's whereabouts with one of his assistants: he's still at Westminster and they're not sure when he'll be back.

I wait.

It's close to midnight when Dad's car pulls in – obviously even the later curfew doesn't apply to him. I go to his office; he always stops here first. I hesitate, then sit in his chair, behind his desk.

A moment later he walks through the door. He's startled to see me – and not very pleased, either.

'Samantha, what are you doing here? Shouldn't you be asleep?'

'It's not a school day tomorrow. And we need to talk.'

'This sounds serious; I'll get the whisky. Hot chocolate?'

Hot chocolate. Sitting on the edge of his desk, feet swinging. Doing as he says, always.

I promise I'll never be bad again.

I swallow. 'No. No, thanks.'

I hear the whisky bottle clink against his glass. He comes back in, sits on the other side of the desk. It feels wrong that we've swapped chairs; why did I sit on this side?

'So, what was so important you needed to ambush me in my office at this hour?'

'I'm fifteen.'

'I'm aware of that; I was there when you were born, after all.' He tips his glass towards me, has a sip.

'So all of these measures you announced tonight apply to me.'

'I'm aware of that, too. Though your birthday is only weeks away.'

'That isn't the point. How can you say everything that happened is our fault?'

'Who is the "our" in your sentence?'

'Everyone my age and younger.'

'The investigations support this conclusion. And obviously none of this is directed at you personally in any way, Samantha.'

'It makes me feel like a criminal.'

'Don't overreact.'

'Well, what about the things that *are* directed at me personally?'

'What do you mean?'

'Like being brought home early tonight.'

'I didn't know that. But security is there to keep you safe; if they brought you home early they must have had a good reason.'

'Huh. How about sneaking around and following me?'

'What are you talking about?'

Could it be that he actually doesn't know? 'Agent Coulson was tailing me from a distance when I was shopping with my friends – in a place that had been cleared for me to go by security, so why was he there?'

Dad shrugs. 'He must have felt there was some risk, that you needed keeping an eye on.'

'If that's the case why sneak about and try to stay out of sight? I felt like I was being spied on.'

'Obviously they felt this was in the best interests of keeping you safe: no one is spying on you, Samantha. What has got into you tonight?'

Am I being unreasonable? It's on the tip of my tongue to apologise, but then that makes me angry again.

'I just want my own life,' I say.

'I just want you to be safe.'

'I don't need to be protected all the time!'

'You don't know the world like I do, Samantha. You and young girls like you, like Ava, too – and boys as well – face a time of terrible uncertainty. Being in the wrong place – taking the wrong step – you don't know what could happen, the consequences it could bring.'

'What does Ava have to do with any of this? Anyway, she's seventeen.'

'Just the same, she still needs someone to look out for her.'

And I'm confused why he's mentioning her now.

'Ava got an additional scholarship; that's why she left and went to board at school. Isn't it?' He doesn't say anything, but then I see it, something I should have seen before. 'That wasn't from the school at all, was it? Did you do that?'

'You're welcome.'

'But Dad – *why* did you do that without asking, without saying anything about it?'

'To look after her. Now let me look after you.'

Looking after *her*? But did it actually have anything to do with what is best for Ava? For whatever reason, he didn't want her in our house any more, so he pulled some strings. It might be what she would have wanted anyway, but what gives him the right to decide things for other people without asking first?

The way he always has for me.

I'm staring back into his eyes and they hold a reflection I don't want to see. A helpless girl who can't make decisions or do anything for herself.

He's wrong.

I get up out of his chair, walk across the room. That's one decision. I close the door behind me: another one.

I go back to my room, each step mine and mine alone. I won't be what he wants me to be, not any longer.

When I open the door to my room, it's in darkness. I thought I left the lights on?

I flick the switch, close the door. I start to walk across my room, and that's when I see it.

There, on my desk: my missing phone.

I stop, the hair standing on end on the back of my neck. How did it get there? Almost holding my breath I look around the room quickly, then in the wardrobes, behind the curtains, anywhere someone could possibly hide.

I'm alone.

I lock my door.

How did my phone just appear there, on my desk? There's nothing, no note or anything: surely if someone had found it and brought it to my room they'd have left a note. There is nothing at all to say how it got here.

At least now I'll be able to hand it in tomorrow.

I turn it on, just to confirm to myself: yep, my contract has been cancelled, too. There's no network.

I go to my photos – I should delete them ...

But there is nothing there. They've already been deleted.

All of my photos have vanished, and not just the recent ones I added.

They're gone.

And with my account closed they won't be saved on the cloud either, will they?

I sit down, pull my duvet around me.

The new government, their new measures. Missing journalists. The brutal response to protests. Hangings. And now my phone reappearing, too, but minus photographs that show the police, army and Lorder brutality for what it is.

And then there is Lucas, and his question.

There has been so much going on, so much confusion in my mind along with it, but now everything is clear. There isn't any need to think where the line should be, what is right, what is wrong. I know, don't I?

Anyway, there's no point in doing things part way with Lucas. Someone – Coulson? – had my phone, saw the photos, deleted them. I'm in this up to my neck already.

I get my tablet. Sure enough the SIM no longer works, but it can still be used on wifi. I message Lucas: one word, and one only.

Yes.

15

Ava

There's a whole school assembly first thing on Monday morning, something that normally only ever happens at the start and end of the year. The hall is packed.

Some government agents are there, wearing grey suits, but they're not doing the talking. Instead it is the head teacher, but she seems to be reading a prepared speech and I've never seen her do that before.

She stumbles over some of the words: she didn't write it, did she? It must have been handed to her to read out to all of us.

It summarises the new rules for under-sixteens, and goes over other changes, too, ones that affect sixteen and seventeen-year-old students like me. We're getting new school photo IDs done today and we have to wear them in public, always, in a holder around our necks – colour-coded red for under-sixteen and blue for sixteen- and seventeen-year-olds. Older A-level students who are eighteen aren't affected.

The grey-suited agents don't seem to be listening to what she is saying. Instead their unsmiling eyes scan the students. Occasionally one says something to the deputy head who stands nearby. She answers, and they make a note. It looks like they're asking her for names.

We're all jammed in here tight but apart from the head's voice the room is quiet. Someone coughs and that seems loud.

At the end we file out by class. The younger ones are handing in their mobile phones as they leave, names being checked against lists, so it takes a while.

Sam goes towards the door with her year group. Even across the room she doesn't look herself, somehow: like she hasn't slept. Her phone is taken, checked off a list, and she disappears through the double doors.

When they finally get to my year group we exit faster since we don't have to hand in our phones, yet we still must walk through the doors in single file, past these government agents. They seem to assess each girl as she steps past, as if they could identify anyone dangerous with a glance: those who can think for themselves, maybe? I force my eyes down just in case.

Later we're brought back to the hall in groups for the new ID cards, and it isn't just a photo. Our fingerprints are taken; retinal scans, too. And a swab of spit: is that for a DNA test? Part of me is furious and wants to argue: what right do they have to know all of this about me, about all of us? But more of me is cautious. It is not the time to stand out in the crowd.

My new photo card drops out of a slot, still warm from the machine. In my hand a serious girl with dark hair stares back, one I almost recognise even though everything around her is changing. It clips into a blue over-fifteen lanyard, and around my neck it goes.

*

There's a commotion outside the boarding house after last bell.

A girl – the one who knocked on our doors last night to get us to come and watch the news – is being taken away, a grey-suited agent pulling her by the arm. She's crying.

'What's happening?' I say to some of the other girls.

One answers: 'Flick didn't hand her phone in, so they came to get her.'

'Why didn't she?' someone else asks.

'Her mum is away at a hospital. They text each other all day.'

Mrs Morgan, the housekeeper, goes up to them; she's saying something, but it's too far away to hear. They brush her aside. Flick – now I know her name – is pushed into a government car. It pulls away.

'What's going to happen to her?' someone asks.

Nobody answers. None of us know.

16

Sam

I record it all. Agents in grey suits, like the ones in assembly earlier – *Lorders* – dragging a small girl away from her friends. Forcing her into a car. And I just watch, safe inside a classroom with my camera up against the glass of a window. I feel sick.

I tuck my camera away. I recognised her vaguely – she's friends with Anji's little sister; Flick somebody, I think. She's maybe thirteen.

Why was she being arrested – if that was even what it was? It doesn't seem the right word to use, not when she is so young; and especially given that 'arrested' makes you think of legal rights and procedures that don't seem to exist any more.

But what could a thirteen-year-old girl possibly have done?

I'm pretty sure Flick is a boarder; Ava might know something.

I open the door to the boarding house and peer inside. A girl walks down the stairs towards me.

'Do you know where Ava Nicholls's room is?' I say.

She looks at me blankly. 'She's tall, dark hair, sixth form. Just moved in.'

She shrugs. 'Sixth formers are all on the top floor.'

I climb up the stairs to the top, and knock on a few doors. No one answers but then I notice faint voices, like radio or TV, coming from the end of the hall. The door is ajar; I peer in. It's a common room, full of chairs and sofas and the TV I could hear. It's empty apart from Ava.

'Hi,' I say.

She looks away from the TV, eyes widening when she sees it's me. 'Hi, Sam.'

'Is it OK if I come in?' I feel awkward, like we haven't spoken properly in ages, though it has only been a few days.

'Of course. Sorry, I can't seem to stop watching the news, even though most of what they say is the same over and again.' She points the remote, mutes it.

'Same shit, different day.'

A quirk of humour finds her eyes. 'Exactly. Why are you here, Sam?'

'Does there have to be a reason?' She raises an eyebrow. 'Well, there is something I want to ask you about.' I walk across the room, sit down next to her.

'This feels weird,' Ava says. 'We used to talk. What has changed?'

And now I'm remembering that I'd decided: no more being careful to say and do the right thing all the time. It might have been my dad that made me think that to begin with, but it applies now, too. I'll just come right out and say what I'm thinking.

'You moved out when I was away.'

'Not my idea.'

'Well, there is something else, too. I was trying to find something in my history on my tablet. I saw that you'd been doing searches about me, my family.'

'I was curious, that's all. And that is all public information that anyone could see.'

'You could have just asked.'

'You're right. Though would you have answered?'

'I don't know. But it'd be good if I had a choice what people know about me.'

'I can understand that. But didn't you get your dad to find out about my mother and why she left without asking me?'

I pause, thinking. That's exactly what I did, isn't it? 'You're right. I'm sorry.'

'It's OK; I needed to know. But what wasn't OK was the other day, by the library. I felt like you couldn't wait to get away from me.'

'I'm really sorry,' I say, about to add *I didn't mean to* – but that isn't completely true, is it? I was waiting for that call from Lucas, but I'd felt uncomfortable being around her, too.

We're staring back at each other, then something in Ava's eyes relents. 'The world is enough of a mess without friends falling out, isn't it?' she says. 'Peace?' She holds out her hand, and I take it. It's warm, a firm handshake. She lets go and I smile and she smiles back, and something inside me eases.

'I've really missed you, Ava. I went to talk to you when we got back and you were gone.'

'Sorry. It got arranged for me.'

In more ways than she knows. Should I tell her?

'What's it like, living here? Is it OK?'

She shrugs. 'It's all right. The things that are bothering me would be the same no matter where I went.'

'Your parents.'

She nods. 'I still can't get my mind around the fact that Dad knew about Mum and never told me. And then there is all the crazy stuff happening in the world around us at the same time.'

'Too many shocks at once.'

'Yes. And it's how they affect each other, too.'

'What do you mean?'

'If Dad hadn't died and I'd found out about my mum, and that he'd known why she left and that she died – and that he'd kept back those letters from her – then I could have got angry with him. Argued. Heard why he did what he did. Part of me is missing him so much I can't stand it and part of me is furious. It feels wrong even to feel that way now, but I can't stop myself.'

My hand reaches out to hers, holds it.

'That just totally sucks.'

'Yes. It does.' She looks at me sideways, eyes thoughtful. 'But maybe you can care for somebody, even though there's no way you can understand something they did. Maybe sometimes a good person can get things really wrong. You don't have to agree with what they did to still care about them.'

Her words are swimming around inside me. Is she still talking about her father? Much the same could apply to mine lately.

And I don't want to talk about him. Not now, maybe

not ever – especially as I can't tell Ava how I really feel without letting her in on Lucas and DIDDSO. That I shouldn't do. Ava has enough to deal with, and anyway, what would happen to her scholarship if she got involved and anybody found out? It's a risk I can't let her take.

'I'm going to have to get going,' I say. 'I've got to make the early curfew.'

'Of course.'

I start to get up and as I do feel the camera in my pocket, and remember why I came here in the first place.

'Oh yeah. There was something else I wanted to ask you about. Was that Flick who got hauled off by agents a while ago? Do you know why?'

'I don't really know her, but what I heard is that she didn't hand in her phone. She was using it to stay in touch with her mother, who is in hospital. They came looking for her.'

I stare back at her, horrified. Surely Flick can't have been arrested for that? Maybe they'll talk to her about it, then let her go. What else can they do with a thirteen-year-old whose only crime was wanting to talk to her sick mother?

We say goodbye, and I rush down the stairs to the pick-up area. My car is waiting, and the driver and Coulson are looking a little stressed about the time.

Staring out of the window on the drive home, I think through what Ava said. As far as her dad goes, I get what she was saying – it makes sense that she shouldn't turn her back on all that he was and did for her because of this one thing about her mother, even though it is huge and hard to understand.

But the things my father has done are in another category. They've led to peaceful protestors being met with violence and arrest; eighteen-year-olds being hanged for trespass. Journalists going missing. A thirteen-year-old girl being hauled away by agents for having a mobile phone. He's changed the lives of every teenager in this country and tarred us all with blame for everything that has ever gone wrong.

This isn't just about Dad, me and my family; it isn't some argument or disagreement we've had, or anything he's done to me directly.

It goes so far beyond that it is hard to see how we could ever come back.

18

Sam

Charlize and Ruth come by the next evening, making much of being allowed out after six p.m.

'What would happen if we dragged you out of the front door?' Charlize says. 'Would you get arrested?'

I shrug. 'How about I lock you in the bathroom until nine p.m. when the next curfew kicks in and do the same to you?'

'I actually can't get my head around all these curfews and stuff,' Ruth says. 'It's insane.'

'What does your dad think?'

She hesitates. 'Keep this quiet?'

'Of course,' we both say.

'He's angry about how things are being put into place, and at these new agents: he calls them Lorders.'

I'm startled to hear that expression has been picked up by the police.

'He says they're taking over, that it isn't right. A lot of the older guys are taking early retirement and clearing out. He's thinking of doing the same.'

'You should get him to talk to my dad, tell him what he thinks.'

'He tried, Sam. Your dad wouldn't see him.'

We don't quite know what to say after that, and they leave not long after. But Charlize forgets her bag in my room and we go back for it while Ruth waits.

Once we get there Charlize unzips her bag, reaches in and passes me a small box.

'What's this?'

'A present from Romeo. Lucas! By the way, I told him about your drawing.'

My mouth hangs open, embarrassment twisting in my stomach. 'Charlize, you didn't! How could you?'

'You can thank me in your wedding speech. Anyway, he asked if I could give this to *Juliet*' – she winks – 'without anyone noticing. I wonder what it is.' She gives a small shake, and there is a slithering sort of noise. 'It sounds like jewellery to me.' She weighs the box in her hand. 'Seriously heavy jewellery.'

'Wonder all you like! It's private. And the car is waiting for you.'

'I'll corner you to find out later.' She gives me a quick hug, runs back out of the room.

Door firmly closed, I go into my studio, then close that door, too.

I can't believe she told Lucas I drew him as Romeo. I cringe. How long has he known?

When I did it I had no reason to think I'd ever see him again or I wouldn't have done it. And I only did so because it made it easier to do the drawing, basing it on a real person, not making one up. It doesn't *mean* anything, not the way Charlize thinks.

I look at the box in my hand. It's small, oblong,

wrapped in blue paper with heart-shaped stickers on it. I tear the paper, pull it away, and inside is a wooden box. I open it, and Charlize was right: there is a necklace.

I unhook it from the box and take it out. It's pretty: a silver chain, with a four-leaf clover hanging from it. Luck would help us, but I'm puzzled why he'd send this the way he did. He could have just put it in the post. I'm even more puzzled why he'd send something like this to me at all.

I pick up the two halves of the box again, then realise the bottom of the box is much heavier than the top of it, even though they're about the same size. The padded part where the necklace was clipped is stuck to the bottom of the box but pulls away with some tugging.

A hollow space is cut into the padding; tucked inside it is a mobile phone.

I turn it on; there is a text message waiting:

Hi Juliet, Romeo here. Thought this might come in handy.

My pulse rate quickens. Me having a phone is breaking all the rules. Does this mean the necklace wasn't some sort of romantic present, it was just a cover – using the box as a way to hide the phone? And he couldn't post it – they X-ray all the post now – so he gave it to Charlize to give to me instead.

I check the phone out completely. It's a basic mass-produced smartphone, small and light enough to easily hide in a pocket. There is nothing personal on it apart from social networking accounts. The accounts are signed in and the username is JulietSays999: no posts have been made. I smile to myself: Lucas is Romeo, he's made me Juliet. And adding 999 – the emergency number – is perfect. Its says, *this is urgent*.

I search for the DIDDSO tag, and there's a post about Lucas's missing mother – posted by RomeoSays999. There's a photo of her and I study it, a woman I've never actually met who has inspired so much; there is also a screenshot of her *The Death of Democracy* article. There are posts about other missing journalists, too.

But that's not all: it's not just Lucas's posts. There are images tagged DIDDSO from all over the country, from different accounts.

This – right now – is the moment. Does JulietSays999 have something to say? Does she dare?

The old Sam would have been too scared; she wouldn't have dared to defy her father. She might have wanted to throw this phone in the river.

Instead I transfer the photos of Flick to the phone, and do a DIDDSO post of my own.

19

Ava

For the first time in my life, I'm popular. Well, my phone is, at any rate. Even though it's kind of an antique, it still works; once the younger boarders realise I don't care about the new rules they can't stay away. They've even stopped apologising about my father's death as if they had something to do with it.

Amelie and Chitra are the two who are here now. 'Did you see it?' Amelie says to me.

'See what?'

'Did so.' Her eyes are round.

'I don't know if I did or didn't; what are you talking about?'

'No, not like that, look: it's a tag.' She holds up my phone. 'There's all this stuff being posted about missing journalists and the government. And Flick is there now, too, so someone from school must be involved!'

'Flick? The girl who was arrested?'

'Yes. But they got it a bit wrong. They said her mum was sick in hospital; that's not true. She's away working in a hospital.'

There are footsteps in the hall and she hurriedly closes

the screen and hands my phone back to me. It's safely on my desk when the door opens. It's Mrs Morgan.

'Girls? Time for sleep.'

She waits until they leave and then comes in, shuts the door.

'Making friends now, are you?' Mrs Morgan smiles.

I look back at her, say nothing.

'Well, there seems to be more traffic to your room lately. I hope you're not letting any of them touch your phone; you don't want to be responsible for them joining Flick.'

'Have you heard anything about what happened to her? Where she is?'

She shakes her head, says goodnight.

Once the door closes behind her I pick up my phone. What were those girls talking about – *did so*?

I search for it and finally work out what they were saying – it's actually #DIDDSO, and comes from DemocracyIsDeadDoSOmething. And there is a post with a series of photos of Flick. *Schoolgirl arrested: her crime? Keeping her mobile phone so she could talk to her sick mother in hospital*. The government agents pushing her into the car in the attached photos are tagged as Lorders.

From the angle, it's not hard to tell which building – maybe even which classroom – they were taken from. The time is also known, so they could work out from the timetable who was in that part of the building on that day. Whoever took these is going to be in trouble if they do.

I search the DIDDSO tag and find more photos, all posted in the last few days. There are a number of posts about missing journalists, like the girls said before; more about other young people who have been arrested and then disappeared – in all different parts of the country. Each one has more likes, more shares; outraged comments, too.

Goosebumps rise on my arms, the back of my neck, and I shiver.

Democracy may be dead, but at last, somebody is at least *saying* something about it.

And if people wake up and see what is happening where they live … ?

Maybe, just maybe, they can stop it.

20

Sam

There's no way I can sleep. This phone in my hand; the photos in my camera. The tag Lucas and I came up with together that is spreading, and the last two words it stands for: *Do something*.

There is risk. I can't ignore it: this could all be traced back to me. But what if these photos I took could make a difference – could even make *the* difference, the one that changes everything?

I have to do it.

One by one I go through my photos and pick the most damning. First the ones I took from the air at Westminster the day the so-called riots began. Most of the protestors look like teenagers, or even younger, and they weren't attacking anybody. They were unhappy about the changes and came out to say so – and they were just bludgeoned to the ground, rounded up. Taken away in police vans – to who knows where.

Next, I go through the ones from Chequers. Again, the people they caught weren't violent, all they really did was trespass and vandalise some government monuments. The photos show them surrendering, hands up. I find

BBC photos of the hangings to include.

JulietSays999.

DIDDSO.

I post them all.

It's only moments before a message comes through: it's Romeo.

OMG. You never said what you had ... you're amazing. Absolutely bloody amazing.

Why yes, I am. And thanks.

We message each other through the night, me trying not to remember how the original Juliet fared. Sometimes I drift off only to wake again and check my posts – the likes, the shares – and message Lucas again. Hundreds quickly become thousands. Tens of thousands. Hundreds of thousands, and going up and still up again. Likes and shares are from all over the world, but crucially they are also *here*.

Until finally, around dawn, goosebumps tickle my neck, my spine:

DIDDSO is trending. It is actually trending.

21

Ava

Entropy: I feel it in the city, working its way out – disorder seeking a path.

I'm out for an early-morning walk, before school. Not a time of day I usually favour, especially with so little sleep last night. I'd stayed awake as post after post with the DIDDSO tag came up: first shocked at what they showed, then silently cheering inside as more and more people got involved.

I wonder as I scan in and out of checkpoints if they'll notice how much ground I'm covering and ask themselves what I'm up to. But all I'm doing is walking, feeling, watching. I've got my sixteen-to-seventeen ID around my neck – coded blue. There's a lot of blue about: I'm not the only sleepless one. Not so much red, since under-sixteens aren't allowed to congregate in groups of more than four, but they are there, too – just more spread out.

Teenagers mill about in groups like swirling particles: they connect here, disperse there, always keep moving. I don't feel strangled like I did before; there is some strange energy in the very air. I can taste it.

Can the authorities as well? They're on edge at the checkpoints, more so than on my last walk.

I'm both excited and scared to think what might be coming. I don't want more violence in this city, it's had enough, but it's hard to see how things can go any other way.

Fever burns in my blood like it did in my dream the other night. I don't want to hide away any longer: I don't want to run away any more, either. This city is mine, my heart beats with its energy. An outsider no longer: I want to be – I *am* – part of it.

22

Sam

The next morning when I go to the car to get to school, Coulson isn't with the driver in the front – he's in the back. He's never been there before, and fear twists my gut. Why is he sitting there?

The illegal phone is buried deep in my schoolbag. I'd thought it made more sense to bring it – to not leave it in my room, given how the last one disappeared – but maybe I was wrong.

The driver holds my door open; I get in.

'Good morning,' I say to Coulson – with an upward inflection. One that asks *why are you here?* He nods, says nothing.

The driver gets in the front, starts the car. We pull out through the gates. The light is on; the one that shows the driver can't hear anything said in the back.

Coulson says nothing, but somehow I resist the urge to babble into the silence, and stare out the window.

'We need to talk,' he says finally.

I turn slowly to look at him. 'Oh?' I say, and there is amusement in his eyes.

'Samantha, have you heard of an online campaign

called DIDDSO?'

I frown, shake my head. 'Should I have? What is it?'

'Dissidents putting up anti-government messages and images.'

I raise an eyebrow, shrug. 'Doesn't sound familiar.'

'I'm glad to hear that. It wouldn't be in your interests – or your father's, or the government's – if you were involved in any way. Yet something puzzles me.'

'What's that?'

'Some of the images posted and tagged with DIDDSO look familiar. I think I may have seen them somewhere before.'

My phone. He did take it, didn't he? And he deleted those photos; he must have. He knows.

I say nothing, fighting to breathe normally, not to react.

'Of course, if you know anything about these dissidents, who is involved, the photos, you should tell me. I'll protect you from the fallout if you tell me the truth. But only if you do so before things go any further.'

'I'm afraid I can't help you there.'

'Samantha – Sam. It is my job to protect you, even if it is from yourself. Let me do my job.'

The door next to me is opening – it's the driver. We've pulled in to school and I hadn't even noticed.

I'm reaching for my bag, trying to stop my hands from shaking.

'Think about it,' Coulson says.

I get out, try not to slam the door.

I fail.

23

Ava

That day there is another whole school assembly. No warning is given; we're taken from our lessons and all brought together.

I'm not surprised to see that Lorders are here again. The name has caught on and when I look at them, in grey suits today, stationed around the room at every exit, it is the name in my mind. If they saw those photos of Flick they'd know they were taken at our school; they'll be looking for whoever it was that took them.

Flick.

Sam came to ask me about her, didn't she?

I told her Flick's mum was in hospital; from what I'd overheard, I'd assumed her mother was unwell, not working away. Whoever put up that post made that mistake as well.

It doesn't mean it was definitely Sam who posted it; someone else could have overheard what I did and made the same mistake.

My stomach does a weird flip when it hits me. The DIDDSO posts: many were by RomeoSays999 and JulietSays999.

Romeo: Lucas was Romeo in her drawing, wasn't he?

Some of the photos were taken at Chequers: Sam was there, too.

My eyes are searching the room.

I find her, rows in front of where I am with my chemistry class. Am I imagining this or is she sitting bolt upright?

An announcement is made. They're searching for and checking all mobile phones. Everyone is to be searched, not just those prohibited from owning them by age.

Please, Sam: don't have done something stupid.

They start at the front. The first row files out through double doors to the adjoining cafeteria.

24

Sam

Can your heart actually stop beating from fear? Mine is slowing, each beat louder in my ears, as the second row is asked to file out.

I'm in the fifth row.

Did Coulson know this was happening today – is that why the talk in the car on the way to school?

Charlize nudges my arm, concern on her face, and I force mine to relax.

Think, Sam.

There are two things I've done they won't like: I've got a phone I'm not allowed to have, and it's signed into accounts that posted to DIDDSO. The latter is definitely the worse.

Can I delete the accounts without anyone noticing?

Quicker and easier to reset the phone.

I glance around the hall. Lorders at every exit are scanning the room. Anything I do is going to have to be subtle.

Charlize is on my right, Ruth on my left. I'm more or less in the middle of a row, not near either end, so anything I do with my hands probably can't be seen – but my bag is on the floor. If I bend to get it they will see. And the room is quiet, very quiet; everyone is nervous. There isn't all the usual foot-shuffling and squirming you'd expect with everyone crammed in together like this. Any sound or movement is a risk.

Someone coughs behind us. In front of us a girl I know vaguely is sniffling in that trying to be quiet but failing kind of way. I think she has allergies; Charlize is leaning back in her seat as if to get away. She's got a horror of germs.

Tissues. There are tissues in my bag. I could give her some, and slip my phone into my hand at the same time. Before I can think about it I just do it: reach down into my bag. Slip my phone into my sleeve; tap the girl in front on the shoulder and pass her a pocket pack of tissues.

The third row is beckoned. They stand, start filing out – blocking my view of the Lorders at the front. If I can't see them then they can't see me.

There is more coughing behind, more like a coughing fit now, and people are starting to fidget, to look around.

I glance down.

Settings.

General.

Reset.

Erase All Content and Settings.

Done. I glance up just as the last of the third row files past in front of me.

I don't dare move again; the phone is under my hand. What am I going to do with it? Time ticks slowly by but still too fast for me to work out what to do next.

The fourth row – the one in front of us – stands now, starts filing out.

Charlize nudges my foot with hers. Her hand: it slips against mine, the one with the phone palmed underneath it.

Did she see what I did?

She tugs at the phone under my hand. She's over sixteen, she's allowed a phone, but I resist. Even though I've reset it, what if it can be traced to DIDDSO somehow? How will she explain having two phones? She doesn't know what she's doing.

Charlize takes it from my hand and slips it into her own pocket.

25

Ava

We're told to put any phones, tablets or other devices we have into a tray. Then a detector of some sort is passed over us, our bags – to see if there is anything we kept back.

I'm so scared for Sam: is she the Juliet responsible for those DIDDSO posts? They were going up last night. If she was using a phone and has it on her now, she can't get through this. They'd find it for sure.

One of the Lorders beckons me forwards.

'Are you feeling better?' she says.

'Sorry?'

'You were coughing before. It was quite a performance, yet you seem fine now.'

'I – have a cough that comes and goes.'

'And it's gone.'

'Yes.'

She has my phone in her hand. Could they see the history, the things I've been looking at?

Her eyes on mine are cold.

She hands it back. 'You can go.'

26

Sam

I'm waiting in the hall. Where is Charlize? Why is she taking so long? She was ahead of me but I was waved through before she was. I feel sick with worry; I'm going in there to tell them the truth – I have to – *right now*. I start towards the door when she steps out.

Her shoulders are straight.

'Charlize?'

She shakes her head slightly. 'Come on.'

It's break time so we head for the art block. She leans back on the radiator like she always does and before I can say anything raises her hand.

'I don't want to know. Don't tell me anything.'

'What happened? Why were you in there so long?'

'They wanted to ask me why I had two phones when only one is registered to my name.'

'And?'

'I said it was one I had for another boyfriend.' She winks.

'Did they believe you?'

'You know I get A-stars in drama. Anyway, they've confiscated that phone, said they'd have to tell my parents

I had an unregistered, but it isn't actually something they can arrest me for at this time. Duh.' She rolls her eyes.

'You shouldn't have done it. But thank you.' I hesitate, not wanting to involve her further but not seeing a way around it. 'There is just one more thing. Could you message Lucas for me?'

'More favours?' She takes out her phone. 'What should I tell him?'

I think fast. I don't want to be too explicit; what if they're monitoring Charlize now? There are things she doesn't know and I want to keep it like that – it's better for her that way. What came with the phone? I touch the chain, its four-leaf clover, hanging around my neck.

'How about this: say *Thank you for the necklace, but the chain is broken. I'll call you when I get it fixed*.'

She gives me a look, shakes her head. Types the message in, shows me and presses *send*. 'There, done. You *owe* me.'

'Big time.'

'Yes. Bigger than big time. I'll think about it for a while.'

She's being all nothing-fazes-me-Charlize but I can tell she was freaked to be questioned by the Lorders. I give her a hug.

We've been friends for ever, but I can't believe she's taken this risk – that she's done it for me. I've felt like we've grown apart for a while now, but maybe that's just me. She's stayed the same, constant; I'm the one who has been changing and keeping things back.

As far as that phone goes she seems to think that's the last we'll hear of it, but I'm not sure. What if they can analyse it somehow, go back past the reset, find out what was done on it? I don't know where Lucas got it from – can it be traced back to him?

Somehow I'm sure this won't be the end of it.

27

Ava

I finally find Sam in a corner of the library.

'We need to talk,' I say.

'Is something wrong?'

'Not here. Come back to my room.' I don't wait for her to say yes or no, I just go – and she follows me across the school grounds to the boarding house, and up the stairs to my door.

I shut it behind us.

'What is it?' Sam says.

'In assembly this morning I suddenly had this conviction about a post I saw about Flick. Actually, some of the girls here mentioned it to me, and then I found it.'

'Flick?' She glances away, as if she doesn't want me to see her eyes.

'You asked me about her the other day: the girl who was arrested for not handing in her phone. And you see, as it turns out I got something wrong. It isn't that her mum is sick in hospital; she works away in a hospital. Strangely enough, whoever put up that post also had that wrong.'

'Oh? I don't see what that—'

'Listen. There was also a post about what happened at Chequers, with photos: I seem to remember you were there that day? So I think it is you: that you are Juliet, and Lucas is Romeo.'

Sam doesn't say anything, either to confirm or deny – but when she finally glances up at me her eyes say it all.

'So I'm right!' I feel both admiration and fear for her at the same time. 'I was really frightened in assembly that you were going to get caught with something you shouldn't have. I even staged a coughing fit to distract them.'

'That was you? I'm sorry I worried you.'

I shake my head; impatient, conflicted and struggling with words in a way that is unusual for me, until finally all that comes out is this: 'It's *brilliant*.'

'What?'

'The idea, the tag, the whole concept of DIDDSO. I love it. It's amazing and brilliant and brave. I want to get involved.'

'No, Ava. It's too dangerous.'

'What – and that's all right for you?'

'Well, maybe what I mean is more that you can't risk a misstep.'

I shrug. 'I don't think even the deputy head would take my scholarship away for posting something online.' I look at her closely. 'There's something you're not saying. What is it?'

'Would you stop that? That reading my mind thing. It's freaking me out.'

'Tell me, Sam.'

'It's about your scholarship. I didn't know until

after you'd moved here, but the school didn't actually increase it to cover your boarding fees. Dad is paying the extra.'

I stare back at her. I'd wondered before if her parents had arranged it to get me away from Sam, then thought it was wrong to suspect such a thing when they'd done so much for me.

'But why the pretence? Why didn't he say anything about it before?'

'Or maybe even ask if that was what you wanted?'

'So, is it kind and generous, or—'

'Controlling and condescending?'

'Er ... yeah. Maybe some of both.'

'Look, we had this big, well, argument, I guess. He doesn't think I'm capable of making decisions or judging what is right or wrong for myself. But it isn't just me, it's everyone under a certain age. We need to be looked after, because clearly we can't be trusted. We're dangerous to ourselves, to each other. It wouldn't have even occurred to him to ask you what you wanted.'

'You're furious with him, aren't you?'

'Yes. For so many reasons. Think about it. They – their generation – are the ones who've really messed up. When there was all that economic and political upheaval in Europe, what did they do? They voted to get out. Even though most people didn't want that, they either couldn't be bothered voting, or voted to leave, thinking it was some sort of protest against the government – and they landed us here. They closed borders, kicked people out; made it so that people like your mother had no real choice but to go. And they just carry on screwing up again and again. Yet somehow they seem to think we're the ones at fault.'

'Exactly. They're blaming us when all we're doing is reacting to what *they've* done. I want to help, to be involved. And it isn't just something I want, it's what I *need*: focusing on this – focusing outside of myself – has made me feel alive again.'

'I can't let you take any risks for me.'

'It's not for you, Sam. It's what *I* want – for me. Anyway, it's my decision.'

She sighs. 'I wouldn't forgive myself if anything happened to you because of me.' She slumps back against her seat, and I look at her closely.

'What's wrong?'

'I had a phone in my bag today at assembly.'

'Sam! What happened to it?'

'I reset it; Charlize saw me do it, and she took it. They questioned her for having an unregistered phone. I'm really scared they'll find some evidence on it and she'll be in trouble.'

'You didn't make her do it.'

'No, but I'm guessing she thinks I just had to be in touch with Lucas.' She shrugs.

'She thinks you're involved with him?' *Are you?*

'We've let them think that,' she says, and there is some discomfort in her about it – whether because of the masquerade, or because there really is something between them, I can't tell. 'Maybe I should have told Charlize the truth. Lucas used her as a go-between to give me the phone in the first place: it was hidden in a parcel, and she didn't know what it was.'

'So it was Lucas who involved her, not you.'

Sam tilts her head, thinking. 'I suppose so. Though I got Charlize and Ruth to set things up so I could see Lucas, and never told them why.'

'That's not in the same category as getting someone to carry an unregistered phone,' I say, and the more I think about it the more I'm uneasy about Lucas's actions. Despite how much I think what he and Sam are doing is amazing, and necessary, was it fair to use Charlize like that when she didn't know what was at stake?

'I don't know. Maybe. But shouldn't I have told her about it all afterwards?'

'Perhaps then it was too late, and knowing what you've been doing would be more dangerous for her? At least now if they ask she can honestly say she knows nothing about DIDDSO.'

'But if I had told her, then at least she'd have known how risky it was to take the phone.'

'There's nothing you can do about it now.'

'I guess not.' She looks tortured. 'I haven't been a good friend to her, not for a while. But you're right. I can't make decisions for her, or for you, any more than you can make them for me.'

'And?'

'Maybe there is something you can do to help. Let me think about it.'

28

Sam

The next day Charlize isn't at school, and my stomach twists with fear. Has something happened to her? Has she been arrested? Maybe she's just sick, has flu or something, but even as I tell myself this I don't believe it.

I message her on the school system: no answer. Email: no answer.

I find Ava, tell her what's happened; we go back to her room to use her phone.

First I try Charlize's mobile; it goes straight to a message. *This number is no longer in service.* I feel the colour drain from my face. I enter Charlize's home number.

It is answered quickly, cutting off the first ring. 'Hello?' A breathless voice – her mother.

'Hi, it's Sam, is—'

'Oh, Sam. She's – Charlize is—'

'What's happened?'

'She's been arrested. Look, I have to keep the line clear. Bye.'

There's a click and then a dial tone, and I stare at the phone in my hand. Give it back to Ava. She must either see from my face or she's carried on with mind-reading.

'She's been arrested?'

'Yes,' I say, feeling the weight of what has happened settle inside, crushing me.

'Oh no.'

'I have to go to the authorities, and tell them the truth. Don't I?'

'Then you'd both be arrested. She'd still be in trouble for lying to them about it being her phone.'

I stare back at Ava, shake my head. 'If they think it's her who has been posting stuff as Juliet for DIDDSO, surely she'll be in far more trouble than she would be just for lying about a phone.'

'You don't know that they've connected that phone with your Juliet posts.'

'But why else would she have been arrested? I've got to turn myself in.'

'Think about it. What is the best thing you can do to help Charlize right now? Keep DIDDSO going. Add her to it: another teen who has been arrested, just for having an unregistered phone in her possession. Another victim of the regime. If you post as Juliet, then they'll know *she* can't be Juliet – because Juliet is still out there.'

My head drops into my hands, following what Ava is saying but still feeling it's very wrong not to go to the authorities – to see if the truth can help Charlize.

'Do it.' Ava holds out her phone.

'I can't post as Juliet; I don't know the password. Lucas set it up.'

'Contact him?'

'If I use your phone, could it be traced to you? I don't want you to get into trouble.'

'Of course all the end-to-end encrypted services were banned years ago. But we could do it on wifi instead of the mobile network; use an internet-to-mobile calling service. Then I can bounce the IP address so it can't be traced.'

I feel my mouth hanging open, then shut it.

'How do you know all that?'

'It's a way to use your phone to call people on wifi without paying mobile charges. Dad used it to call me all the time with his taxi wifi.' She flinches when she says *Dad*, then does some things to settings on her phone, and holds it out. 'It's ready.'

'OK. I remember his number – I memorised it the other day. What with my other phone going missing and the new one being illegal I thought I should in case I ever needed it, and I guess I was right.'

Ava shows me how to use the internet-to-phone service. 'Can I do this on my tablet at home, too?' I say.

'Yes. See, it's an internet account? So it comes from that, not my phone number. You can call or text using this, and it can't be traced. Unless your tablet is monitored.'

'It might be.' If I were Coulson – and saw my photos – it would be, so that isn't a chance I should take.

I enter Lucas's number – it rings and rings out to message. Should I leave a voicemail? I'll go for something vague.

'Hi, it's me,' I say. 'I haven't got a phone any more, but you can reach me on this number.'

Seconds later he texts back. *Can't talk now. Molly and Dad have been arrested, I'm in hiding with Nicky. Only just got away. Got what I assumed was your message from Charlize, but when I tried to get in touch with her to find out what was going on the number was disconnected.*

I beckon Ava over to look. Her eyes widen.

I answer: *What — arrested? Why? Phone reset but confiscated at school assembly; C had it; she's been arrested, too.*

Lucas: *That may be how they found us — if they managed to restore that phone and link phone records from C to me.*

Me: *Oh no ... I'm so sorry. Are you all right — where are you staying?*

Lucas: *Not sure yet. Have some friends I can try, but don't want to put them in that position.*

'Our flat,' Ava says, still reading over my shoulder. 'It's empty; the rent is paid for another two and a half months. They could stay there?'

Me: *Ava's here; this is her phone. She is boarding at school, and the flat she had with her dad is empty and the rent paid for a few more months — she says you can stay there.*

Lucas: *That'd be awesome. Ava, are you sure?*

Me: *Yes! She says yes.*

I hand the phone to Ava; she enters the address, and door code: *Aristotle383bc.*

I take it back and message again. *I can't believe this is happening. I'm so sorry.*

Lucas: *No one knew they were going to start searches at schools like that; it's happening everywhere. But this won't stop us. Will it?*

Me: *No. Which reminds me: I need login details for J.*

He texts back with the password. *Stay strong. I've got to go.*

Me: *Keep safe. You can reach me via Ava on this number.*

Lucas: *OK. I'm going to ditch this phone now & get another so will be a different number. Take care xxx*

I look back up at Ava, unable to speak.

I find a photo of Charlize on the school website to include, and Ava helps me compose @JulietSays999's latest:

Sixteen-year-old schoolgirl arrested, her only crime having an unregistered phone. Stop the madness! #releaseCharlize #DIDDSO

'This *has* to make them realise it isn't Charlize who has been doing these posts,' I say. 'And once they know that, they'll let her go. Won't they?'

'I hope so.'

29

Ava

There's a knock on my door; it opens without waiting for me to answer. It's Chitra — one of the younger boarders who has been sneaking looks at my phone. I'm just about to apologise and say sorry, you can't use it any more — what if Lucas contacts me for Sam when one of them has it? — when she bursts out.

'Quick, you have to help. Can you open the side gate?'

'Why? What's going on?'

'Come on. I'll explain on the way.' There is such panic on her face that I get up and follow her, half running down the hall and then the stairs.

'It's Amelie,' she says through gasps. 'She's out with a bunch of girls, and the bus was late, and it's almost six.' Six, as in curfew time. 'It'll take them too long to get let in at the front gate.'

We get to the side gate just as the clock starts striking the hour. Only staff and sixth form students are given the code and I'm hitting the numbers into the keypad, fast.

But when I hit *enter* the gate doesn't open. Have they changed it?

Maybe I made a mistake.

I do it again.

This time the gate lock clicks open on the fifth chime of the clock, and they tumble through – four girls, only one of them with a blue ID who can be out later than six, panic and tears on their faces. If they'd had to go to the front gate, ring and wait to be let in they wouldn't have made it. They're panting from running and fear.

'Thank you, Ava,' Amelie says and throws her arms around me in a hug, and I pat her back, awkward, and we all walk back to the boarding house.

Mrs Morgan is waiting at the door when we get there, relief all over her face when she sees us. 'Please be more careful in future, girls,' she says. 'You don't want to be arrested – especially now.'

'Why *now* – has something happened?' I ask.

'It's just been announced. They're lowering the minimum age for the death penalty from eighteen to twelve.'

30

Sam

'Any word on Charlize?' Ava asks as she closes her door behind me.

I shake my head. 'Nothing on her, but her mum has been fired from the BBC. I tried going to my dad, asking if he could do anything for Charlize, and he just blanked me. And can you even believe about the death penalty age being lowered? Things seem to keep getting worse.'

'They couldn't do it, could they? Hang a twelve-year-old child?'

'I'm starting to think they could do *anything*.' I glance at my watch. I'm early; it's another twenty minutes until Lucas told Ava he'd call. He's got his own internet account now to bounce from instead of using his mobile directly: if only we'd had Ava with us and done that from the beginning.

I slump down on Ava's bed.

'You look exhausted.'

'I can't seem to sleep much lately.'

'Because of Charlize?'

'Yeah. And Lucas's sister and dad, too. They're all in custody, and it's my fault.'

Ava sits on her chair next to me. 'It's the government's fault. It's those who stand by and do nothing's fault. That isn't you; you're trying to do something.'

'Thank you for saying that. But—'

'No buts. Close your eyes until the phone rings.'

I lie down properly this time and do as she said. Her hand is on my shoulder, then my hair, and her voice is soothing. She starts explaining what they're doing in sixth form chemistry and my mind is soon wandering, drifting. As you'd expect.

When her phone finally rings I jump, startled from sleep, nerves jangled.

She hands it to me to answer, but I beckon her close so she can listen.

'Hi,' I say.

'Hey.'

'Ava's here with me, too.'

'Hi,' she says.

'Thanks for the place, Ava. You've really got us out of a tricky spot. And it's just outside the central checkpoints.'

'No problem,' Ava says. 'Any news on Molly or your dad?'

'No. How about Charlize?' he asks.

I sigh. 'No. Cheer us up?'

'We're getting a huge response with DIDDSO – likes, shares, comments. But we've been talking and think we need to take things to another level to make them take us seriously or change anything.'

'We – who is we?' I say.

'Me and Juro, Molly's boyfriend. He was at Kenzi's protest.'

'I've met him,' Ava says.

'Anyway, we think we need to escalate, do something big,' Lucas says.

'Something big – but peaceful, right?' I say.

'Of course. Anyway, have a think about what it could be, and we'll talk again soon.'

'All right. Take care,' I say.

The three of us say goodbye. I hand Ava's phone back to her, slump back down on her bed. *Take things to another level?*

It's the most important part of DIDDSO:

Do something.

31

Ava

'Be careful, Sam. It's one thing putting anonymous posts up online; I don't like the sound of this *something big* of Lucas's.'

'I can't hide away and let other people do things that I won't.'

'I know you feel you have to stand up against your father – and I understand why – but doing anything publicly against him can't go well. And it won't undo what has happened – whatever it is – to Charlize. Or Lucas's family.'

Sam looks down, lashes dark on pale cheeks. 'I know,' she says, sighs. I touch her hand and she reaches and grips mine.

'Just promise me you'll think about it before you agree to anything. Try to get some actual sleep and then, when your mind is clear, think about it properly.'

'I will, I promise,' Sam says, and her eyes meet mine. I remember trying to draw them and not being able to get what I could see on the page.

'Have you been drawing or painting lately?' I ask.

Sam's eyebrows go up a little. She shakes her head: no.

'Why not?'

'A mixture of things. I've been distracted, busy. I've been using my camera instead. But mostly nothing I was drawing ever felt real enough, not real like a photograph.'

'Maybe if you go back to your art it would help you see things more clearly? If nothing else, it might help you relax so you can sleep.'

She tilts her head to one side. 'Maybe. I don't know. Thank you, Ava. Anyway, there is something else we should talk about – Saturday.'

I shift, uncomfortable in my seat: Dad's cremation ceremony. I sigh. 'That's the thing *I've* been trying not to think about.'

'I know. Are you going to say anything?'

I shake my head. 'I feel like I should, but I'm too mixed up about everything with Dad and Mum. I just can't.'

'That's OK. You don't have to. But no matter what, I'll be there. Penny is coming, too. We'll collect you in the morning, all right? I think Penny said we'll get you at ten.'

Sam leans in, gives me a hug. I want to hang on to her tight and not let go, but I force my arms to loosen.

She pulls away. 'You were right about at least one thing.'

'What's that?'

'I think I need to pay a visit to the art studio.'

32

Sam

I knock once on the art studio door, open it and look in.

Mrs Jenson looks up from sorting out paintbrushes.

She smiles. 'Sam. I haven't seen you outside of class in ages.'

'I know. I haven't been in' – I shrug – 'whatever zone I need to be in to want to paint.'

'Great artists don't need to be in a zone. They are compelled, even in the face of great adversity – perhaps then even more so.'

'I'm not a great artist.' I wander in, the smell of paint drawing me.

'Maybe not. But you could be. Don't you have another lesson now?'

'No, I've got a free.' I'm lying – I should be in English now – and I'm guessing she knows it, but she doesn't say anything.

'Help me with this?'

Soon we're cleaning paintbrushes, the smell of solvent mixing with paint. She doesn't feel the need to talk about nothing while we work and it's quiet. The windows are open because of the fumes, but it's not cold. It's the sort of autumn day that makes you forget winter is coming, and I'm looking at the turning leaves on the tree outside the window, listening to birds. There's a faint hum of distant traffic but other than that it's hard to tell we're even in the city.

Then two large black cars come in through the front gates and pull up below. Doors open and government agents get out, dressed all in black like they are sometimes: Lorders.

Who are they after this time? I sigh. I wonder if I should distract Mrs Jenson somehow and take out my camera: record whatever happens next to get more images for DIDDSO.

They go towards the English block.

Some of them go in through the main doors, and some go to the side doors on the left of the building. The ones that only open into one particular classroom.

The one I'm supposed to be in.

Time seems to stop, the leaves on the trees to still, as if the wind is holding its breath like I am.

The agents that went inside come out through the side door. They speak to those outside. Then one of them takes out a radio, speaks into it.

Then they spread out to look around.

If they're still looking ... they didn't get who they wanted, did they?

I should have been in that classroom, the one they were checking.

Two of them start to head towards this building, and I step back from the window.

'Sam? What's wrong?'

Mrs Jenson walks across, looks out of the window, sees who is there and swears under her breath. She looks at my face, and her eyes widen.

'Sam? Are you in some sort of trouble?'

My eyes are pleading with hers.

'Come.' She pulls me towards the art supply cupboards at the back of the room, yanks out easels and other things. She pushes me inside, puts the easels back in front of me and shuts the door.

It's dark, pitch dark, and the automatic panic from that combines with the real, rational fear, both rising inside me until I want to scream, to push it all away and get out of here—

'We're looking for Samantha Gregory,' a cold voice says, and now I'm frozen, still.

'She's not here,' Mrs Jenson says. 'Her art lesson was yesterday. They could give you her timetable in the office?'

'We have it.'

'Well then, you know: she isn't here.' She sounds nervous – she's talking too much. Then I hope I just hear that because I know her so well.

Footsteps – heavy footsteps – come across the floor.

They're getting closer.

Doors creak open to my left; a moment later they shut again.

Then this door – the one I hide behind – opens. There's light but then I shut my eyes tight as if somehow that'll stop them from seeing where I hide.

Then the doors close again.

The footsteps move away and the relief is so strong I

sag back, and the stack of easels against me shifts and clunks against the door.

Fear rushes through me again, a wave of dread. Do the footsteps pause? Did they hear?

No. They don't come back.

33

Ava

'Can I help you?' It's the librarian's voice, but her tone is wrong and too loud in a space she likes to hush.

I glance around the stacks.

Lorders: two of them. One stands by the door, the other at her desk.

'We're looking for Samantha Gregory. Is she here?'

Fear and adrenalin flood through me. They're looking for Sam? I didn't see her when I came in – *is* she here?

'No, I haven't seen her this afternoon,' the librarian answers. 'Perhaps check her timetable in the—'

'We have,' he says.

The one by the desk then checks through the library, around every stack, in each study carrel. When he gets close to me I stare at the book in my hands, will my eyes to stay down and not look up and challenge.

Moments later they go back out through the doors.

There's a buzz around the room now – stray words connect in my ears.

Really? Sam?

Charlize hasn't been in school.

What have they done?

There is dismay and maybe some delight as well at who looks to be in trouble – they were at the top of the social ladder, and now this?

They would have gone to Sam's scheduled class first. If she wasn't there, where is she? Did she see them coming, somehow get away and hide?

And now they're searching the school.

Sam, where are you?

34

Sam

Once again I'm trapped in darkness.

The smell of paint is one I usually don't mind, but now it is so strong that, combined with breathing in and out too fast with panic, I feel dizzy.

The floor of the boot is rough against my cheek; the car moves slowly across the staff car park.

We pause. Turn right, continue on, and then stop. We must be at the back gates. The automated ones without a guard that only staff can use.

It's taking too long; why is it taking so long?

A metallic clanging sound: is that the gate? We move forwards. We're out.

We go faster now. The fumes – paint and car now, too, I think – the darkness, the fear – are overwhelming. We stop, start, turn corners; carrying on for so long I'm going beyond dizzy to faint, and my thoughts are random, disordered.

Where am I going to go?

To Lucas – Ava's flat. I think I can remember the address from when we gave it to Lucas.

Mum is going to go completely mental. Dad – he'll

have a different kind of freak-out. He'll be embarrassed; absolutely furious, too. Will he have to resign?

What's going to happen to me?

Did Charlize tell them that it was my phone?

Maybe when I posted as Juliet when it couldn't be her it made them realise she might know who it was. Maybe they made her tell them where she got the phone.

I hope she's OK. Maybe they worked it out some other way – from the photos at Chequers and from the helicopter, the ones Coulson must have seen before they were posted.

Through it all, Ava's face floats in and out. I hope that none of this will come back to her.

35

Ava

Not knowing where Sam is, if she's OK, is twisting me up inside.

They've probably found her and arrested her by now; how would we know? When people disappear in the backs of those big black cars no news bulletins follow: they just vanish.

The minutes tick slowly past. It's time for my chemistry lesson now and I don't want to go, but a sense of self-preservation says to do things as normal. Not to stand out.

I walk to the science building, feet dragging. Everywhere around me it seems girls are talking in hurried whispers about Sam.

I sit down, blankly copying chemical equations that are the starter, but unable to solve them. Unable to think at all.

The door opens at the back. 'Excuse me. Is Ava Nicholls here?' It's a nervous-looking receptionist from admin.

'That's me,' I say.

'You're wanted in the deputy head's office.'

First fear then dread fills me – what is it now? Maybe there is news about Sam? My feet feel heavy as I walk to the admin building.

When I get there half a dozen other students are in chairs in the waiting area, including Sam's friends Ruth and Anji. Are the others friends of hers, too? I sit down and a few more girls arrive.

Then the office door opens, but it isn't the deputy head who stands there: it's a Lorder.

'Anji Addington?' he says, and Anji gets to her feet and goes through the door. It closes.

We're all sitting, waiting, looking around at each other with apprehension in our eyes … but no one says anything. What's happening in there?

Perhaps ten minutes later the door opens and Anji steps out. Her face is white; she leaves through the other door without saying anything.

One by one names are called; a girl goes in; time passes. They come out and leave with varying degrees of distress on their faces. There are only a few of us left now.

'Ava Nicholls?'

I get up, walk, go through the door, and sit down when gestured to do so in a chair opposite the desk.

The one who called my name stays standing by the door; there is another Lorder in the deputy head's chair. He's looking at a tablet in his hands, and seconds of silence stretch.

Finally he looks up. 'How do you know Samantha Gregory?'

'Everyone at school knows Sam. And I was asked by the school to tutor her.'

'You are friends now.' He says it as a statement, not a question.

'Sort of. I mean, we're not exactly in the same social circles. I haven't seen much of her since I started boarding at school.' True.

A pause. 'Yet you must be close. You stayed with her family at first when your father died.'

'Well, yes. It was her mum and a housekeeper who asked me to stay, though. Sam wasn't there when I called.'

'But when your father died it was Sam that you called for help?'

'I didn't call to ask to stay there; I called to talk to her.'

A blank face stares back at me. 'Tell me what you know about JulietSays999,' he says, finally, and my mind is racing. Do I admit I know what it is? Really, everybody does – there'd be no point in lying.

'It's an account on social media. It posts stuff about the government.'

'And do you know who it is in real life?'

'I have no idea,' I lie.

'I see,' he says, and somehow manages to convey a world of doubt in two words. 'And when was the last time you spoke to Samantha Gregory?'

Do they know she came to my room? They might. Lots of people probably saw her come and go.

'Yesterday. She visited me in my room.'

'Why?'

'About me tutoring her some more,' I say, lying again.

He nods slowly, staring at me, and it's all over his face: he doesn't believe me. I'm scared, and then I'm angry that I'm scared of them and their questions. But maybe they are just fishing – trying to frighten us all into telling them something, anything?

'It's a very serious offence to lie to an investigator. Is there anything else you'd like to tell us now?'

'No,' I say.

'You may go. But if you hear from her, you must call us.' He hands me a card.

I take it and get up, head for the door, making myself walk normally when all I want to do is run.

'And Ava?' he says, and I turn my head, face him. 'If we find you've misled us in any way, you will be prosecuted.'

The other Lorder holds the door open now, and I step out. Into the waiting room, straight across and through the other door to the outside.

I breathe in deeply, greedy for fresh air. Gradually I start to feel calmer, more myself.

If they didn't believe what I said, they might be watching me.

And my flat.

I go straight back to my room and message Lucas, using wifi and a bounced IP address. I hope I'm right that it can't be traced.

Get out of my flat fast: it's not safe any more.

36

Sam

Finally the car stops.

The boot creaks open, and Mrs Jenson pulls away paint cloths and easels that were covering me.

'Are you all right?'

'I think so,' I say, and sit up, feeling shaky but glad to gulp in fresh air and daylight, even though the light is fading.

What time is it? Curfew is at six. I have to find somewhere to hide before six.

She helps me out.

'I've taken you beyond the central London checkpoints. Do you have somewhere to go?'

'Yes.' But what do I do now? Where am I? How can I get there? But I don't ask her these things; she looks scared, poised to run – to get as far from me and this trouble as she can, and who can blame her?

She wraps her arms around me in a quick, fierce hug.

'Thank you. For everything,' I say.

'Stay safe, Sam.'

She gets back into her car, pulls out of the lane in a hurry and is soon gone from sight.

I wait a moment, walk to the corner, and look around. There are shops, cafés. It's nearing the end of the working day and people are marching about on their way home or wherever it is they are going, and it's been so long since I've been anywhere on my own that just standing here is frightening.

But no one is looking at me. They're all focused on their own concerns and wherever they are rushing to, and as long as I don't do anything weird no one is going to give me a second glance.

What next?

If the authorities start hunting for me at places other than school, I need to change the way I look. This school uniform has got to go for a start.

I walk up the road until I spot a second-hand shop, and go in. It's not one of those vintage kind of shops Anji likes, either; it's cheap, basic stuff, maybe not even that clean. I almost walk out again but then make myself hunt through the racks.

I find some jeans that almost fit, a jumper, a hat to cover my hair. Mum would be horrified if she saw this outfit. *Mum*. She'd be horrified now no matter what I was wearing.

A last check in the mirror in the changing room: I try to look nonchalant, older than I am. If I were taller I'd have a better chance of pulling it off. I go through my schoolbag, find my purse. Best not use cards. I count my cash. After I buy these clothes I've only got about £90. I shove it in my pocket, put my ID into my purse: I'll find somewhere to dump it.

It's almost six p.m. If I still had my red ID around my

neck a glance would be all anyone would need to know I'm under sixteen and subject to an early curfew. My birthday is only weeks away, but even assuming I was sixteen already I should still be wearing a blue ID. There's no way I can pass for eighteen: anyone in authority who sees me is instantly going to be suspicious.

What now? Hide somewhere until morning? And then what? I have no idea how to get to Ava's flat. I have no idea how to do anything on my own.

Internet: that's what I need. I ask before I leave the second-hand shop; there's a café with wifi, the girl says – they have some tablets customers can use. She tells me where to find it.

I hurry, wanting to get off the street before six. When I find the café, it's reassuringly dimly lit. I get some coffee, borrow a tablet and head for a table, one in a back corner where I can watch the door.

I go to a map website, enter the address of Ava's flat, ask for directions from my current location, and ... oh. It's twelve miles.

Do I dare take the tube? I'm not sure I know how to do it on my own. How pathetic am I? I think back to the time Ava took me, to how she used the tickets, the gates. There was security, too; changing lines. Not looking at people.

I go on the Transport for London site to see if I can work it out. It looks like I'd have to go into central London and then out again; central London above ground means checkpoints, ID scans. Do they have them on the underground now, too? I don't know but don't dare risk it.

I could walk twelve miles — if I have to — but it's nearly six now. Even assuming no one challenges me after six, once it hits nine p.m. then it's a complete curfew and the streets will be empty. Can I walk twelve miles in three hours? I don't know, but I stare at the map until I think I know the way.

I feel sick inside. Somehow I have to get through tonight, get to Ava's flat, hope Lucas is at home or that I can remember the door code. Aristotle-something. Then we have to plan our next moves, flood the internet with DIDDSO and hope things change before I get arrested.

None of this seems likely. We're crazy, aren't we? I'll probably get arrested tonight and that'll be it, and no one will ever know what I was trying to do, or why. I'll just disappear.

Artists sign their work; to say, *here: this is me. I did this*. I want to sign this, too — to own it.

I log into all the networking sites as Juliet, link them together and go to my profile.

The names listed are all the same as the usernames at the moment: *JulietSays999*.

Do I really want to do this? Yes. Anyway, I don't think it could get me into any more trouble than I'm already in.

And this is me: it's mine. I made this — with a little help from Romeo. I change the profile name to Sam Gregory. I find a photo of myself I don't totally hate online, and put that up as my profile picture; then an image of Westminster and Big Ben for the banner on top.

This is it. Save, or cancel?

Save.

And now I write a new post:

I'm JulietSays999: I'm also Sam Gregory. Today Lorders came to my school to arrest me, but I got away. My crime? Social networking posts they don't like. This, in the UK? #NotMyUK #DIDDSO.

I log out quickly, wipe the history. I don't know if a DIDDSO post uploaded in a place like this will flag attention somewhere, so I'm getting out of here – now.

37

Ava

I go back to my room before dinner to check my messages: there's no reply from Lucas. I hope he and Nicky are OK.

I'm idly looking at DIDDSO posts when a new one drops in at the top.

From JulietSays999.

It's Sam? She must have got away! Then, at least right at this moment, she's OK, and the relief is so strong that it's a moment before the words of her post register.

She's telling everyone who she really is?

Tears well up in my eyes. That's a line in the sand, one that can never be washed away by the sea. She can't come back from this.

It only just went up. Is she still there?

Quick now, Ava. I create a new profile for myself. Hesitate, then make my username AristotleSays999, and hope she'll remember the door code and work out it must be me. I send her a friend request.

Then I wait.

And wait.

There is no response.

38

Sam

There's a clock I can hear striking in the distance – perhaps on a church – and I count, even though I know what it will be.

Six chimes.

It's six p.m.

I don't know what else to do so I keep walking, still heading towards Ava's flat.

It's cold and I pull my charity-shop jumper closer around myself, wishing I'd left my school uniform top on underneath or got something warmer.

The full curfew isn't until nine p.m. and there are still plenty of people walking about; some give me glances, probably wondering how old I am, why I haven't got an ID badge around my neck.

The streets get narrower. There's rubbish on the pavement, boarded-up shops. There's a broken manhole cover and I stop, pretend to do up my shoelace and let my purse with all my ID fall into the drain. There aren't many working street lights and the fear, the darkness, are starting to get to me. It's hard not to run. People stare at me more openly now. I keep walking.

There's some commotion up ahead, people are bunching up on the pavement. My instinct is to go back the other way and I push through people back the way I came, but then it starts to bunch up that way, too.

Police cars. There are two of them at the next junction. I go to the edge of the pavement, look up the road back the other way and they are there, too. They're at both ends of the road.

Are they looking for someone? Are they looking for me?

Don't be daft. How could they possibly know to look for me here?

They're checking ID, that's all it is: an ID check. But I haven't got any, and even if I hadn't thrown it away it was red and it's after six. They don't have to know who I am for me to be in trouble. I could get arrested for any of that.

Panic is rising inside me and I try to melt into the crowd away from the road, looking for a place to hide.

'Lass – over here.' A door is open in a building, boarded-up windows on both sides of it. 'Come on, I'll help you.' A man is looking at me, beckoning. He is thirty or so, narrow eyes, and there is something about him that makes me want to get away from him, to run.

Run where – to the police?

No choice.

'Hurry, before they see you,' he says.

I go through the door and he shuts it behind me.

It's too dark inside and panic rushes through me even more – there are some candles, no electric lights – and it smells, or he does. My eyes adjust; the place is derelict, rubbish on the floor.

'What's your name?' he says.

'Juliet,' I answer.

'Welcome to my palace.' He laughs.

There are vague rustling noises – rats? – and I'm thinking I'd rather chance it with the police. I move towards the door but he gets in the way.

Run.

I dash across the room into a hallway and it's dark but there is fresh air – there must be a door, a window? I run, he's coming behind me, I can hear him. There's a door, it's broken. I push and it gives. I'm outside. My foot catches on something and I trip, sprawl and land on the dirt outside.

Then he's there, grabbing my arm and yanking me to my feet.

There's a flash of movement. A thud.

He lets go of me, falls heavily to the ground. Behind him stands a girl with a plank of wood in her hands. She throws it to the ground.

A skinny girl, maybe my age. Another girl, younger, stands behind her. Then they're walking away, across an overgrown garden to a gap in the fence at the back. The man groans on the ground, then is still again, and I'm too scared to move, too scared not to.

'Wait,' I say. 'Please.'

'Why?' the older girl answers.

'I don't know where to go. Can you help me?'

She turns, faces me. 'Just did. But that was more for personal satisfaction.'

'Please.'

She sighs, checks me over. 'I like your bag.'

'Here. It's yours.' I hand her my schoolbag.

She takes it and starts going through it with interest – my school blazer, books. Then she looks back at me, assessing. 'First night out?'

'Yeah.'

'Not much to do until tomorrow but stay out of sight. Curfews, huh?' The younger girl nudges her, looking back at the still form on the ground. I can see blood on his head now.

'In case he wakes up we need to clear out of here,' the older girl says. 'Or I could hit him again?'

'No! Let's go.'

39

Ava

When the phone rings I'm asleep but shake it off in an instant to answer: 'Hello? Hello?' I'm praying that it's Sam, that she's all right.

It's Lucas.

'What's happened?' he says. 'I got your message, and we've left the flat. Have you seen the Juliet post? Sam has said who she really is!'

'Lorders came to school this morning to arrest her, but she got away: I don't know how or where she went, but somehow she did. The post went up some time after that; she must have figured they already knew, so why hide it?'

He swears softly. 'Do you know where she'd go?'

'No. I mean, she has loads of friends, but I can't see her going to any of them. She'd be scared to get them in trouble.'

'Family?'

'Same answer; besides, they might be on her dad's side, how would she know? And this afternoon, Lorders were questioning some of her friends at school – including me. I'm not sure they believed what I said about not knowing what she was doing or where she was, which is why I said to get out of there. If they didn't believe me they might check the flat.'

'You're right. We're with a friend now; we can't stay here, but we'll work something out tomorrow.'

We continue to talk uselessly in circles for a while, but there is nothing we can do to help Sam, not now. She's never been on her own, not anywhere. Lorders are one danger, but there are so many more, dangers she'd have no experience of at all. I'm scared for her into my core.

40

Sam

I follow them, stumbling in the half-light. I stick with Juliet as my name; the older girl is Megan – the younger one Rosie – but Megan tells me Rosie doesn't talk.

We're going to another empty building they know, slipping between shadows, down hidden ways. I keep bashing into things in the dark and soon I'm cut, bruised. Megan hisses at me to be quiet but I'm clumsy with cold and fear. I want to cry but somehow I'm past actual tears. I'm numb, exhausted, hungry and the most scared I've been since I was kidnapped when I was so little. And I could be home, warm and safe: what was I thinking? Why have I done this to myself?

Megan stops behind another derelict building. She pulls aside a piece of wood in a broken wall, making a space that they slip through easily. It's only just big enough for me to push my way through and my jumper is caught, my arm scratched, before I make it.

It's dark, cold, damp. There is the dim flickering of a candle in one corner, and as my eyes adjust I see others in the dark. There are boys, girls, all ages – about a dozen. Megan and I are probably the oldest.

She pushes into the midst of them, makes a space for her and Rosie, looks at me still standing there and sighs. 'Get some kip if you can.'

Something touches my leg and I jump, look down. A small boy with dark eyes is smiling up at me. 'Mummy?' he says, and I drop to my knees, then sit next to him. He puts his head on my arm.

'He calls everyone Mummy, daft brat,' Megan says.

No one says anything else. There are the sounds of breathing, someone snoring a little. My nose is assaulted by smells. A girl gets up and squats in the corner, then goes back to where she was. The little boy falls asleep against me, but I can't bring myself to close my eyes in this place. Every time there is a noise I jump, look back at the loose piece of wood where we came in.

That man – I shudder. What would have happened if Megan hadn't hit him on the head? I don't know.

What if he woke up, followed us here?

He'd never fit through the gap in the wall. Maybe that's why they come here – to hide away from people like that.

41

Ava

The next morning my head is in a fog. I make myself get up, try to get myself together: Dad's cremation ceremony is only a few hours away. I want Sam to be safe more than anything, but my own selfish longing is still for her to be there with me.

After I shower I check my phone again for any new posts from JulietSays999: there's nothing.

At first I don't notice the likes, the shares – across platforms. People everywhere are talking about Sam: the girl who had it all risking everything seems to have caught the public imagination. She's trending. New posts are going up and tagging her, too: #makenotmyUKchange; #Julietisourgirl; #Sambyanyothername – and all of it is linked with #DIDDSO. Expectation seems to tingle in the very air – that something is going to happen. But what?

A message comes from Lucas: he's found somewhere for him and Nicky to stay for a while, and he'll call me as soon as he can.

I go to breakfast; it's being whispered about there, too. The numbers of likes, shares and new posts tagged to

Sam and DIDDSO is *still* climbing.

She is achieving more than I could have ever imagined, but where is she?

Please be all right, Sam.

42

Sam

I'm in that dream, in the darkness, but now something has changed. Someone new is there. Lass, he calls me; he says he'll help me, but he doesn't want to help ...

'Wake up.' Someone is shaking me and I'm thinking I'm at home, I've overslept and it's Mum or Penny – or anybody, really, but who it actually is and where I am. I open my eyes.

'You were screaming,' Megan says.

'Sorry.'

She shrugs like it's a usual thing.

I ache, everywhere – I'm stiff, cold. I sit up and somehow manage to bang my head on the wall next to me and swear. Then say sorry again.

She laughs. 'We have no anti-swearing rules, trust me.'

It's light – sunshine pours through the broken wall and shows this place and those in it up for what they are more clearly: dirty, hungry children and teens clinging to each other to stay warm in a filthy wreck of an abandoned building. Yet, like Megan, they're laughing, too; squabbling with each other. Just being kids.

If they got caught on the street at night after six p.m. they'd be arrested as criminals, but they're just hungry kids with nowhere to go: maybe if they were arrested they'd be looked after better? But maybe not.

All I want now is to go home, a home I took for granted. I see more clearly now how lucky I was to have it.

But there is no going back. I know it. Even if at some point there was a chance that between them Coulson and Dad could have got me out of things, that time must have passed by now, especially since I've posted that I'm Juliet.

That's why I put that out there really, isn't it? So I can't change my mind and try to creep home.

'I don't know about the rest of you, but I'm hungry,' Megan says.

As if that was some sort of signal everyone is getting up now, squeezing out through the wall. It's easier this morning now that I can see what I'm doing and I manage it without any more scratches or splinters.

'What do you fancy for breakfast today?' she says. 'Full English?' There's a chorus of yeahs. I get the feeling this is a morning ritual.

'What do you do for food?' I say.

'We know places where they throw stuff,' Megan says. 'Some people who'll give us things. We take what we can.'

I put my hand into my jeans pocket, and extract most of the money that was there. Her eyes widen when I hold it out.

'Take everyone to have a full English somewhere. My treat.'

'Don't you need this? Aren't you coming?'

I shake my head. 'I've got somewhere to go.' And I have a feeling whatever happens once I get there, money won't help.

Megan shows me the way to a main road. I orient myself, and start walking. And as I walk, I think of Ava.

I'm so sorry I'm not there with you.

Today of all days, she shouldn't be alone.

43

Ava

I'm getting ready for something there is no way to get ready for, when my phone rings.

Unknown number?

My mind is racing: please, *please*, let it be Sam.

'Hello?'

'Hi, Ava? It's Penny.'

'Oh. Hi.'

'This must be a very difficult day for you, and … well, I'm really sorry, but I'm not going to be able to come to your dad's ceremony today. I'd really meant to.'

There is genuine concern in her voice, and despite everything else going on I'm touched.

'Thank you, Penny. I understand.'

'I've arranged a car to collect you from the school front gates at ten a.m.'

'I was going to get the bus; it isn't necessary.'

'It's already been done; don't argue. They'll wait and take you back afterwards. Is there anything else that I can do?'

'No, thank you. You've done so much to help already.'

'Oh, and Ava? We're all so desperately worried about

Sam. I know you must be, too. If you'd heard from her, you'd let me know, wouldn't you? And tell her to call home. Her mother is beside herself.'

We say goodbye soon after that. As I go back to the first thing I was going to wear – black skirt, a sky blue shirt that might not be on theme with the colour, but it's my nicest one – I wonder. Did she really call about my dad? Or maybe it was to find out if I know anything about Sam.

44

Sam

A full English isn't usually my thing but ever since Megan said it I can't get it out of my head. By the time I've walked for an hour or so – stopping to look at maps in bus shelters now and then so I don't get lost – my stomach is a gnawing empty thing it has never been before.

The café I choose to go into isn't impressive-looking, but it is busy – it's full of what look like students, college or university. I stand in the queue, get a heaped plate, pay and see how little money I have left. Megan and her friends needed it more than me.

It's long communal tables, everyone sitting and eating together – in a companionable silence. No one seems to notice me so I ignore them and eat.

I'm concentrating on this plate of food in a way I've never done before. Eating too fast, I force myself to slow down, afraid I'll make myself sick. The joy of toast, butter, fried eggs, bacon …

At first I don't notice the hush – it's more something I become aware of gradually, like the growing unease that comes with it.

I look up and the greasy food twists in my stomach.

Police – two of them. They're scanning the room as if they're looking for somebody, and they're between me and the door.

I slouch down a bit more. There's a tall boy opposite, he might block their view.

They stop here and there, checking ID badges – scanning them into a handheld gizmo. If I ignore them maybe they'll ignore me?

But they're coming closer.

One of them comes up behind me now; the other is still between me and the door.

'Where's your ID?' he says.

'I'm eighteen.'

'Sure you are.'

He pulls me by the shoulder and I twist and pull to get away; he uses both hands to grip me tight. I'm struggling, he's dragging me across the room towards the door. My hat falls off my head, my hair spills down.

'Look – it's Juliet!' somebody says. Other voices say *Juliet* and all eyes are orienting on us now.

'Let her go!' someone says.

'Yeah, let her go!' someone else says.

And now they're up out of their seats, pushing and shoving, and the police and I are caught in the middle of this mass of people. I'm being pulled in different directions, crushed too, feeling by turns scared and sick. The grip the policeman has on me doesn't waver as I'm dragged slowly out of the café door.

But outside the café even more people are rushing towards us – where did they all come from? We're getting crushed, I can hardly breathe. And then—

It happens.

My stomach twists, an involuntary shudder clamps and goes through my body. I throw up, violently – all over the policeman holding me. His grip loosens.

I'm swept away from him now in a crowd that is still growing.

Then there are sirens in the distance.

'Everybody – run!' a voice says, and people are scattering in all directions.

A girl grabs my hand.

'Come on, Juliet: *run*!'

Fear gives me energy and with a group of a half dozen students we race down a lane, then an alley, to the back door of a house. They start to rush through the door, but now I'm remembering the last time a stranger helped me get away from the police. I start to back away.

'Quick, before anyone sees us: get inside.' Two boys not much older than me are waiting for me and the girl who urged me on to go in first, eyes darting back the way we came in case the police are in pursuit.

They aren't like that man last night: they're a group of students, scared and risking everything to help me.

I go through the door.

45

Ava

The government car is there at ten, like Penny said it would be. And despite what I'd said to her I'm really grateful not to be on the bus, not to be worrying about connections and being on time.

I sink into the seats in the back, and we're soon on the way.

Staring out the window, I twist the hem of my shirt and think maybe I should have worn the black one, but who cares what anyone thinks about what I'm wearing? Assuming anyone even comes.

Of course the only person I wish were here by my side is Sam.

The rest of the morning is a blur. There are more people than I thought there would be, including some girls from school: Chitra, Amelie and some of their friends – the ones I let in through the side gate that day. There are a few old friends of Dad's that I almost recognise from when he used to teach at King's College, but many more are black cab drivers.

Dad had always said they were an interesting lot. He wasn't the only PhD driving for a living in these times, but he said it had always been that way – characters and misfits, philosophers and classicists, those who claimed they knew every street and lane of London and scoffed at anything computer-assisted. And I soon learn that only some of them knew Dad personally: the rest came today to send off one of their own.

Penny had found the civil celebrant – is that the right title? Dad was an atheist, and I guess I am as well, so that was the one thing I'd specified. He said a few words about Dad, his life. And how proud he was of me. But no mention of the wife he loved, who everyone thought had left him.

I stare at the coffin at the front when it moves on little tracks to go behind a curtain, and then off to the fires.

Goodbye, Daddy.

I'm dizzy, choking on pain and confusion too much to breathe.

Gone. He's really gone.

Then someone is helping me to my feet: a kind-faced cockney cabbie, one who'd been round with whisky once at Christmas.

He helps me to the door, to shake hands with people, to thank them for coming, until finally I can leave.

Outside I gulp in fresh air, wait as the car Penny arranged pulls up.

Before the ceremony began, once I was inside, every time the door opened I looked for Sam.

But now I realise I probably wasn't the only one. Off

to the side stands a man with a face I recognise. He was one of the Lorders at school who questioned Sam's friends.

He sees me looking at him and nods his head as I get into the car.

46

Sam

The students follow closely behind me through the door, shut it and turn the deadbolt. We stand there, panting. With the others who went in before us there are four boys, two girls and me.

One of the girls peers through the slats of a window blind. 'We just made it. They're coming around the corner now. I don't think they saw where we went.'

Then they're all talking at once, while I stand there, dazed at everything that has happened.

'What now?'

'Hide?'

'No! They'll do searches.'

'Quick: out through the front. It'll take them time to find the way around.'

'Not long!'

'So *hurry*.'

I'm being pulled down a hall – a girl runs ahead, goes up some stairs and then runs back down them a moment later with some things in her hands. I'm dizzy, probably both from lack of sleep and from what I've eaten coming up again. I go along, unable to process thought enough to think what is or isn't a good idea, but they're on my side – they got me away, didn't they?

'Take that off,' she says. My jumper? I look down; I'm covered in vomit.

Then she's pulling it over my head, and something blue is tugged down in its place before we run down the hall. There is a beanie in her hands and she helps me put it on, stuffing my hair underneath.

'Bring that,' she says of my jumper. 'We can dump it on the way.' One of the others stuffs it in a bag.

Now we've reached the end of a hallway, and go down some steps. The girl who has been calling the shots pauses with her hand on the doorknob.

'Act calm, don't all go at once. Slow down,' she says.

She opens the door; there's a busy road, with shops and cafés across from us, terraced houses this side with the same student look.

One of the boys links his arm firmly in mine as if he can tell I might fall over, and we cross the road.

There are sirens, they're getting close now, but we walk at the same even pace. We go through an open doorway to a shopping arcade, then speed up a little as we go past the shops. At the end is another door and we step out to a lane. It leads to markets. We make our way through crowded stalls, leaving the market on the other side.

And so we keep going, zigzagging from one street to another, down lanes and backways, leaving the sirens fading behind us. They know the area well; we never hit a dead end. I have no idea where we are or how much longer I can keep going, and I feel myself leaning more and more on the arm linked with mine. Then he pauses, puts it around my waist and holds me up even more.

There's a quiet discussion between the few ahead of us as to where we should head to next; some phone calls are made.

A park; we've reached a park. We're waiting for a call or something and I sink on to a bench. A few minutes later a phone rings, and then we get up, head to another exit.

A car is just pulling up. Doors are opened and we pile in.

47

Ava

Mrs Morgan is waiting at the doors of the boarding house when I get back to school.

'Are you all right, Ava?'

'No. I mean, yes.' I shake my head, desperate to say whatever I need to say to get away from her.

She says she'll make tea, that we can talk; I'm guessing this is in her job description, since she seems relieved when I say no, that I need some time alone.

At last I rush up the stairs, shut my bedroom door.

I'd so wanted Sam there; I'm so glad she didn't come. Did that Lorder really think she might?

I didn't dare look at my phone when anyone else was around, or in the government car – who knows if there were some hidden CCTV inside of it. At last I take it out, switch it back on, hurriedly check to see if there are any new posts from JulietSays999: but no.

I sigh, flop down on my bed. I start to check for anything new and interesting tagged to Sam or DIDDSO, and … there are pages and pages of posts. I sit up again, heart beating fast, scanning through them rapidly. Everyone is going completely crazy – she's been seen?

There are images with some of the posts – many are blurry – but it's Sam, I'm sure of it! She's OK – at least she was when these images and snippets of video were posted – it looks like it was happening around the same time as Dad's ceremony. She threw up? I'm hoping she's not ill even as I'm applauding how it made the policeman holding her lose his grip. She was swept away from them by the crowd.

From the posts it seems the police found her because of random ID checks; they didn't know who she was, just saw someone they thought was underage without an ID. Now they must know who slipped through their hands: how about those who helped her get away? Will they be able to identify them from these photos? And now I'm wondering if they were made blurry on purpose before posting, to try to hide who they are.

She was lucky only two police officers were there, without backup nearby; also that no Lorders were involved. They're always armed.

But where is she now?

48

Sam

Toast and butter: truly the most amazing combination in the history of food. I'm making myself focus on it and eat it slowly, licking butter off my fingers. It's delicious.

Though I may never eat a full English ever again. The thought makes me feel instantly queasy, and I push it out of my mind.

'More?' one of them asks – the one with the car, who brought us here, to his flat. Nasir; I think he said his name was Nasir.

'Ah, I want to say yes? But in case I get sick again should probably say no. Thank you.'

'No worries.'

Now that the toast is gone and my head is feeling clearer, I'm looking up at the four boys – including Nasir – and two girls: my rescuers.

They all seem to be staring at me, in a weird way: like I'm something amazing and not quite real.

'I don't understand what has happened: people were calling out my name – Juliet, that is – and got me away from the police. Which is obviously awesome, though I hope no one gets in trouble for it. But how did so many people recognise me and know who I am?'

'You're famous,' Daisha says – her name I remember, the one who organised everybody and got us out and away, fast. And I don't think she means your-dad-is-deputy-prime-minister sort of fame.

'What are you talking about?'

'You're everywhere: all over the internet. Hang on, I'll show you.' She gets a phone out of her bag, finds the post I did outing JulietSays999 as actually being me, Sam Gregory, and on the run. She points at the figures underneath and my jaw drops. I blink my eyes a few times, and look again.

Millions of people – actual *millions* – have liked and shared my post? That's way too many for me to get my head around what it even means.

'No way,' I say finally.

'Way. And that's not all.' She shows me some of the comments, the different tags linked to me, the cries for change – all tagging JulietSays999 and DIDDSO – and I can't take it in. Is this really happening?

There are photos and footage from just after my interrupted breakfast this morning, too – from different accounts and vantage points. Of the policeman dragging me through the café, then everyone reacting – surrounding us – the push-and-pull match that more or less ended when I chucked up all over him and he lost his grip.

Nice. I shudder, the images making me feel sick all over again.

'Thank you, all of you; for everything. I wouldn't have had a chance of getting away without you.'

'We're all glad we could help,' Nasir says.

'Can I send a message?'

'Of course,' Daisha says, and hands me her phone. I log in as Juliet, then send a private message to Lucas as Romeo: *I'm safe and with new friends. We need to talk. When/where?* Then I stop, think. Can I message Ava, too? Should I? I so want to see her, talk to her, tell her I'm OK. But even more I want to keep her away from all of this. Keep her safe.

Instead I add another message to Lucas: *Tell Ava I'm OK.*

'What is the plan now?' Nasir says.

I look around the room, and I can see it – feel it. They're all looking to me, up to me, for the answers – ones I don't have – along with any sort of plan. My gut is twisting.

'Sam?' Daisha says. 'You've really started something; brought so many people to their senses. Brought them together. It could be amazing.' Her eyes hold mine, and part of me wants to run away from all of them, and their expectations.

I'm just one girl. What can I do?

But maybe, just maybe, that is the point.

I swallow. 'I'm just one girl. But you're right. Look at all the crazy fuss I've managed to kick up: imagine what we can do together. Not just us – but everyone who has been sharing these posts and making ones of their own. There are too many of us for them to ignore.'

Daisha smiles. '*This* is our moment.'

'Yes. We may only have one chance before they shut us down. We need to do something, make an impact that can't be ignored or forgotten. But it isn't up to me, it's all of us: here, across London and everywhere in the UK.'

'What should we do?' Nasir says.

I'm thinking, and then remembering another night in London, when everything really started for me. The first time I dared stand on my own was also the first time I stood with so many others – holding hands for peace. For Kenzi, an innocent boy mistakenly shot by the authorities. I'll never forget how that felt – being connected to so many other people – before it went wrong.

A line of people like that was too vulnerable. We need to multiply that, again and again; hold it strong and firm. Co-ordinated action here in London and everywhere – across the UK.

I gather myself. Nod. About to tell them what I think we could – *should* – do, when something rings. Everyone jumps.

'It's the intercom,' Nasir says. 'Someone is at the door.'

'Are you expecting anybody?' Daisha says.

'No.' He gets up and glances down the side of the curtains to the street below. 'It's one person. Male, about our age probably. I don't recognise him.'

The intercom rings again.

'Wait and see if they go away?' he says.

A phone dings: it's Nasir's.

'I've got a message,' he says. 'From an account with username *LibertySays999*. He says will we please open the door?'

A hurried DIDDSO search shows that LibertySays999 was one of the first – and most prolific – to post with the DIDDSO tag.

'Let him in,' Daisha says. 'He's been part of this all along.'

'If it really is him,' I say.

'How else could he message from that account?' she says.

'But *why* is he here?' I say.

'Let him in and ask,' Daisha says.

In the end we all agree – but they insist I stay out of sight.

Nasir buzzes him in. I'm behind the kitchen door, listening. Moments later there is a knock, the sound of the front door opening.

'Hi. You're probably wondering why I'm here.' A voice I don't recognise.

'You could say that.' Nasir.

'We've been trying to track down Juliet. She was seen running away with your sister, Daisha – neither have been seen since. It was a guess that she'd come to you here.'

'Who is this *we?*' Daisha asks.

'The original DIDDSO group – me, Lucas, a few others.'

'Coming here was a good guess,' I say, curiosity having got the better of me, and I come out from behind the door.

There stands a boy, perhaps eighteen; he has dark, straight hair, wide-set eyes and pale skin. He's completely unforgettable-looking and I know I've never seen him before.

He grins. 'There you are! Juliet – Samantha – Sam. So happy to finally meet you. I've heard so much about you.'

'And you are?'

He laughs. 'Sorry. I'm Juro, a friend of Lucas's,' he

says. And I remember Lucas mentioning his name before, as someone he was making plans with. 'His sister Molly is my girlfriend.' A shadow of anger crosses his face when he says that – Molly, who was arrested along with her dad.

'Have you heard anything – is she all right?'

'No word. The best we can do for Molly and her parents is carry on, and put an end to this government. But first we need to get you out of here; if we could work out how to find you here it won't be long before the authorities do.'

Nasir and Daisha exchange alarmed glances.

'I'm so sorry,' I say to them.

'It's not your fault, but he's right,' Daisha says. 'We all need to leave.'

'I've got a van around the corner,' Juro says. 'Let's go.'

'Wait,' I say. 'How do we know you are who you say you are?'

'Lucas said you'd ask that.' He takes his phone out of his pocket, shows me the messages between the two of them. Lucas's last one is a photo of Lucas and Juro with Molly.

'OK then,' I say. 'Let's go.'

49

Ava

I can't breathe, can't sit still. Fear and hope are all mixed up inside me. Is Sam still free? Is she all right?

The likes and shares keep growing.

So many people seem to have so much love for her online, but they don't even know her, the real her: the funny, sparky girl. The sad one, too – such a talented artist, yet somehow afraid to strive to be great. Goosebumps go up my back when I remember why she said that was: that she couldn't see herself much beyond now.

When a message comes in from Lucas everything twists inside me.

I open it.

She's OK! I've had a message, she's on her way to me now.

And now, for the first time in a long, draining, sad and confusing day, I can cry.

50

Sam

Juro unlocks his front door, and there, inside, are Lucas and his little brother, Nicky.

Lucas grins. 'There you are, at last! You remember Nicky?'

'Of course. Hi, Nicky. And Lucas, this is Daisha.' Juro took the others to another friend's house, saying there wasn't enough space for everyone, but I'd asked Daisha to come with us. I've only known her a short time but there is something about her. I trust her judgement, and with the things we need to talk about that will be important tonight.

'Come on, Nicky,' Juro says. 'Let's give them a minute.' He, Nicky and Daisha leave the room: I guess when you're called Romeo and Juliet they think you need time alone.

Lucas comes closer, takes my hands in his. He studies my face as if trying to read in my eyes where I've been. He hugs me and I hug him back.

'I've been so worried about you,' he says. 'Ava told me what happened at your school. How'd you get away?'

'It's a long story, but I was heading for Ava's flat,' I say, leaving out the details to keep my promise to Mrs

Jenson: to keep her help a secret.

'Once you were on the run Ava thought we should leave the flat, so we came here. She was questioned by Lorders at school; they spoke to loads of your friends.'

My eyes widen. 'Oh no. Poor Ava. And other friends, too?' I shake my head. 'None of them knew anything, apart from Ava. I hate that my friends were targeted like that; I never thought that would happen.'

'It's not your fault. It's this government, these agents. Anyway, where have you been?'

'It hasn't been a great few days. But I'm OK.'

'All right, mystery girl, have it your way: keep your secrets. But I hear you threw up all over London's finest this morning. Actually, I've seen the images on social media: good one.'

'Yeah, well, clearly that was a strategy, you know?'

'Of course. Should I be nervous? If I get close to you?'

'Only if you feed me breakfast.'

He smiles. 'We've got to save the world first; let's keep that for another day,' he says and I get now he thought I was suggesting something – what might happen in the night *before* having breakfast together – and feel colour rising in my cheeks. Before I can think how to react he takes out his phone. 'There is something I want to show you.' He goes to his account – RomeoSays999. His real name and photo are there now.

'Lucas! Are you sure you should have done that?'

'It feels good to be who I really am. Anyway, I'm already wanted, so what could it matter? Now it must be about time to get this strategy meeting going.' He taps on the adjoining door.

The four of us sit down to talk together: Lucas, Juro, me, Daisha.

'It's time,' Lucas says. 'We've got to take the next step, stand up, united. Now, while there is so much focus on DIDDSO – thanks to Sam.'

'There'll never be a better moment,' Daisha agrees.

'But what should we do?' Juro says.

'I've got an idea,' I say.

'Tell us,' Lucas says.

'The demonstration for Kenzi was amazing in so many ways, everyone holding hands and standing together like that. But a single line of people was too easily torn apart by riot police, too easily disrupted by other elements. We need something that'll last longer and get as much attention as possible. How about a sit-in at government property, timed to be co-ordinated – at the same moment – all over the country?'

'Just because we're sitting down it won't be that hard to drag us away,' Daisha says. 'It'll just take longer if there are more people.'

'Not if we're all linked in a grid,' Juro says.

'How so?' Lucas says.

'Have rows of people with linked arms, but also link each row, in front and behind, using our feet?'

'Let's try it.'

We sit on the floor, in two rows of two – Lucas and me at the back, Juro and Daisha in front. Our feet around their middles.

'If we have multiple rows like this – as many people as we can get – it won't be easy to get us all apart,' Lucas says, helping me to my feet.

'It'd be even better if half face out and behind them another half against their backs face the other way – that way it is feet out all the way around,' Juro says.

'Can we get enough people?' I say.

'Going by all the online action, yes!' Daisha says.

Juro has found a notebook, pens. 'We need a list of key local people who can co-ordinate this in each city. Then a list of government sites that we can occupy, in order of priority. Then each core organiser in each city must use their contacts to gather and ready key participants.'

'Wow. OK, how long will it take to do all of this?' I say.

'Look, it's like studying for an exam,' Daisha says. 'If you have weeks, you take weeks. If the exam is tomorrow, you find a way to get ready for tomorrow.'

We exchange glances.

'Can we really do all this for tomorrow?' Lucas says. 'Isn't that a bit crazy?'

'Where's your sense of adventure?' Juro laughs. 'We have momentum, and the sooner we do this the less chance we'll get found out ahead of time and stopped.'

'How do we know who to trust?' I say. 'What if some of the DIDDSO posters are fakes – government agents pretending to be one of us to find out what we're doing?'

'How about no one is allowed in without an introduction from someone we know already,' Lucas answers, but I'm still nervous. If it is like A know B knows C knows D, by the time you get to Z, does anyone really know anyone any more?

'All it would take is one person making an error in

judgement recommending somebody for it to all go wrong,' I say.

'Trust me,' Lucas says. 'We'd spot a government agent a mile off – unless they've started recruiting teenagers.'

'You're right that we must be careful, but the problem is there are so many people that would exclude,' Daisha says. 'Me, for example, if I hadn't happened to go out for breakfast this morning in the same café as Sam. How about just a moment before it takes place it is posted up everywhere – so anybody who wants to take part – or just cheer us on – can come out?'

'Great idea,' Lucas says. 'We can schedule posts ahead of time.'

'Also, we need images and video to get out everywhere. Some of us should be in the crowd ready to film,' I say.

'Better yet: to livestream it – across platforms,' Lucas says.

'What time?' Daisha says.

'I think it should be at six p.m.,' I say. 'The time of the early curfew.'

'As far as where, top of the London list of places has got to be Westminster,' Juro says. 'All four of us should be there.'

'Last time I saw footage of Westminster there were rather a lot of armed guards about the place,' Daisha says.

'That's true,' I say. 'I've seen them.'

'But there are also huge crowds of people. They're not going to start shooting at a bunch of teenagers sitting on the ground with an audience like that; trust me,' Juro says.

I'm uneasy, remembering what Ava said – about my

dad. There is no other place I could be that would be more of a direct challenge to him. It's his personal territory. But how can we *not* include Westminster?

'So is everyone in favour of a countrywide co-ordinated sit-in to take place at six p.m. tomorrow?' Juro says.

I shake off my misgivings. Like Daisha said, this is our moment. Literally millions of people are behind us. We all grin, and then we're laughing, giddy and excited.

And then Juro gives us each a to-do list.

My job is to message a list they are drawing up of all their trusted contacts, tell them what we're doing and enlist their support: they think people will jump on it more readily if it comes from me.

But first I do a public post once again as @JulietSays999:

Thank you, everyone, for your love and support! I'm safe with friends now #UKstillrocksjustnotthegovernment #changemustcome #DIDDSO #seeyousoon … ?

It doesn't matter what has happened to me the last few days – what will happen to me next – if what we do changes everything. There is something like a drug rushing through my blood: it makes me light-headed, reckless. I can feel its warmth from my heart out to my arms, legs, to the tips of my fingers and toes: excitement. Pride at being part of this.

And *hope*.

51

Ava

I read Sam's Juliet post over and over again.

They're planning something. Aren't they?

What is it?

I'm terrified for her – excited – full of hope for what they might achieve. These feelings are all jumbled up in a knot inside me, and not knowing more is an agony: what are they going to do?

She hasn't accepted my AristotleSays999 request. Either she didn't see it, or she didn't realise it's me.

I sigh. I can't sit still, checking for messages that aren't there over and over again. I need to get out of here – get some air. Time for a walk.

Out through the school gates moments later, I walk fast, not going anywhere in particular. Remembering to pay enough attention that I don't get lost.

It's warm; clouds hang heavy and dark in an otherwise clear sky. It feels like it does in late summer before a thunderstorm but it is months too late for that.

There are footsteps behind me but I'm so lost in my thoughts I only really notice when they quicken, come closer.

At a corner I glance back and my breath catches tight. It's that Lorder – the one from both the deputy head's office and outside Dad's cremation ceremony. It's definitely him, although now he's dressed in jeans, a shirt – undercover, I guess. He's following me?

I wait for him to catch me up. He's youngish, early twenties perhaps. He was the one who didn't talk at the interviews, who stood back and listened.

'Hello, Ava,' he says.

'Are you following me?' I raise an eyebrow, and he grins.

'Yes. I was hanging back to start with, but frankly, I was getting tired. And I'm getting the impression you're not going anywhere because you keep doubling back.'

'It's called exercise.'

'I see.'

'Is there something you want?' I say, and even as I say it I wonder if I'm pushing him too far. Will I make him angry and land myself in trouble? But he's amused.

'Actually, I was wondering if you know what has happened to Samantha Gregory.'

'Only what I've seen online,' I say.

'I got the impression that you were friends – true friends. If you care about Sam, tell her to call if you hear from her. We can still get her out of this mess before it's too late.' He reaches into a pocket, gives me a card, then walks off.

The card gives his name as Agent Coulson. I frown. There is something familiar about that name. Was it the same agent Sam said saved her neck at Kenzi's demonstration, and then took her home to her dad?

Now that he's gone my reaction to what just happened is setting in, and I'm shaking. Will I always have to look over my shoulder, see if someone is following in my steps?

Or maybe now that he's fronted up with his card, he'll leave me alone.

I go back to my room.

52

Sam

I take a break from the endless messaging of 999 accounts while Lucas goes to check on Nicky. I scan through messages I've been sent, posts I've been tagged in.

There's a friend request from someone with the username AristotleSays999.

It has to be Ava. Doesn't it? I look at the profile: all it says is '383BC'. That was the other part of her door code: it must be her.

I accept the request, and two messages ping in from her account.

The first was sent yesterday: *I need to talk to you – are you OK?*

And the other was sent today: *Is something going on? I want to be involved.*

I *so* want to see Ava, to talk to her. It was her dad's cremation ceremony this morning; what with the police and the mob and all that I wasn't thinking about her as much as I should have been. But she wants to be involved? No; *no way*. I don't want her to be there.

I send a message back: *I'm so sorry I wasn't there this morning. I hope it went OK. But stay safe: keep away from this and me for now. I want to see you, too, but we can talk afterwards.*

Lucas comes back in. 'Juro thinks we should stay in different places tonight, go in separately tomorrow. Just in case, well, something happens to one of us.'

'That makes sense.'

'Nicky and I are going to stay with a family friend tonight; it's near where we need to go tomorrow, so he can stay with them there. We need to leave soon, before curfew. But first there is something I want to show you.' He holds out his hand. 'Come with me?'

We go up some narrow stairs that are more like a ladder at the end of the hall; there is a hatch at the top. He swings it open and it leads to a surprise roof terrace – there's a small garden of plants in pots, a bench with cushions, and a view across London that may be mostly blocked by blocks of flats but is still awesome.

There are dark clouds hanging low in a sky that is also strangely lit by patches of sunshine breaking through in places. For the first time in a while my hands itch for a paintbrush.

We sit down, and Lucas reaches into a bag that was over his arm. He takes out a bottle of champagne.

I laugh. 'Isn't it a bit soon to celebrate?'

He shrugs. 'Maybe. But I was remembering when we first met,' he says. He rips off the foil over the cork, then twists the wire key to loosen and then remove the cage.

'The charity dinner.'

'And the champagne.' He holds the bottle in one hand and twists the cork in the other until it flies through the air with a bang. I wince, remembering.

'And then there was the headache.'

'Only a taste, you'll be fine. Sorry, I don't have any glasses. Ladies first?' He hands me the bottle and I hold it up. The bubbles fizz up as I take a sip and I laugh again as it spills over the top; I push it away to stop it getting over my borrowed clothes.

He takes it back, has a longer drink than I did, then coughs. 'Smooth,' he says.

'Oh, yes.'

'Who would have thought that day that things would lead us to now, to this moment?'

I take the bottle back, have another drink from it and the bubbles tickle my nose. 'That's it for me. No more.'

He puts it down on the roof by the bench and leans in, and without any warning he's kissing me.

I'm kissing him back. I'm not even sure why, it isn't something I wanted to do: is it just to see what it would be like? Another thing to tick off a bucket list when time might be running out?

Part of me is here, kissing Lucas, fizzing with the champagne, the nerves and excitement and fear of what is about to happen – but the rest of me somehow knows that this moment, this kiss, isn't real. It is part of all these other things, rather than anything that is truly who I am.

Then there's a creaking noise and a face peers up through the hatch. It's Juro.

'Sorry to interrupt. Your lift is here, Lucas. Time to go.'

53

Ava

I read Sam's message over and over again, so happy she's answered, at last – but she doesn't want me involved. She doesn't even want to *talk* to me until whatever it is she's doing is over.

But I can't leave it alone. There are too many *what if*s. What if something goes wrong? What if something happens to Sam? What if I never get a chance to see her again? Not knowing what they're going to do is an agony, but if she doesn't want to tell me, how do I find out?

Lucas.

I message him before I go to bed. *Please call, doesn't matter if it's late*.

I'm sure I'll never sleep. I toss and turn, trying and failing. But then when my phone finally rings it wakes me, and I realise the sleeplessness was just an annoying dream.

I fumble for my phone in the dark, afraid I'll disconnect instead of answering.

'Yes, yes?'

'It's me. Lucas. Sorry, I only just saw your message now.'

'Is Sam there?'

'No, I was with her earlier; she's fine. We've been busily planning things for tomorrow.'

'Planning what?'

'Didn't Sam tell you? We're staging sit-ins. At government sites in cities across the UK.'

'Tomorrow? That's fast.'

'Yes. We decided the sooner the better: while DIDDSO is trending, and Juliet – Sam – is, too. We need to make an impact while attention is on us. Before they track us down and put an end to it all.'

'That makes sense.'

'Do you want to come?' Lucas says.

This is the moment. The one where I tell him no, that I'm not a revolutionary – it's not who I am.

But all I see is Sam. All I hear is her voice. All I want is to be near her, but where is she now? Where will she be tomorrow?

'*Yes.*' I hear my voice say the word – the one that draws my own line in the sand, and could change my world for ever.

54

Sam

I have a borrowed ID: a girl with my approximate height and hair colour, and just a little older so the ID is blue. Emily is her name. She seemed relieved that giving me her ID was the extent of what she could now do today, since she can't get through roadblocks without it.

We're travelling in small groups, twos and threes; I'm with Daisha and Juro. We'll all meet up again close to Westminster.

I'm nervous. How closely will they look at the photo on the ID? After everything that has happened to lead me to this moment, this day, if I get stopped by a checkpoint and can't get there – well. It would all have been for nothing.

Juro carefully picked which checkpoints we should go through to get to the centre even though it meant a longer trip around – so we go through ones that are manned by police, not Lorders. They are slowly taking them all over but there aren't enough Lorders to go around.

Yet.

They have to be stopped before their grip can get any tighter.

We're in the queue at the first checkpoint. 'Stop looking scared,' Juro says, his voice low. 'Try to act natural.'

Easy to say. But the queue is moving quickly; they can't be studying faces too closely, can they? And I make myself breathe normally, pretend I'm somebody else: somebody named Emily who isn't wanted by the authorities.

Juro goes first. A policewoman scans his ID, waves him on. Then Daisha: she's through, too.

I hand the woman my ID but somehow before she grasps it I have let go, and it falls to the ground. She clucks with annoyance.

'Sorry, sorry,' I say, bend to grab it and hand it to her, feeling colour rising in my cheeks.

She scans it and hands it back to me. I walk through.

55

Ava

I pause in my doorway. It's time: to leave this room, and then school. To enter the code to go through the gate, walk – get the bus. The tube. All allowing extra time to double back and forth and make sure I'm not followed before I head for the place Lucas told me. We're all meeting there by five p.m. at the latest.

And from there, we go on to Westminster.

I don't know what will happen; I don't know for sure that I'll be back here afterwards. The chain to my mother's locket is around my neck – a talisman. I kept putting it on and taking it off, not wanting to risk anything happening to it, then decided I had to have this small reminder of her with me. But when I went to put it on for a last time I saw that all that taking it on and off had tangled the chain. I sat there for ages trying to tease a small knot in it free but couldn't get it, and couldn't shake off the feeling that it was an omen of what was to come.

I keep hearing my father's voice. He was always the cautious one – work hard, stay out of trouble. He'd be the one to say, *Don't go, Ava. Don't take the risk. Be safe.*

His words are still buzzing in my ears like an annoying mosquito as I walk across school and punch in the gate code.

The lock mechanism clicks open. I take a deep breath and step out through the gate.

Will Sam be there when I arrive?

I hope so.

I'm doing this for her.

That's simplistic; things are never as clear as that, are they? There are so many reasons to be there, but she is the most important one of all. I can't miss what might be my only chance ever to see her again.

Maybe I'll even tell her the truth.

56

Sam

The rest of the journey – checkpoints, tube, changes underground – all goes without a problem. We climb the stairs from the underground to air and daylight above, then it's a short walk to the meeting point: a house where one of the other triple-9s lives.

We're soon there, ring the bell and are let in. It's busy. People are arriving to check in, find out where they're to go next. Some are leaving already as we enter.

And there, at the back of the room? It's Ava.

There is a rush of joy when I see her; I've missed her so much. But it is mixed with dismay at the same time: how did she know to come here?

She sees me then, raises a hand – starts to make her way across the room and I run to her – our arms go around each other, a tight, fierce hug. I take her hand, pull her to a corner away from the others.

'How did you know, Ava?'

'I messaged Lucas,' she says, and I realise, too late, that I should have asked him not to tell her.

'Why are you here?'

'Why are you?'

'I'm caught up in this now; you aren't. You don't have to be here.'

She hesitates. 'Somebody named Coulson asked me to tell you that you can still get out of this if you call him.'

I'm shocked. 'Coulson? He spoke to you?' I shake my head. I might have been tempted a day ago, but not now. 'I could never back out of this, Ava. But you can.'

She doesn't respond. There is something she's not saying, something her eyes still hold back.

When I tried to draw Ava before, I always felt there was something I couldn't quite grasp that I needed to know to really capture her, to know who she is. Something she kept close.

There is this sense of time running out: that everything that needs to be said, to be experienced, to be known, has to happen right *now*.

And more than anything, in this moment, I want to know Ava – know her completely.

'There's something you're not telling me, isn't there? Whatever it is, Ava, you can trust me. Tell me. Please.' She looks down, doesn't say anything; for a heartbeat, two, three …

Her eyes meet mine. 'When the Lorders came looking for you at school I thought I'd never see you again. Then when I realised you'd got away – I … well, I had to come. I couldn't risk not seeing you again.'

I smile again, so glad to see her, too, even though I still wish she wasn't here. I want her to be safe. There are all these feelings mixed up together inside me and her eyes are on mine – and now they're open, full of emotion

– and I *feel*, everywhere; at once. Like my skin is on fire, each breath is electric, and her eyes: now they are saying what, somehow, I always knew.

'Sam, Ava!' I jump, turn. It's Lucas. He walks over, bends and kisses my cheek, then goes to speak to Juro.

I'm shaking my head slightly but Ava doesn't see; her eyes are cast down again.

'That's not – I mean, he's not…' She looks up again. 'I don't like him like that,' I say, finally understanding why things never felt right with Lucas, or with any other boy before him. 'Not like I like you.' I say the words quietly. And her eyes shine at mine.

'That's why I want you to go,' I say. 'I *need* you to go. Please?'

Then there is a commotion behind us; a child's voice. It's Nicky.

'I told you to stay with Auntie,' Lucas says, upset in his voice.

'I ran away. I want to go!'

'You *can't*. I said I'd keep you safe – I promised. You're too little.'

'I am not! I'm coming with you.'

'No, Nicky.'

'There isn't enough time to take him back,' Juro says. 'He'll have to come with us.'

Even though I can hear these things happening around us, they seem remote – as if I'm alone with Ava. We're in our own space, apart. We hear the other voices but focus only on each other.

My eyes are still pleading with Ava. 'Please go,' I say again.

'Will anyone volunteer to take Nicky back to our friends?' Lucas says.

'There's no backing out for me, but no one knows you're involved,' I say, my eyes on hers still. 'Go. Please, Ava. Do it for me.'

'I'll do it,' she says, but this she says louder, not to me – to the room. She turns to Lucas. 'I'll take Nicky.'

Lucas calls his friends, tells Ava where to take Nicky to meet them. There are more people arriving, talking about what we're about to do, how to do it. More groups leave to spread out around the area – I'm to be in the last group to go, with Lucas and Juro – and I hear the plans, but through it all there is only Ava.

'Thank you for doing this,' I say.

Ava's hand is touching something at her throat – she's wearing a necklace?

'I don't think I've seen you wear jewellery before.'

'It's a locket – it was my mother's.' She pulls it out from under her top, and holds it in her hand.

'Does it have photos in it?'

'It did. There was one of me, and a lock of my baby hair. She must have taken those when she left.'

I reach to touch it in her hand: an oval of silver, delicately carved, hung on a box chain. The chain is tangled a few inches above the locket on one side.

'There's a knot in it.'

'I can't get it out. I've tried.'

'Let me. I'm good at these things.'

She hesitates, slips it over her head and hands it to me.

57

Ava

Somehow I find myself walking away, a small hand in mine.

Nicky is protesting; he seems to think he's missing out on some game. Maybe I was playing one, too; I don't know. I couldn't not go today – I had to see Sam, to speak to her. But once I did she seemed to know, somehow, that I needed an out.

The locket is back around my neck, under my shirt, against my skin. She did undo the knot; it hangs free on the chain.

It's her way, isn't it? Somehow Sam makes me feel all problems – mine, and the world's – can be solved.

That the impossible can come true.

Part 4: Consequences

There are few true moments when taking an action – or not taking it – may change history. And even fewer when the same choice will change all that you are; where no matter what you do or don't do, it is wrong.
This is one of those moments.

Deputy Prime Minister Gregory,
personal communication with Prime Minister Armstrong

In the carefully orchestrated dance, freedom of movement is an illusion.

MP Astrid Connor,
private diary

Part 4: Consequences

1

Sam

We're milling about, part of a vast crowd – no pattern to our movement.

Not yet.

Even though Lorders and their guns guard Westminster, the tourists are still out in force with their cameras. Maybe there are even more of them now than there have been in a while: perhaps with all the checkpoints and curfews they feel safer? And some of us mix in with the tourists, cameras and phones ready to livestream whatever happens.

Gradually we move in closer, tighter; careful eyes on the time. Ready to form Juro's grid, with inner rows facing Westminster, outer rows facing out. He uses subtle signals to guide groups into place. Lucas and I stay close to Juro and Daisha – we're to be in the centre, together.

The eerie sky: mixed light and darkness.

A low murmur of voices against the louder ones that surround us.

Big Ben begins to strike – it's six.

Now we move fast.

My right arm is linked with Lucas, my left with Daisha; Juro is in the row behind ours and facing the other way, towards Westminster, his back against mine. There are rows and rows of us forwards and backwards and when we sit, all at once, we link our feet, too, around the person in front of us, locking us together.

There is an almost lull, of shock and silence.

And then there is noise.

People who have nothing to do with us are running away, mostly – scared of what might happen next. But not all. Some stay, and are cheering; ragged cheers that become stronger as more voices join in and the crowd begins to swell beyond us.

We are our country; *we* matter. We are all linked together and stronger than they know.

There are sirens. Shouting.

We're drenched with bursts of cold water – water cannons. On our own we'd be knocked over, swept away; together we are coughing and spluttering but still holding on to each other.

Riot police are moving in. We know what they are, what they can do – I've seen it first-hand before, and I taste my own fear, acid in the back of my throat.

But if everyone, everywhere, is watching this: it is worth it. It means something. Everyone will know: all we did was sit in around Westminster. This is our country, it should be *our* government, but it isn't, and that's wrong. Surely if this is witnessed it'll all change? When everyone sees what is happening here, now?

That is why we have to hold on.

A voice – amplified – calls for calm, for reason.

I recognise who it is, can just see her now at the edge of the crowd in front of us: she's an MP, she's been to our house once for a dinner.

Then Juro's warm back pulls away from behind me.

What's happening? I twist, turn to look.

What I see, it can't be, it can't …

His whole row are turning, crouching; jackets pulled off as one – red slogans on their T-shirts:

A4A.

And … and … in their hands –

Guns?

Blasts thunder in my ears. They're firing over us into the police, the screaming crowd beyond. The MP who was speaking: she's been hit, she falls.

Police officers are shouting, returning fire; we flatten ourselves to the ground, trying to pull away but we're all caught together, tangled. There is nowhere to go. And Juro and his row – he designed it like this, didn't he? – they're protected in the middle of all of us.

Riot police led by Lorders in Kevlar with shields make a charge into our edges, trampling or grabbing those they can reach and peeling them away like an outer layer of skin.

Fear: I can taste it, smell it, hear its cries all around me now – more layers are peeled away, each more painful than the last.

Screaming – gunshots – truncheons.

Blood.

Lucas's arm is yanked from mine. He's dragged away, struggling; there's a blow, more blood.

An arm pulls around my neck, yanks me away from

Daisha. Screaming: I'm screaming, struggling.
My head explodes –
jagged lights –
pain –
Darkness.

2

Ava

I'm on the tube at six, heading back to school after dropping Nicky to Lucas's friend's family. I take out my phone – a mix of fear, hope and excitement rushing inside me – but the underground wifi isn't working. I frown, impatient, desperate to know what is happening.

I fly up the stairs at my stop, phone already in my hand.

But when I emerge on to the street there's no signal.

That's odd; I'm sure I've used it around here before.

I wait at my bus stop, checking my phone again and again; nothing. Has this old phone finally given up?

My bus pulls in; I get on, find a seat. Look around at the other passengers. Puzzled and annoyed faces are peering at phones – tablets, too. It's not just mine; nothing is working.

There's a twist in my guts. What's happening?

My stop. I get off in a hurry, and almost run back to school. My hand is shaking as I punch in the gate code.

I'm running past the library when I see that the lights are still on, and bang at the locked door.

The librarian opens it. 'Is something wrong? We're closed, Ava.'

'I know, but please, just for a moment: can I use a computer?'

She shakes her head. 'The whole school system is down.'

'Down, how?'

'We're not sure. There's no internet signal. Nothing is working.'

Nothing?

I run back to the boarding house, and burst into the common room.

'Does anyone have a signal?' I say, and heads shake no. I'm gasping for air, not just from running but from panic. 'When? When did everything stop working?'

'It was at six, exactly,' someone says. 'I know because the news was just coming on.'

'Ava? What's wrong?' It's Amelie.

I can only shake my head, say nothing. I close my eyes. Hands guide me to a chair, push me to sit down.

Everything is spinning inside.

It seemed too easy, didn't it? Everyone getting there. Sam and some of the others who were wanted using borrowed ID and not being challenged. Everything went right, and I thought it was Sam's magic: the way everything always goes right for her.

But something has gone wrong, so wrong. This can't just be some random tech failure. Somehow, the Lorders must have known something was up; they must have. And they let it happen, but they made it so nothing could get out. No phone signals, no internet — so no DIDDSO posts, images, livestreaming. Nothing.

Nobody knows what happened.

What happened?

3

Sam

Fractured images, sounds. Pain.

Movement, and now the agony is even greater.

It fades to black.

I promise! I'll always be good.

He's shaking his head sadly. Walking away.

Daddy! I'm screaming, but I'm alone.

A sharp drawing in of breath. It was just a dream. Wasn't it? I stir, and pain explodes in my head. I force my eyes open.

Where am I?

Dim light. I'm in a bed; there are metal bars above, curtains hanging down from them. Like around a hospital bed. Am I in a hospital?

I try to sit up and can't – something holds me down. I turn my head a little, gasping with pain.

Handcuffs. I'm handcuffed to a trolley bed.

Distant sounds, a door. Voices. I'm struggling, pulling to be free.

'Ah, you're awake now, I see.' A hand holds my eyelid

open and a bright light shines briefly into my eye several times; then the same is done to my other eye. I'm blinking, tearing up.

'Where am I?' My voice is croaky, my throat sore: it wasn't just in my dream that I was screaming, was it?

'New London Prison infirmary.'

4

Ava

That night I watch the news every hour.

They say technical faults caused widespread issues with the internet and phone signals. Yeah, right. A serious-faced reporter says that a violent protest at Westminster led to the murder of an MP, half a dozen police officers and more innocent bystanders; numerous others were injured. There is a brief mention of linked violent protests in other cities. Promises from a government spokesperson that all perpetrators will be dealt with to the full extent of the law.

The *law*? How can they even say that with a straight face?

How can a sit-in be called a violent protest?

If there was violence, I'm sure Sam, Lucas and DIDDSO didn't start it.

What happened?

It's on the ten p.m. news bulletin.

'This just in.' The newsreader's face is flushed, like she can't believe what is in her hands.

'Two of the ringleaders of the co-ordinated violent

protests that took place earlier today across the UK have been identified. Codenamed Romeo and Juliet, they are Lucas Economos, son of disgraced journalist Giana Economos, and Samantha Louise Gregory, daughter of Deputy Prime Minister Merton Gregory.'

Their images fill the screen. Hungry for Sam, I stare. They've chosen a rare shot where she hasn't got her politician's daughter's face on. She looks annoyed, a bit sulky. Lucas just looks angry.

'They were well known online and stirred up a large contingent of young teens to commit extreme acts of violence against authority. And now we go live to Downing Street.'

The view changes: they pan out to Downing Street, then focus on the door. Armstrong emerges, with Gregory following behind him. They walk up to a prepared podium.

'Violent dissent cannot be tolerated in a free and fair society, no matter who is involved,' Armstrong says. 'It will not be tolerated.'

Gregory is pale. I can imagine an echo of shock, of distress, but all my eyes really see are ice-cold fury and determination.

5

Sam

Coulson is my first visitor.

He shakes his head. 'I tried so hard to help you, and look what you've done. You've made me a failure. I don't fail.'

I say nothing.

'There may still be a way I can help you.'

I look away.

'We can prove that the JulietSays999 accounts weren't set up by you. We'll say you were forced to go along with the rest, that you were there under duress. You'll have to back us up, renounce the violence that was committed in your name.'

'The only violence that was committed was by the police, and A4A. And they weren't part of us. Their aims weren't ours.'

He nods, doesn't argue. 'I believe that is true, but you were part of a group that committed violent acts in a joint enterprise; you were one of those who led the group. Whether you controlled their actions or not you are culpable in law. You say you don't support A4A, so why not say so publicly?'

'But you want me to renounce all of it – not just A4A. I can't do that.'

He sighs. 'You let them play you, don't you know that? Lucas Economos might not have known that Juro Adachi – and Lucas's own sister, Molly, too – were in A4A, but he was their puppet. It was their idea to target you, to get you involved from the beginning. They needed a face people would follow; one that would shock people, make them pay attention. Your face.'

'I don't believe you,' I say, but he's making me think, and question things I hadn't before. It all seemed to happen naturally at the time, but did it? Lucas sought me out at the charity dinner where I first met him. And I remember Ava saying something like it was weird that Lucas made the long trek to a party at Charlize's that night when his friend, Kenzi, had just been shot. And he confided in me straight away. He barely knew me, but I was the one he called when Kenzi died; when his mother was taken, too.

Lucas told me the things most likely to make me want to help him.

I hide the shock that I feel to think about later.

'That's not all. Juro has told us – he bragged about it, really – that you were specifically targeted to destroy your father. That everything they did at Westminster with you there was aimed squarely at him: to put him in an impossible position, and to undermine the government.'

Now I'm horrified. For the first time in my life I stood up for what I believed in – I made my own decisions – even though it meant going against Dad. But was I actually being manipulated into place all along because of who he is?

How could Lucas do this to me?

I shake my head. No. Even if Lucas sought me out to be some sort of figurehead for the cause, this was still *my* cause: one I believed – *believe* – in. And Lucas didn't know about Juro and Molly's involvement in A4A. He couldn't have. I'll never believe that.

'Even if that is true, it doesn't change anything. I did what was right.'

He shakes his head. 'I don't understand you.'

'I know. I've got integrity.'

He shakes his head again, dismissively this time, like that is a trait not worth having. 'You all thought you were so clever. We knew something was being planned. We didn't stop it – we let it go ahead. Do you really think so many suspected dissidents could go to places like Westminster and not be noticed? That you could use fake IDs at checkpoints? You only got through because we let you.'

Now I'm shocked again, and this time I can't hide it. 'You knew, and you let it go ahead? What about the people who died?'

He hesitates, like he's deciding what to say, then shrugs. 'We weren't any more aware that A4A had infiltrated your group than you were, or we would have treated the situation differently. We let your sit-ins go ahead so we could get all the dissidents in one place, to identify and deal with all of you at once. And we also blocked everything, stopped it from getting out.'

'Blocked everything? What do you mean?'

'The internet – phone signals – all of it. Nothing got out. Not a single image.' He stands to go. 'If you change your mind and want to talk, tell the guard. But don't leave it too long.'

I'm reeling from too many shocks, the last one most of all. Coulson walks across the cell; now he's at the door. I have just enough grip on myself to remember there is still one more thing I need to know – even though I'm afraid of the answer.

'Wait.'

He turns.

'What happened to Charlize? She wasn't involved in any of this. She just tried to help me by taking my phone.'

'I know.'

'Please tell me.'

'She still lied about the phone she had. But she has since been released for time served.'

The door clangs shut behind him.

At least that is one thing off my conscience: Charlize is OK. I sit on the floor, draw my knees in close and wrap my arms around me.

Is the rest of what he said true? About Lucas targeting me? About Juro and Molly getting him to do so because of my father?

I was sure we were doing what was right, what was important. I'd felt free, but was I fated to take these steps all along?

And Coulson said they blocked all the phone networks, the internet.

I'd been holding on inside to hope: that everyone in the UK and around the world knew exactly what happened – that peaceful protestors were attacked with violence. Even though there was an element of A4A that messed it all up, if they'd seen the actual footage of the day surely they'd have been able to tell that we were as shocked by that as anyone? And maybe, just maybe, if they could see that, people would stand up, stop this, overthrow the government and reinstate democracy.

And free us, too.

And nobody knows what really happened?

Coulson said we're all responsible for what A4A did because we were there together. Can it really be true that the crimes they committed fall on all of us?

They *killed* people. Does that mean all of us will be tried for murder?

I'm rocking myself, trying to shut it out. This small cell – these cold walls – are pressing in on me in a way they didn't before. Is this all there is for me now, for ever? I want to scream *let me out* – but not Coulson's way – never that.

Nobody knows?

Nobody knows.

6

Ava

The trial begins days later. Whatever happened to legal teams and months of preparation?

It's not televised; only the sentencing will be. So all we can do is wait.

School is there is to distract me, but even that usual certainty feels wrong. The anticipation and energy that were in the air before – the sense of anything being possible – are gone. And we carry on, because what else is there to do?

So students walk quietly to and from their classes, barely raising their eyes. They sit there, dutifully taking notes or moving test tubes around the chemistry lab.

There is a sense that the students, the school, the entire city, are all holding their breath: waiting with me. Waiting to see what will happen.

7

Sam

'Samantha Louise Gregory, Lucas Daniel Economos, Daisha Salah Khan and Juro Adachi, please rise.'

The heavy chains around our ankles clunk and clang as we stand. My head spins, the pain still there from being hit. We all have injuries from that day.

The four of us were charged and tried together. Like Coulson said, it was considered to be a joint enterprise, so everything that happened was our fault together – though little of what was said in court bore relation to anything that actually happened, and we weren't allowed to speak. Not even to each other, though I've felt Lucas's eyes, seen the anguish: almost heard the words *I'm sorry* in how he looks at me, the same way I look at Daisha. She was only there because of me. Juro often seeks me out with looks that are derisory, triumphant.

'You have been found guilty of the following crimes.'

The list is long.

Seven counts of murder. Many more of attempted murder and grievous bodily harm. Incitement to murder. Aggravated criminal damage. Violent disorder. Riot. Incitement to riot.

There's a pause when he gets to the end of the list.

'You are all sentenced to be hanged by the neck until dead.'

'*No*. You can't do this!' It's Lucas. Even with chains he manages to twist, turn, to face the cameras: to implore those watching to honour DIDDSO: *do something*.

He's dragged away to the sound of Daisha's stifled sobs, and Juro's laughter – is it mocking, or tinged with hysteria? Perhaps both. In some twisted corner of his brain, Juro seems to think he has won. But he'll die, too. Maybe that's what he wanted.

I'm numb.

8

Ava

I ask to see Sam at New London Prison where they are being held. They're not allowed visitors.

I call her father again and again, both at home and at Westminster, and no one will put me through. No one will even speak to me.

Finally, I go there: to their home. I ring the bell at the gates I was welcomed through as Sam's tutor, and then as her friend.

'Yes?'

'It's Ava Nicholls. I want to speak to Merton Gregory.'

There's a pause.

'He's not here. Do you have an appointment?'

'Can I make one?'

Another pause.

'Wait a moment.' And there is hope inside, that he is really here; that somehow he will see me now.

But then an outer gate opens, and out steps Penny.

'Ava. Hi. Why are you here?'

'I have to see Sam. I *have to*; please help me. I can't get through to her parents, or into the prison—'

'Leave it, Ava. Go. Don't call or try to come here

again.' There is real sympathy in her eyes. 'For your own sake, Ava. Sam wouldn't want you to get in trouble, would she? Now go.'

'But—'

'Go.'

She steps back through the gate, and I half stumble, half walk away.

9

Sam

'You have a visitor.'

'What?' I'm startled. We'd been told we weren't allowed any since the day of the sentencing. Of course the only one I had before that was Coulson. 'Who is it?'

'Deputy Prime Minister Gregory.'

'You mean my father.'

He doesn't say anything to that; he's waiting for me to stand and follow him through the door he's unlocked. I'm tempted to say no. What is there to say to my dad, after all?

But what point is there in keeping arguments going now?

I follow the guard down the hall.

He opens a door. Dad is inside a small room. The guard doesn't come with me when I go in, and I'm surprised. Aren't I supposed to be a dangerous, violent criminal?

'Samantha,' Dad says.

'Dad.'

We look at each other.

He shakes his head. 'How could you?'

It's on the tip of my tongue to counter with a few *how*

*could you*s of my own, but I shake my head. 'I'm not sure there's any point in having that conversation now.'

'I suppose not.' He sighs. 'My own daughter. Undermining everything we hoped to achieve.'

'Yep, that's me. The underminer minor. You've got to watch out for us; we're dangerous.' I almost giggle, feeling weirdly giddy.

He shakes his head. 'I don't know why I came.'

'Neither do I.' And I stare at him and I want him to, I don't know, *cry*, maybe. Say he had no choice, Armstrong made this happen, there was nothing he could do.

Just like he probably wants me to beg for his forgiveness. And neither is going to happen, is it?

'There's something I need to tell you,' he says. 'It's, well – I mean – I don't ...' His voice trails away. Whatever it is, he doesn't know how to say it, and that isn't a problem he normally ever has.

'What is it, Dad?'

He swallows. 'Armstrong offered to pardon you. It was Sandy, his daughter, apparently. She convinced him.'

My eyes open wider, shocked. 'A pardon? But how? And what about the others?'

'I said no.'

I stare back at him, finally say, 'No? You said ... no?'

'We can't do it, Samantha. No one would respect our authority if we did; everything we've achieved so far would be undermined.'

This is what Juro wanted, isn't it? To put my dad in an impossible position. He probably expected that Dad would save me, that the government would collapse or something as a result. But he didn't know my father.

Neither did I.

I stare back at the man who has always kept me safe. It was his job, wasn't it? Not just when he was a policeman, rescuing me from kidnappers. It's what parents *do*: what they are supposed to do, at least. Some don't, true, but I'd have bet my life on my dad being the one guy in the world who would always be there to rescue me if he could.

He is the one who looked in my eyes and said *no one will ever hurt you when I'm around*. But they are going to do more than just hurt me, and he could have stopped it.

He carries on telling me *why* – why he hasn't saved me; pleading with me to listen. Now he is the one who wants forgiveness, I guess.

But even though what he is saying is all about the bigger picture, the consequences he fears if he saves me, I don't think that's really it. I'm not just his daughter any more; I'm one of *them*. Even as it is tearing him apart inside, something has changed and he sees me being what he hates the most, in every fibre of his ex-policeman core:

A criminal.

He could never save a criminal, could he? Not even his own daughter.

I turn my back and start to walk to the door.

'Samantha, please. Don't leave like this. Isn't there anything I can say to make you understand?'

I pause, turn, face him. 'It's not a question of not understanding; it's more not believing in the one person I always believed in any more.'

His face is stricken. 'I had no choice.'

'Does it make you feel better to think that? Then do so.' I almost feel sorry for him.

'Is there anything I can do?'

I bite back the mix of emotions I can't even name: anger? Hurt? Betrayal? Maybe all three. I hesitate.

'There is something, isn't there? What is it, Samantha?'

'I want to talk to Lucas.'

'No! No way. He's the one who put you in here.'

I sigh. 'It might surprise you to learn that I make my own decisions.'

I turn back to the door, knock.

The guard opens it. 'We're done,' I say.

The guard looks at my dad.

'Take her!'

His voice: it sounds wrong. Is he actually crying now?

I thought I wanted him to, but it doesn't make me feel any better.

10

Ava

I don't know why I'm doing this now. Maybe it's because I'll wrap my arms around myself and scream if I think any more about Sam, and what is getting closer as every minute ticks slowly by. Or maybe it is because her dad has done nothing to help her.

It makes my own dad seem not so bad.

So far I've only read one of his letters: the one he wrote to Mum after my birthday. Now I take them all out of their place at the bottom of the box. I sort through the two piles – Mum's letters, Dad's – and put them together in date order.

I'll pretend. I'll read them like they were written by somebody else's parents. No, not even that: as if they've been made up in some author's head and published in a novel. They're characters in a story; a sad one maybe, the sort that is hard to read but you make yourself finish it because you have to know what happens.

The early letters start with practical things, like about the hospice where Mum is, how she got there. Dad's are full of longing for her and stories of me, as if he's trying to keep me in her life.

So why didn't he keep her in mine?

Before long Mum is asking him to tell me the truth: to get me to write back to her. But he never did. He never even gave me the letters she wrote to me.

Why must be hidden somewhere in these pages. When two people have a conversation about things they both know, they don't spell it out – there is no need. But maybe I can work it out.

I steel myself to read on, trying – mostly failing, but trying – not to feel, just to look at it like a puzzle that must be figured out.

One thing stands out. There are so many mentions of my school, mostly by Dad but by Mum, too. And Dad doesn't just tell her how I'm doing; there's stuff from him that looks like he's taken it from the school newsletter, things like academic achievements by other students, sports team victories. He even goes on about the unusually high number of girls leaving our school that got into Oxbridge the year I started. Why would he bother Mum with that kind of thing? When he was writing to her university was still years away for me.

And then, finally, in Dad's familiar handwriting are these words: *I don't want Ava to blame herself.*

Why would I? For what?

Mum left because she needed medical treatment she couldn't get here. What could that have to do with me?

I scan through them again, and then I see a line I'd skipped over before. In one letter early on Mum says her sister was sorry not to meet me after all. *After all*: that implies she thought we were going to meet, doesn't it?

Maybe ... we were going to go with Mum. To Sweden.

But then why didn't we?

The disparate pieces resolve and move in my mind, then snap together. Just before Mum disappeared – my scholarship. I got offered this amazing scholarship to the best girls' school in London.

They were so proud, both of them. But there was something weird about their reactions, too. I remember picking up on it, thinking they weren't going to let me go there for some reason, even though I couldn't imagine why.

I cringe when I remember. I said I'd *die* if I couldn't go to this school. Didn't I? I was a child – eleven years old – but still. Thinking about it now that I know how ill Mum was then, it makes me feel sick inside.

This is insane. Isn't it? I shake my head. Could it really be that we didn't go with Mum because I had been offered a scholarship? Dad was always so insistent about school, study, making sure I succeeded, but even so: it seems crazy.

I reread all the letters carefully from the beginning. All the little references I didn't notice the first time slot into place. The way Dad went on about the stupid school and the opportunities it gave me; how Mum said they did the right thing, that it was right for me to go there.

That's it, isn't it? That's the reason I never saw her again: so I could take up my scholarship, go to this school. I wanted to go here, but no one ever told me what was at stake: the biggest decision of my life was made without me.

How could they do that to me? Put my education ahead of being with my mum?

It seems beyond extreme.

But Dad had lost his job at the university. We were barely getting by. So many people were homeless, starving – not just here, there was economic collapse all around Europe, too. Maybe this scholarship *was* the one chance – the only chance – I was ever going to have to make something of my life.

They did it for me, but if they had asked I would have said no. I would have said we ought to stay together.

What would it have been like, moving to Sweden?

Being with my mum when she needed me the most. Holding her hand when she died.

Sam is going to die soon now. I can't be with her either, or hold her hand.

Despair is so deep and murky, it holds me fast. I can't move, I can't even cry any more.

The only way I know that I'm still breathing is that it just goes on and on.

11

Sam

I'm lying on the narrow bed in my cell, staring at the ceiling. It will be lights out in less than an hour, and when they go out here it is properly dark. A thin bit of light comes from the narrow window in the door from the hall and that's it.

I seem to have lost my fear of the dark. I'll never like it, but the unreasoning panic it used to bring is gone. Maybe that's because there are too many other things to be afraid of? When I wake up tomorrow – if I sleep, that is – it will be for the last time.

How much will it hurt? Will it be like slowly suffocating, or sudden, overwhelming pain from a broken neck? Maybe both.

'Tomorrow, I die,' I whisper into the quiet, but hearing it doesn't make it seem any more real.

There are footsteps in the hall and I glance at the door. It's not time for the guard's next check.

They stop by my door; I sit up. I hear the key scrape in the lock, and then it opens.

Next to the guard stands Lucas.

My eyes open wide in surprise. Did Dad do this

last thing for me after all?

'You've got ten minutes,' the guard says, and nudges Lucas in, then locks the door behind him.

Lucas is pale, dark circles like bruises under his eyes – eyes he can't seem to raise to meet mine.

'Hi,' I say.

He stumbles to me and holds out his hands, drops to his knees next to my bed. I don't reach out in return and his hands fall by his sides. He finally looks up, eyes glistening with tears.

'Sam, I – I'm so sorry. It wasn't supposed to be like this.'

'No, being hanged wasn't really in the plan, was it?' There's a silence that stretches. 'Come on, get up,' I say finally. 'Sit next to me.'

He does so and I can feel him wanting to hold me, see it in eyes that now they have found mine can't seem to let go, even to blink.

But seconds are ticking by.

'Lucas, there are some things I need to know.'

'Ask me anything.'

'Was Kenzi really your friend?'

His eyes open wider; he's surprised I ask about him? 'Well, no, not really. I mean, I knew him by sight from school. But—'

'Yet you said he was your friend. It was all part of a set-up, wasn't it? To hook me in. Get me involved.'

'I – well – it wasn't my idea. It was Molly, and I guess Juro. When they heard you were going to be at that dinner I was going to. But I had no idea about them being in A4A; I swear it.'

'But all along, you were lying to me.'

'I wanted to tell you the truth; I was going to after the sit-ins. I wanted – I *want* to be with you, Sam. You must know how much I care for you. I'm sorry, so sorry.'

He is crying properly now, and I let his head go against my shoulder, his arms around me. My body is rigid at first but I sigh, let myself relax again him.

I know he's sorry. I know he had nothing to do with A4A. But when I thought he wanted to be my friend, he set out to trick me, trap me. He lied and used me, didn't he? And even when he decided he had these feelings for me that he says he has, he still didn't tell me the truth. He said he was going to, but would he have done, really?

And tomorrow, we're both going to die.

I'm hurt. Angry. He drew me in; he didn't give me the chance to be outside it all and decide where I stood, and then act. But if I'm honest it wouldn't have changed anything. I still think what we did was right.

I even let him kiss me that day. It didn't mean anything to me, not like he probably thinks it did; I just wanted to see what it was like. In a way kissing Lucas made me see why he – why any boy – wasn't for me. So maybe I used him a little bit, too.

I don't care enough to try to tell him the truth about everything I feel. But I do care, just enough, to give him a lie of my own:

'Sssssh, Lucas. It's all right. I forgive you,' I say.

12

Ava

The sun rises just like it does every other day, and that seems wrong. How can it?

When I get to the area reserved for friends and family, I'm shocked – deeply – to see Nicky here. Lucas's little brother. The woman with him is the family friend I'd taken him to that day; she must be caring for him still.

I go to her. 'Can't you take him out?'

'No. The Lorders insisted he must see the consequences for what they are.' Her face is set, stony with anger, but she doesn't dare oppose them.

No one does any more.

13

Sam

My last outfit. I wonder if Mum will be watching? It's hideous – a shapeless, thick dark shirt and trousers.

Then I hope she isn't here. She doesn't deal well with anything ugly, unpleasant. How is she coping? Does she know Dad stopped Armstrong from pardoning me? Could she ever forgive him if she does?

Or maybe she agrees with him.

My hands are cuffed behind my back.

Somehow, I walk: one foot goes in front of the other. *One step ... two ... three ...*

As I walk I stand tall, and breathe.

Every sense is alive, magnified. The cold air in and out of my lungs; the rough cloth of these clothes; the jar of the floor through my shoes as our steps echo down the hall. There is an odd smell, too; one I can't identify – it's not quite but almost like antiseptic, and seems to be coming from the guard who walks behind me.

Twelve steps ... thirteen ... fourteen ...

I'm not sorry for what I did, not any of it. But I'm sorry to leave Mum; even Dad. He may think he knows what he's doing, but somehow I think he doesn't, that this will impact him in ways he hasn't even imagined.

Twenty … twenty-one … twenty-two …

I'm sorry, Ava; I don't want to leave you. Be strong.

As I walk and count, I hold her in my mind – her eyes the way I finally saw them. This is what I want to see as I die.

14

Ava

Sam's parents have arrived. They are to one side, government agents – Lorders – next to them so no one can get too close. Her dad stands tall, rigid; he's holding up his wife. She's wearing dark glasses but even though I can't see her eyes through them, still something about her doesn't look quite right. Is she medicated to get through this?

We see the four of them step outside: Lucas, Daisha, Sam, Juro.

They are across a field; too far away to really see their faces. This is the first time the new law allowing the execution of anyone so young is to be used. In deference to their ages they decided no close camera work, and that family and friends would be kept at this distance. As if somehow that makes it OK.

Even from this far away you can tell that Daisha is crying. She has to be taken to the gallows; she can't or won't walk on her own. The other three do, but Sam's head is down. Her feet shuffle and she sways a little. It somehow doesn't feel like how I thought she would be, but how do I know – how would anyone be in this situation?

The four of them go up the steps; now Daisha is standing straighter and managing on her own. On to the small platforms.

Should I be here? I don't know if it will make it better or worse for me to watch, but I have to be here for Sam. For her last moments. I'm not sure how aware she is of her surroundings right now, but if she looks up this way, she'll see me – standing here – and know that I came.

But her head stays down.

The ropes – they are put around their necks.

The trapdoors are opened.

They fall, and jerk and flail in the air. And as if a rope is around my own throat I can't breathe, I can't – not until it is over.

It seems to take for ever before they are still. They don't seem real any more now – just dolls on Lorder strings. Where there were four young people, full of life and possibility, energy and risk – drive to change things and make them better – four forms hang, still and lifeless. There is nothing to say who they were as individuals, or what brought them to this moment; there was so much secrecy in their trial that we'll never really know. They could be anybody from here.

Cries of pure anguish swell and grow – intense, almost animal – it's Nicky. Who thought bringing him here could possibly be a good idea? And it takes me out of myself, helps me tear my eyes away from what they will never stop seeing. I go to him, try to hold him, but he pushes me away.

'I'll make them pay. I will; I'll get them,' he says, with all the pure fury a five-year-old can feel etched on his face.

The woman who brought him takes his hand. 'Come, Nicky. It's time to go.'

She yanks him along, but as they go past the Gregorys he breaks free, launches himself towards them. Gregory turns and flinches just as Nicky screams, '*I hate you!*' and then, just for a moment, I wonder – does everybody? – does his young life hang in the balance?

One of the Lorders grabs Nicky and drags him back to his keeper, and Gregory turns away. But not before I see the tears on his face.

15

Sam

I'm coughing. There's a horrible smell – what is it? Something was held to my face, and I must have blacked out ...

Where I was going floods back to me. I struggle to sit up.

I'm in the back of a van; at least, I think it's a van. There are windows, but they're covered with something so there's only thin light at their edges. We're moving, driving along at a fair clip.

I can't work it out. What's going on? My thoughts are so fuzzy.

Think, Sam: focus on what you know.

Fact 1: I was on my way to be hanged.

Fact 2: something made me pass out.

Fact 3: I'm in the back of a van going who knows where.

Dad; it must be Dad. He must have decided he couldn't let them hang me and got me out of there. Who else would have been able to do it?

Lucas, Daisha, Juro: what about them? I know what I don't even want to think about must have happened by now, and my tears come.

When the doors finally open, natural light dazzles my eyes. I'm hungry, thirsty.

'Get out,' a voice says.

I stumble forwards, out of the back of the van. It's bitterly cold, raining. I'm inside fences, tall fences, with barbed wire on top. It's bare and bleak, with grey stone and slate rising above where we stand.

It's another prison. I'm in prison.

'Where's my dad?' I say, an edge of something like panic in my voice.

'Your dad?' Someone steps forward. I shake my head as if to knock sense into it. It's Astrid Connor – the MP I suspected of engineering the deal between Armstrong and Dad; if she did, she's the one that landed the whole country in its current hell. What is she doing here?

'What's going on?'

'Your dad has no idea where you are.'

'Tell him!'

'As far as he knows, he watched you hang this morning. I suspect he's far into a bottle of whisky by now.'

'What? But I thought he—'

'No. Your dad didn't let them pardon you, and he didn't rescue you, either. I did. But you might not thank me.'

'I don't understand. What's going on?' I say again.

'Your dad is getting all the kudos from the Lorder party now: we've decided we rather like that term you rebels applied to us, by the way, so we're keeping it. Anyway, he nobly sacrificed his own daughter for the greater good, and showed the country how serious we are about imposing law and order. He'll be the successor, the next in power – there can be no doubt. And at some point, when it's my turn, I'll use you to knock him back: make it look like he deceived everybody and saved you, hanging some innocent in your place.

'But that's the long game. In the meantime, welcome to Honister Slate Mine Prison. Your new home.'

16

Ava

I'm cold through, as though I'll never be warm again.

I sit on my bed, walk across the room, sit down again. I want to scream, to rage, like Nicky did: to promise a violent revenge against everyone who did this to Sam.

My hands are shaking, they flutter up and down like they're not attached to me. One brushes the locket around my neck.

The last time I saw Sam she touched this locket; she undid the knot in the chain. She held it close in her hands. Now, I hold it close in mine.

I wish I had a photograph of Sam I could put inside it – one that I'd taken, when she was just being who she was and not how the world saw her.

I push the little catch on the locket, and it springs open.

Something falls out, into my hand.

It's soft, and that fair almost-white blonde: that impossible colour. A lock of Sam's hair? She must have put it in when she undid the knot. It has been in my locket all this time, here, against my skin? I didn't know.

But she knew, I think: that something like this would

happen. Or at least that we wouldn't see each other again. She put it in here for me to find.

I remember her saying – it feels like another lifetime ago, now – that she didn't see herself becoming an artist or anything else, because she couldn't see beyond *now*. As if somehow she knew that she wouldn't grow up and go beyond what we already are.

Before I knew her, I watched her. I couldn't help it. She was so beautiful, and I always saw her as the girl who had everything, could do anything. That her life was effortless and perfect and always would be, and part of me hated her for that.

Then I got to know the real Sam, and I saw how her life wasn't easier than mine, it was just different. And I couldn't hold how I felt away any more by hating her, because I didn't.

Careful not to miss a single strand, I slip her hair back in the locket and close it again. I wrap my fingers around it.

I shut my eyes, and I remember: her smile, the warm feel of her against me when she hugged me that last time. Her voice saying she didn't like Lucas, not the way she liked me.

Here in my hand is my mother's locket, concealing a lock of hair of the girl I loved. Because I did, didn't I?

The two lost ones will stay together, against my skin – near my heart.

My dad knew me better than I knew myself. His voice was in my head that day telling me to go home and be safe, but it was also *my* voice. I'm not the brave one, the one who can stand against authority; at least, not the way they did. Sam knew it, too.

But I *will* find a way, my own way, to make a difference.

I clutch the locket close in my hand, and finally the tears come.

Epilogue

Five years later

1

Ava

I'm studying, concentrating – it's neurology, my favourite subject, and there is elegant joy in both the simplicity and complexity of neurons, neural pathways, brain structure. There's also an exam tomorrow. But despite my focus, gradually I become aware that there is an increase in background noise in the college. Not just the usual ebb and flow that I am used to ignoring.

I frown, listen. It's not quite excitement, not quite fear. Some of both? Has something happened?

I open my door, look into the hall. There are voices in the common room, and I walk towards it. Someone hisses *be quiet*, and the TV is turned louder as I enter the room.

'Breaking news. We can confirm that Prime Minister Armstrong and his wife Linea Armstrong have both been killed in a terrorist attack this afternoon on their way to Chequers. The time was exactly four p.m. – five years on from the signing of the agreement to form the Lorder government.'

The facts – as they choose to tell them – unfold on the screen. There is shock and grief on the newsreaders' faces, a mixture of shock and hastily suppressed glee in the students around me. The prime minister and his wife were on their way to a celebration to mark five years of Lorder power; their children had gone ahead and have been informed.

Sandy, their oldest, must be about the same age now as Sam was when she died.

There is footage taken from the air of burning motorway below; speculation as to method, perpetrators. Mention that the prime minister had called a press conference to take place on their arrival at Chequers; theorising as to why.

Then there is some grainy footage shown, a boy – maybe ten or eleven years old – his face turned away. They suspect him of involvement and ask for the public's help in identifying him; his first name is believed to be Nico. The side of his face is frozen on screen for a moment, and I draw in a sharp breath.

Is it – could it be – Lucas' little brother? Could this Nico be Nicky? I frown, look again when they replay it – but no. I can't be certain, and even if I was – no. I'll not say.

Then they go live to Gregory – Sam's dad. He's making a statement – sadness at this atrocity, guarantees of swift justice. He's not deputy prime minister any more, they say: of course. With Armstrong's death he is now the prime minister.

I stare at him as if by doing so I can see inside him, past the greyer, thinner hair, the lines by his eyes that weren't there before. Gregory isn't the man I remember. But who was he, really, even then? Not who I thought. I couldn't believe what he did – what he didn't do – and I still can't now. I can't reconcile who and what he is with some of the other things he did – like paying for my dad's funeral, and increasing my scholarship to school, too. Without it, could I have ever got where I am now?

And then how he stood there when Sam died, and cried.

I can't see him without remembering all of it, and soon I have to retreat back to my own four walls, away from eyes.

Safe in my room, door shut, I'm leaning against it and threatening to lose it now, completely. I do what I always do when that happens:

I hold my mother's locket in my hand.

I open it. The lock of Sam's hair is there as always, a bright talisman that doesn't fade. And the engraving I had put in tiniest print inside the locket – one for both Sam and my mum:

> *We live in deeds, not years;*
> *in thoughts, not breaths;*
> *in feelings, not in figures on a dial.*

I recite the rest of the quotation that wouldn't fit inside, changing the pronoun as I do so: *We should count time by heart throbs. She most lives who thinks most, feels the noblest, and the best.*

I close the locket again, let it slip back against my skin. It hangs near my heart, this locket of silver with its slip of hair, these words of a dead poet because I couldn't frame my own. Philip James Bailey may have died over a century ago, but what he said was just how I felt.

After that dark time I'd eventually found my solace between the pages like I always do; I'm studying medicine now. The Lorder government made all university free, admission based solely on ability, which got me this place at Cambridge. I'd wanted to save people like someone could maybe have saved my mum: I even legally changed my surname to hers, to remember her and to remind myself every day why I'm doing this.

But my motivation has grown so much wider than that now. Because although this government has done much that is good, the order they've imposed has been on the back of the deaths of girls like Sam, and boys like Lucas.

When Gregory's own daughter was hanged, it was like suddenly everybody believed the new Lorder government – they took them seriously. People were afraid, with good reason. Lorders meant business, and anyone who didn't obey their rules followed on the gallows. And they did wipe out anarchist groups like A4A, just like they said they would – groups that were behind so much of the trouble that started it all.

None have dared to oppose the Lorders publicly the last few years – until today – and why would any rational person do so? The UK is safe, secure, prosperous now in its isolation. Everyone – those over twenty-one, at least, with the latest changes – is equal now, no matter where they came from or anything else. And anyone who stands against the Lorders in any way soon disappears – or is hanged.

I guard my memories fiercely, despite the pain they bring. Sam's smile: not the plastic, public one, but the real one that lit her up from inside and warmed her eyes. The way she moved, quick and light, like sun shining through trees – there and beautiful, but fleeting. How in the end she risked everything for what she knew was right. The artistic talent she had, but denied: where could it have taken her if the world had been different?

Where could it have taken *us*?

This senseless, stupid waste of life. I'm not a revolutionary, despite how close I came to being one for her – but I will find another way. A way to stop it.

I swear it, or my name isn't Ava Lysander.

2

Sam

So little of the outside world finds us in this place that when it does it's a shock.

One of the guards tells us at dinner. Prime Minister Armstrong and his wife: they're dead? Killed by terrorists?

There's a spontaneous cheer amongst the women, and we lose our free hour as punishment.

I liked her, Mrs A, and manage to feel a pang of regret, but only for her and her children; not for her husband – a man responsible for so much misery.

Does this mean that my father will take power, that Astrid will have her moment at last to destroy him – to dangle my existence in the public eye?

Will I get out of here? Please, God. *Please*.

Though maybe if I do I will be hanged: that was my sentence, after all.

Next to me, Giana catches my eye: she knows what I'm thinking about, what I'm hoping for, and she squeezes my hand briefly as we're herded out of the dining room and back to our cells. I'd found her here – Lucas's mum – recognised her soon after I arrived. Then had to give her the painful news about Lucas.

So, Armstrong's five years in power have come to a fitting end. I've been here almost all that time. It feels both for ever and moments ago since I arrived in the hell that is Honister – a slate mine that was reopened as a women's working prison. *For ever* in that each minute of each day stretches endlessly with backbreaking and dangerous work. *Moments ago* in that the things that happened that day at Westminster – the sense of joy and possibility that turned to pain and despair – are as clear to me as if they were happening now.

The cell doors clang shut and lock, and the lights go out.

Astrid was right: I don't thank her for saving my life, leaving me here to rot. But would I rather a rope around my neck now?

I have learned two – no, three – things since I got here.

I'm strong. There is steel enough inside me to withstand anything. As much as I hate to admit it, maybe I got this from Dad.

Friends can be found in unlikely places. Honister's prisoners range from journalists who wouldn't keep quiet like Giana, and protestors like me, to real thugs and murderers – but there is also kindness, friendship, and failing that, often respect.

And I *am* an artist. Ava was right. Mrs Jenson, too: what was it she said? *Artists are compelled – even in the face of great adversity. Perhaps then even more so.*

My hands are cold, raw from rough work; the only light is dim from the hall through the bars in the door.

But it is *my* time now. My sketchpads and pencils are earned from guards – by drawing their children or pets from photos, or whatever else they want me to do.

I sit on the cold stone floor and lean against the door, the best spot to catch the light, and flip through the pages. None of my subjects have been here; they aren't copied from what my eyes see, but come from my heart, my memories, my feelings – good and bad. Mum is here, friends, places, too, even Dad, and somehow they are all more real now, drawn this way.

But most of all, there is Ava.

I touch her face on the page, and know I wouldn't choose the rope over this moment – breathing, feeling, longing – even now.

No matter what happened to Lucas, to me, to so many others – I still believe. One day, it may not be soon, but one day someone *will* come along who can find the way to change things where we failed.

In the meantime, I wait. I hope.

And I know this: despite the bars, when I put pencil to paper, I am free.

Acknowledgements

Fated was the story I had to write. I wasn't entirely sure it was a good idea: did people actually want to read about an alternative-but-very-like-our-own world where things go horribly wrong after the UK leaves the EU? Yet I felt compelled to give a voice to teenage characters who can't vote in key decisions but are stuck with the results.

To *Slated* fans old and new around the world: thank you! Your enthusiasm for Kyla and her world were part of what brought me here. I know it isn't the sequel some had been hoping for, but there was so much to say about Sam, Ava and the political situation that led to the world in *Slated*. I hope it doesn't disappoint you.

Thank you to my agent Caroline Sheldon and editors Megan Larkin, Emily Sharratt and Rosie McIntosh for helping me realise my vision – and for their names! – and to designer Thy Bui for yet another amazing cover.

Special thanks to Ann Giles – also known as blogger the Book Witch – for suggesting the Willow Song to be sung by Ava's Swedish mother, and for letting me borrow the endearment she used for her own daughter.

Nick Cross, thank you for being both the source of

Nicky – Nico's – name, and occasional technical advisor (of course any errors are my own).

Thank you to all those who entered a competition to have a character named after them, and congratulations to winners Ruth Miller and Anji Kilvert-King.

Finally, thank you to Graham, Scooby and the guys for reminding me of the important things. Even in the midst of chaos, our corner of the real world is still a beautiful place to be.

'A gripping thriller' – *Bookseller*

Available in paperback, ebook and audio

TERI TERRY

MULTI AWARD-WINNING AUTHOR OF *SLATED*

DANGEROUS GAMES

Available in ebook and audio

TERI TERRY

MULTI AWARD-WINNING AUTHOR OF *SLATED*

BOOK
OF
LIES

A TRUTH, A LIE
TO LIVE, OR DIE

'[An] excellent psychological and
supernatural thriller' – *BookTrust*

Available in paperback, ebook and audio